CARR, J.D.   F

Fire, burn!

FIRE, BURN!

One October night in the middle of the twentieth century, Detective Superintendent John Cheviot got into a taxi, bound for New Scotland Yard. When he stepped out it was from a horse-drawn cab, the year was 1829, and a beautiful woman was beckoning him in from Old Scotland Yard. There were things he couldn't remember — and things he didn't know — like the state of his romance with Lady Flora. Then Cheviot suddenly found himself and his lady accused of cruel murder . . .

Books by John Dickson Carr
Published by The House of Ulverscroft:

THE HOUSE AT SATAN'S ELBOW
IN SPITE OF THUNDER
DARK OF THE MOON

JOHN DICKSON CARR

FIRE, BURN!

Complete and Unabridged

ULVERSCROFT
Leicester

First published in the
United States of America

First Large Print Edition
published 2002

British Library CIP Data

Carr, John Dickson, *1906 –1977*
   Fire, burn!.—Large print ed.—
   Ulverscroft large print series: mystery
   1. Detective and mystery stories
   2. Large type books
   I. Title
   813.5′2 [F]

   ISBN 0–7089–4606–2

Published by
F. A. Thorpe (Publishing)
Anstey, Leicestershire

Set by Words & Graphics Ltd.
Anstey, Leicestershire
Printed and bound in Great Britain by
T. J. International Ltd., Padstow, Cornwall

For Sir Allen Lane

1

'Then Who Will You Send
to Fetch Him Away?'

The woman couldn't have been killed in the broad corridor with the fringed lamps. She couldn't have died before the eyes of three witnesses. And yet she had.

In short, as Cheviot will tell you, the most baffling murder case in his experience occurred in the year 1829.

Now that was fully eight years before Queen Victoria came to the throne. It flared up during the last sunburst of the dandies, and of the prettiest courtesans with white skins and enigmatic mouths and rooms full of rich *bijouterie*, in the dance of scandal before old, obese King George the Fourth gasped out his life against a table at Windsor.

Therefore, since Detective-Superintendent John Cheviot is very much alive in these years of the nineteen-fifties, being not yet middle-aged, some explanation of such statements ought to be made.

At about ten o'clock on an October night, present-day, Cheviot hailed a taxi in Euston

Road. To the driver he said, 'Scotland Yard.' Then he slammed the door and sat back.

Cheviot was Superintendent of C-One. Under the Commander of the C.I.D. there are nine C-departments; and C-One is the Murder Squad. Cheviot owed his position to the fact that the present Assistant Commissioner believes in promotion by ability rather than seniority.

Nowadays it is no disgrace to have entered the Force by way of Winchester and Trinity College, Cambridge. And, provided a man does his work well, nobody will object if he rummages much in the ancient police-records preserved at Scotland Yard Central.

Then, too, Cheviot had learned to control his over-imaginativeness; to appear as stolid as everybody else. Public-school austerity is no bad training for the semi-military discipline of the police. If he was saved from what swooped down on him, he was saved by a woman and by his own sense of humour.

Cheviot, let it be repeated, got into a taxi in Euston Road and told the driver to take him to Scotland Yard.

It was a muggy night, though not warm, and with a slight mist. He did not notice where they were going. His thoughts were absorbed in a case which does not concern this narrative. To this day he swears that he

2

had no cold premonition, no warning that a bit of the dark world had pierced through and pinioned him, when the cab drew up and stopped almost at the place where it should have stopped.

'Now if that charwoman,' he thought, 'is telling the truth . . . '

Stooping down towards the left, he twisted the handle of the cab's door. He opened it to step down. And the top of the door-frame knocked off his hat, which fell off backwards on the floor of the cab.

Startled out of his thoughts, he stood humped in the doorway. He was wearing a soft felt hat. It should not have hit the floor with such a heavy bump and bounce, or rolled when it did.

Instead of glancing over his shoulder, he looked ahead. Through the mist he saw a dim gas-lamp, in a sort of glass coffin, where an ordinary lamp-standard should have been.

Well, that should cause no shock at the heart or even any surprise. Many parts of London were still lighted by gas.

Carefully he bent down and picked up the hat by its hard, curled brim. He climbed out: not to a running-board, but to a high step. The cab in which he had travelled bore two brass-bound carriage-lamps, burning oil. Beyond the light of the offside lamp he could not see either the driver or the horse. But he could smell the interior of the cab now, and smell the horse too.

Cheviot did not say anything. The expression of his face remained unchanged. He jumped down into an inch of mud, which spattered and was more unsavoury still, over a cobblestone road. But his voice was too loud when he spoke.

'What's the fare?'

'Shilling,' said the driver.

That was all. But, more than any of these discrepancies, of the night or of a disaffected brain, Cheviot was startled by the hatred and vindictiveness in the cabman's low voice.

'A shilling. Oh,' Cheviot said mechanically. 'Where did I hire you?'

An invisible whip cracked, pouring more hatred.

'Euston Road. Yer said 'Scotland Yard.' But yer meant 'Great Scotland Yard'; w'ere else? And yer meant number bloody four White'all Place.' The whip cracked again. 'Well! There 'tis!'

Cheviot looked at the hat in his hands. It was something like a modern top-hat, but much higher and heavier, its nap of beaverskin with a furry gloss. There seemed to be something damnably wrong with his hair, which was far too thick, when he

4

carefully jammed the weight down on it.

His right hand slid down to his right-hand trousers pocket. His coat, of fine broadcloth, was too long; he had to push it completely aside before dipping into the pocket of rather tightly fitting trousers, and fishing out a handful of change.

Silver coins glimmered between mist and cab-lamp light. When he saw whose head was on every one of those coins, Superintendent Cheviot stood very still.

And, all the time, that eerie invisible voice still poured hatred at him.

'Quite the nob, ain't yer?' it jeered. 'Fr'all I knows, yer may be one o' the two new Commissioners of Bobby Peel's brand-new ber-luddy p'leece . . . '

'*What's that?*'

'You 'eard!' The voice grew softly frantic. 'Got coloured clothes on, ain'tcher? And, for all that, you'd try to gammon me out of me fare. Wouldn't yer? Say I didn't pick yer up in — '

Cheviot looked up.

'Be quiet,' he said.

Once upon a time a female reporter had written that Superintendent Cheviot, of the Murder Squad, was 'quite distinguished-looking, with rather sinister light-grey eyes, though to me he seemed good-natured enough.'

No doubt this was gush. And yet, as those same light-grey eyes were raised now, they held a look so sinister that the cabman's voice stuck in his throat. The eyes were set in a lean face, above the two white points of the collar and the casually tied black-satin stock.

'Walk-er!' thought the driver. He didn't want no row. He didn't want no real trouble with a nob who looked as dangerous as this 'un.

'Here; take this,' Cheviot said mildly. He handed up two shillings to a cabman who should already have jumped down and held open the door.

If the fare all the way from Euston Road happened to be only a shilling, then that extra bob was an enormous tip. The cabman seized at the money. Almost soundlessly, muffled in mud, the cab backed and shuffled and clopped away down Whitehall into an eerie night. But the invisible voice still cried two words of hate.

'Peeler!' it said. '*Spy!*'

John Cheviot turned and strode left into the little turning where, beyond the gas-lamp bracket, was the only brick house showing a few furtive lights on the ground floor. The chill mud clogged his trousers and oozed unpleasantly across his shoes.

That was reality, surely?

But it wasn't. Cheviot knew better.

'This is Old Scotland Yard,' he thought, 'exactly as it ought to be. Only a few hundred yards up from where I want to go. It hasn't changed, of course. It's *my* eyes, *my* senses, *my* brain.'

And then, in sheer terror and despair:

'Oh, God, it's happened. I never really thought it would, even when I was over-worked. But it's happened.'

That was when he first saw the woman.

A closed box of a carriage, painted in dark lacquer, with gilt wheels and glossy bay horses, had been drawn up close to the windows of number four Whitehall Place. Cheviot hardly saw it, because the carriage-lamps had been turned down to mere blue sparks, until a top-hatted coachman in red livery sprang down from the box.

As the coachman twisted a tiny wheel under the lamp, its flame blossomed up bright and yellow. The carriage-door was opened. A woman put one foot down on the step and hesitated, waving away the coach-man. She looked steadily at Cheviot from a distance of only ten feet away.

'Mr. Cheviot!' she called gently. Her voice was very soft and sweet, with a hint of demure formality. She lowered her long eyelashes in confusion, and sat back into the carriage.

Again Cheviot stood still.

This was worse than ever. He had caught only a brief glimpse of her. And yet, though he had never seen her before in his life, he thought he knew who she was.

She was no girl. She may have been thirty, or perhaps more. The hint of maturity in that slender figure only added allure. She wore a gown of white brocade, with faint yellow stripes, well off the shoulders and cut low at the breast, with bare arms.

Her hair, clear golden, was parted in the middle and drawn across the forehead so as to expose the ears, ending in flat round plaits well behind her head. It exposed the soft beauty of face and neck, faintly coloured despite a dusting of rice-powder. Her mouth, unpainted, was small but full-lipped, like her rounded chin. Most of all, beyond her gracefulness, you noted the eyes: large, long, heavy-lidded, of a clear dark blue, outwardly as innocent-looking as those of a girl of fourteen.

But she was not in the least innocent.

One of the hardest tasks in Cheviot's life was to walk straight across to that carriage. Out of the corner of his eye he noticed that the top-hatted coachman in red livery again sat straight-backed on the box, staring ahead. 'I am blind,' the coachman's back seemed to say. 'I hear nothing; I see nothing.'

Cheviot removed his hat. He mounted the step of the carriage, and bent his head inside.

This was no hackney cab. It smelled of jasmine perfume, even its claret-coloured cushions. The woman was leaning back, her innocent-looking blue eyes half closed; but she sat up as he entered.

'Dearest!' she said, in a voice so low it was barely audible.

Then she lifted her mouth to be kissed.

'Madam,' said Cheviot, 'what is your name?'

The blue eyes flashed wide open.

'Isn't your first name Flora? *Isn't* it?'

'As if you didn't know!'

'You are Lady Drayton. You're a widow. You live at — '

Even at her most intent or her most passionate, as he was to discover, she would colour with that air of timidity or even shyness.

'I live,' she whispered, 'where I am waiting to take you home. As always.'

Cheviot, the outwardly stolid, never quite understood his behaviour then. Dropping on one knee, he locked his arms tightly round her waist and put his cheek against her breast.

'Don't laugh at me,' he said. 'For God's

sake don't laugh at me.'

Flora did not answer that she would not laugh at him. She did not say he was hurting her, though his grip did hurt. Instead her arms went round his neck, and her own cheek was pressed against his hair.

'My dear! What is it? What is the matter?'

'I'm out of my senses. I'm mad. I'm a cursed Bedlamite! You see . . . '

For perhaps thirty seconds he whispered or shouted wild words. It is doubtful that Flora, who could remember everything he said and repeat it to him afterwards, understood one tenth of what he spoke.

But the black fear-sting was being drawn out of his brain, slowly, as he talked. He could feel the soft, perfumed flesh rise and fall under his cheek. He felt the pressure of her arms round his neck.

'This is one fine position,' he thought, 'for a police-officer on duty.'

Cheviot stumbled to his feet, inadvertently treading on the hem of a white-and-yellow gown tight at the waist but wide in the skirt according to the prevailing mode. He could not stand upright in the carriage. Bending over, he put his hands lightly on her shoulders as her head went back.

Flora's neck seemed too slender to support the weight of the heavy golden hair. Her long, large, innocent-seeming eyes were blurred with tears, and she trembled. Her presence was so sensually disturbing that —

'You are not mad,' she told him gently. Then she made a wry mouth, turning her head away. 'Except, to be sure, that you wish to become Superintendent of their Central Company, or Central Division, or whatever name they give it.' Back turned the disturbing eyes. 'And, if you be mad, what am I?'

'Oh, you're out of a picture-book!'

'Dearest?'

'To be exact, from a folio of coloured drawings at . . . '

About to say 'the Victoria and Albert Museum,' he checked himself.

'Nobody-knows,' he said, 'how long I have loved you. Nobody will ever know.'

'Well. I should hope not.' Yet she took fire at his mood. 'Oh, how I wish we were at home now! But — but are you not late for your appointment?'

'Appointment? With whom?'

'With Mr. Mayne and Colonel Rowan, surely?'

Beside Flora, on the cushions, lay a large Leghorn hat and a red cashmere shawl. Cheviot studied them in the dimness. As one who had delved much in ancient records, he knew that the names of the first two Police

11

Commissioners, acting with joint authority, had been Mr. Richard Mayne and Colonel Charles Rowan.

He knew their portraits, their histories. He knew —

'You refer,' he said, and cleared his throat, 'to Sir Robert Peel's . . . ?'

'*Sir* Robert?' Flora looked perplexed. 'I had heard old Sir Robert was very ill, and not expected to live. But has he died? And has Mr. Peel inherited his father's baronetcy?'

'He hasn't, he hasn't! Not yet!' Cheviot cried out. 'Forgive me,' he added more mildly. 'It was only a mistake.'

'We-el,' murmured Flora. 'I suppose you must go. But don't, please *don't*, remain away too long.'

And once more she lifted her mouth.

What happened in the next few minutes need not be told here. And yet, as Cheviot left the carriage and strode confidently towards the door of number four Whitehall Place, the fit of horrors had departed.

'Come, now!' crackled a satiric voice in his own brain. 'Isn't this only the other part of your dream, the secret dreams all men hide and cherish? Didn't you want to see, in action, the first Scotland Yard in history? When the mob was a tiger, when gangs were more murderous, when the police were hated and attacked as interferers with personal liberty? When puzzling crimes, of house-breaking or murder, could be solved only by a blunder of luck or the whisper of the informer?

'Murder, let's admit,' whispered that same satiric voice, 'is always sordid; usually dull; not at all the stuff of novels. Still! Didn't you want to amaze them by solving some such mystery, with fingerprints or ballistics or modern deduction? In your heart, now, don't you still want to astonish them with what can be done?'

'Yes!' Superintendent Cheviot muttered aloud.

Number four Whitehall Place was a handsome brick house, showing glimmers of light through drawn curtains of windows on either side of its door. Cheviot lifted the knocker and rapped sharply.

Was it only in his imagination that someone, close at hand, uttered a laugh?

Cheviot whirled round. Yes; it was illusion. There was nobody there.

The door was opened by — yes, by the sort of person Cheviot expected to see.

The man was of middle height, red-faced, and by his stiff military bearing clearly an ex-Army ranker. His coat, stretching halfway to his knees, was of dark blue and had a line of metal buttons to the waist. His trousers were dark blue. Few would have guessed that his tall hat was reinforced inside by a leather crown and supports of heavy cane, against the lash of clubs and bottles.

As he eyed Cheviot's bearing and clothes, he became more stiff and respectful.

'Yes, sir?'

'My name is Cheviot,' the latter said carelessly. 'I believe I have an appointment with Colonel Rowan and Mr. Mayne.'

'Yes, sir. Will you follow me, sir?'

The Peeler's hardwood truncheon and rattle were hidden by the skirts of his coat. In fact (as was Mr. Peel's strongest wish) you could see little to distinguish him from an ordinary civilian, except for the blue-and-white band round his left arm, which indicated merely that he was on duty.

Cheviot sauntered after him, into a wide and spacious hall with doors on either side. But the passage was going to ruin from its smell of damp, from the spreading patches on its scarlet wallpaper.

The policeman, stiff-backed, marched across to a door on the right. He threw it open.

'Mr. Cheviot,' he announced in a hoarse brandy-voice.

Cheviot felt a second's blind panic, worse than any he had known. He was committed. For good or ill, for ease or death, he must walk the path to God-knows-where. Well! All the more reason why he should walk it with good grace, as Flora would have him do.

He caught only a glimpse of a good-sized room, its oak-panelled walls cluttered to confusion with military trophies. Colonel Rowan, he vaguely remembered, was a bachelor and kept living-quarters here. Then, throwing back his shoulders and with a lazy smile, Cheviot strolled in.

'Good evening, gentlemen,' he said.

2

A Problem in Bird-Seed

Actually there were three men in the room. But, since one was sitting at a writing-desk in a far corner, Cheviot at first saw only two.

On the floor lay a red-patterned Turkey carpet, so spattered and trampled with tobacco-ash that its original colours remained dubious. A polished mahogany table, much burned at the edges, stood in the middle. On it, amid scattered documents and a paper of cigars, was a lamp with a fluted red-glass shade and a red-glass bowl burning a broad flame of petroleum oil.

Cheviot wondered, not for the first time, why petroleum-burning lamps didn't blow up; and was soon to learn that they often did.

Sideways to the table, in an easy-chair of padded purplish silk, sat a tall, slender, rather handsome man in his late forties. His thinning and greying fair hair was brushed up and curled back from a high forehead. What you first noticed were the large eyes and wide nostrils; they added an air of sensitiveness and intelligence to the thin face.

16

This was Colonel Charles Rowan, of course. Except for the absence of sword or sword-belt, he wore dress uniform: his scarlet coat, with heavy gold epaulettes, bore the buff facings and silver lace of the 52nd, a Light Infantry regiment. His white-trousered legs were crossed. His left hand held a lighted cigar; with his right hand he slapped at the chair-arm with a pair of white gloves.

Cheviot glanced across the table at the other man.

Mr. Richard Mayne, a bouncing barrister in his early thirties, was also smoking a cigar. At first glance his face appeared to be perfectly round. This was because of his shiny black hair and shiny side-whiskers. Though the side-whiskers did not completely encircle his face and meet at the chin, they came within an inch or more of doing so. Out of this frame peered dark eyes, also shiny and shrewd, above a long nose and a wide mouth.

Mr. Mayne's clothes were much like Cheviot's own, though of less fine quality. Mr. Mayne wore a sombre-hued coat, pinched-in at the waist but long and loose almost to the knees. The high sides of his collar showed above a white neckerchief. His trousers were of brown velvet, strapped under the shoes like Cheviot's.

17

'Now steady!' thought the latter. 'I'm perfectly cool.'

And yet he kept on clearing his throat as he bowed formally.

'I — I must apologise for my lateness, gentlemen.'

Both his companions rose to their feet and returned the bow. Both of them threw away their cigars into a china spittoon under the table.

'I beg you won't mention it,' smiled Colonel Rowan. 'Speaking for myself, I was rather gratified at your application. This, I take it, is your first visit to Scotland Yard?'

Slight pause.

'Well! — ' said Cheviot, and made a noncommittal gesture with his hat.

'Ah, yes. Kindly be seated, in that chair there, and we'll consider your qualifications.'

Mr. Richard Mayne, who had sat down, bounced to his feet again. His face, circled with the dark hair and whiskers, was not at all unfriendly; but it was dogged.

'Rowan,' he said in a deep voice with a faint trace of Irish accent, 'I have no liking for this. Forgive me, Mr. Cheviot,' and his dark eyebrows twitched back towards the Colonel, 'but this gentleman is too plainly a gentleman. Rowan, it won't do!'

'And yet,' mused the other, 'I am not sure.'

18

'Sure? Damme, it's against the express orders of Peel himself! The Force, in general, is to be composed of ex-Army privates, commanded by non-commissioned officers. *Non*-commissioned. Peel don't want gentlemen, and says so.' Here Mr. Mayne squeezed up his eyes in memory. ''A sergeant of the Guards at two hundred pounds a year',' he quoted, ''is a better man for my purpose than a captain of high military reputation who would serve for nothing, or if I could give him a thousand a year.' What do you say to that?'

Colonel Rowan's thin, fair-grey head, atop the high black-leather stock which gave his courtesy so stiff-backed a look, turned slowly towards Mr. Mayne.

'At our very first parade,' he said, 'we were obliged to dismiss five officers for being drunk on duty. Not to mention the nine men we dismissed for complaints at what they called the long hours.'

'Drunkenness?' scoffed the young barrister. 'Come, now! What else can we expect?'

'Better than that, I think. One moment.'

With another polite bow, Colonel Rowan walked to the desk in the far corner of the room. There he exchanged a few words in a low voice with a man sitting behind the desk. This man, whom Cheviot could not see very well, handed him a long sheet of foolscap.

Colonel Rowan returned to the table.

'Now, sir,' he added, looking at Cheviot. 'Your record.'

He sat down. So did Mr. Mayne and Cheviot, the latter turning round and round the brim of his hat in unsteady hands.

Under the eye of Colonel Rowan, light-blue and mild as it appeared, he felt very small. He remembered, ghost-like, the painting of Colonel Rowan with the five medals across his coat. This man had fought in every major battle of the Peninsular War, and had commanded a wing at Waterloo.

'I believe,' continued the Colonel, glancing at the foolscap-sheet, 'you served in the late wars?'

He meant the Napoleonic Wars, of course. But Cheviot could speak truthfully about the only war he knew.

'I did, sir.'

'Your rank?'

'Captain.'

Mr. Richard Mayne grunted. But Colonel Rowan was not ill-pleased.

'Yes. In the 43rd Light Infantry, I think.' Then he spoke of Cheviot in the third person, as though the latter were not there at all. 'Served with distinction at . . . hum! I will not embarrass him.'

Cheviot said nothing.

'Lives,' pursued Colonel Mayne, 'in chambers at the Albany. Is of independent means: intelligence kindly supplied us by his bankers, Messrs. Groller of Lombard Street. Moves in the — the *beau monde*. Noted as pistol-shot, wrestler, and singlestick-player.' He glanced with approval at Cheviot's shoulders, and looked at Mr. Mayne. 'His private affairs . . . hum! These are no concern of ours.'

Cheviot's voice rang out loudly in the smoky, dirty room.

'If you don't mind, sir, I should be interested to hear what you have gleaned about my private life.'

'You insist?'

'I request.'

'Is at times a heavy gambler,' read Colonel Rowan, without looking up, 'but goes for months without touching cards or dice. No friend to temperance societies, but is never observable as being drunk. His friendship with Lady Drayton is well known — '

'H'm,' grunted Mr. Mayne.

'But is, I repeat, no concern of ours.'

And he dropped the sheet of foolscap on the table.

Too many shocks were having on Cheviot just the opposite effect. They induced in him a mood of exhilaration, a don't-give-a-damn high-heartedness; he was ready to seize at one

21

dream amid dreams.

This was just as well, because Mr. Mayne's deep voice came driving in.

'Now, Mr. Cheviot!' said the barrister, thrusting an arm so suddenly across the table that Cheviot feared the lamp would singe his whiskers. 'By your leave, I'll ask the question Rowan was about to ask.'

Mr. Mayne rose to his feet, putting his hands under his coat and waggling the coat-tails. This disclosed a velvet waistcoat, in which arabesques of black dominated arabesques of green, and which was crossed by a gold watch-chain with a bunch of seals.

'Sir,' he continued, 'you have applied for the post of Superintendent at our Central or Home Division. You are, we hear, of independent means. But your emolument would be only two hundred a year. You would be on duty twelve hours a day. Your work would be hard, dangerous, even bloody. Mr. Cheviot, why do you want this post?'

Cheviot also sprang to his feet.

'Because,' he retorted, 'the duties of the police comprise more than suppressing brawls, or hauling away drunkards and prostitutes. You agree?'

'And if I did?'

'Well, what of crimes committed by a person or persons unknown? Thievery?

House-breaking? Even,' and Cheviot rounded the syllables, 'murder?'

Mr. Mayne frowned at the table and flapped his coat-tails. Colonel Rowan did not speak.

'Such crimes, I believe,' said Cheviot, 'are now dealt with by the Runners. But the Runners are corrupt. They can be hired by a private individual, or rewarded by the Government with prices according to the scale of the crime. Oh, yes! Bow Street can always produce a victim to be hanged. And how often do you hang the right man?'

Colonel Mayne interposed with unusual sharpness.

'Seldom,' he said. 'Damned seldom! — In good time, a dozen years or so,' he added, 'we shall abolish the Runners altogether. We shall then create a new force of our own, to be called the 'detective police'.'

'Good!' said Cheviot in a ringing voice. 'But why shouldn't *I*, in addition to my ordinary duties, become the first member of your detective police? And begin those services *now*?'

There was a silence.

Colonel Rowan looked startled and even displeased. But in Mr. Richard Mayne could be sensed a new and different mood.

'Eh, and why not?' exclaimed the barrister,

firing up. 'We live in a new age, Rowan. Of steam, of railways, of power-looms for the mills!'

'And therefore,' the Colonel retorted, 'of worse and worse poverty. This cry for Reform will cause riots; remember that. If we can assemble seventeen divisions by this time next year, we need every man. You go too fast, Mayne.'

'Do I? I wonder! Always provided, that is, Mr. Cheviot could manage this work. What makes you think, sir, you could manage the work?'

Cheviot bowed.

'Because I can prove it,' he said.

'Prove it? How?'

Cheviot had been looking quickly round the room.

The blood-red glass of the lamp cast a dim, rather ghastly light. Patterns of swords, pistols, muskets, and metal cap-badges glimmered with dull polish round the walls. In the back wall, beside a white marble mantelpiece, loomed up a stuffed and moth-eaten brown bear; the bear stood on its hind legs, forepaws out, seeming to leer and listen with one glass eye gone.

Cheviot addressed Colonel Rowan.

'Sir,' he said, gesturing round, 'is there a loaded pistol among all these trophies?'

'At least,' the other answered gravely, 'I have one here.'

Colonel Rowan drew open a drawer of the table. From it he produced a medium-weight, medium-bore pistol; the whole of its handle, Cheviot rejoiced to see, was plated with pure silver bearing Colonel Rowan's initials.

Just as gravely its owner drew back the hammer to half-cock, above the percussion-cap on the firing-nipple. Then he handed the pistol to Cheviot.

'Will that do?'

'Admirably. With your permission, sir, I will try an experiment. You gentlemen will be the two witnesses. Stop!' Cheviot looked at the figure behind the desk. 'I see there is a third. Three witnesses would make my task more difficult.'

Colonel Rowan craned his neck round. 'Mr. Henley!' he called.

There was a bumping noise, and the rattle of an unlit lamp, as someone pushed his way clumsily from behind the desk. Out of the shadows emerged a shortish, stocky man in his middle fifties.

He was partly lame in the right foot, from a wound at Waterloo, and supported himself on a thin ebony walking-stick. But he had a merry brown eye, a flattish nose, and an amiable fleshy mouth. Even his thick side-hair and short-cut-side-whiskers, reddish in colour, could not hide the broad runnel of baldness in the middle.

You would have thought him something of a ladies' man, a dasher, a lover of good food and wine. You would have thought so even despite his very dark clothes and the air of portentousness he assumed under Colonel Rowan's eye.

'May I present Mr. Alan Henley, our chief clerk?'

'Your servant, sir,' intoned Mr. Henley, portentously and in a cultured voice which had not always been quite so cultured.

He directed at Cheviot a private grin which Colonel Rowan did not see. Then he propped up his stick at the narrow end of the table, assumed an air of deep wisdom, and leaned on the table with both hands.

'But, I say!' burst out Mr. Mayne. 'What's this demm'd experiment? What does the fellow mean to *do*?'

'Observe!' said Cheviot.

With an immense and vari-hued silk handkerchief, whipped from the tail-pocket of his coat, he had been polishing the pistol as though only to give it a higher gloss. Next, left forefinger on the muzzle and right forefinger under the handle, he put it down under the lamp.

'Out in the passage,' he continued, restoring the handkerchief to his pocket, 'you have a constable on duty. I propose to go out there. Tell the constable to engage my attention; at any event, be sure I cannot possibly see what occurs in here.'

'Well? Well? Well?'

'Then close the door; lock it. One of you gentlemen, I suggest, shall take up the pistol. Let him fire a shot, from any distance he likes; say at that stuffed bear beside the fireplace.'

All swung round to look at the brown bear, which leered back with one glass eye.

'Finally,' said Cheviot, 'give me a sign to return. I will then tell you which of you three fired the shot, from what distance it was fired, and what the man in question did before and afterwards. That's all.'

'All?' echoed Mr. Richard Mayne, after a stupefied pause.

'Yes, Mr. Mayne.'

Mr. Mayne smote the table a blow with his fist.

'Man, you're mad!' he almost yelled. 'It can't be done!'

'May I try?'

'Poor old Tom,' Colonel Rowan said rather sadly, and looked at the brown bear. 'I got him in Spain many years ago. One more bullet won't hurt him. — At the same time,' the Colonel added with some sharpness, 'our guest may well be able to tell us at what distance a shot is fired. By reason of the powder-burns.'

Cheviot's heart seemed to turn over. These people couldn't possibly . . . ?

His momentary consternation was shared by the chief clerk as well as the barrister. Mr. Alan Henley rolled up his heavy, half-bald head, opening his eyes wide. A drop of sweat trickled down beside one reddish side-whisker.

'S-sir?' he demanded.

'Come, Henley, you have been to the wars! Have you never observed the nature of wounds?'

'No, sir. Can't say as,' here Mr. Henley coughed and instantly corrected his grammar, 'can't say I have.'

'If a firearm is discharged close against the body, there will be black burns on the uniform. Even at ten or a dozen feet, granting a heavy charge of powder, there will be faint marks. Otherwise, if Mr. Cheviot will forgive me, I find his offer incredible.'

'Incredible?' cried Mr. Mayne. 'I tell you it's impossible!' He looked at Cheviot. 'A small wager, perhaps,' he suggested, 'that you can't do it?'

'Mr. Mayne, I — '

Cheviot paused.

A wave of revulsion, almost like nausea, rose up in his throat. What he intended was a trick, and a very cheap trick at that. It is all very well to imagine yourself dazzling the ignorant with your superior knowledge, and playing the great omniscient. But, when you are face to face with this, you shy back and find you can't do it.

'Five pounds?' inquired the barrister, diving into his pocket and waggling a banknote. 'Shall we say five pounds?'

'Mr. Mayne, I can't take your money. This is a certainty. You see — '

Rat-tat-tat. Rat-tat-tat. Rat-tat-tat.

It was only a sharp knocking at the door to the passage. Yet none of them realized how great had grown the tension. Mr. Mayne jumped. Even Colonel Rowan, the imperturbable, jerked up his chin.

'Yes, yes, what is it?' he called out.

The door opened and closed behind the constable. The constable's tall hat seemed even taller in this light. Standing stiffly at attention, he saluted. Then he marched towards Colonel Rowan, holding at arm's length a four-folded sheet of paper sealed with a conspicuous crest in yellow wax.

'Letter for you, sir. Personal, and by 'and.'

'Thank you.'

The red-faced constable marched backwards stiffly and stood at attention by the door. Colonel Rowan, after glancing at the letter, swung round again.

'Billings!'

'Sir.'

'This letter has been opened. The seal has been pried up from underneath.'

'Yessir,' instantly and hoarsely replied Billings. 'I reckon it was the lady, sir.'

'Lady? What lady?'

'The lady, sir, has got her kerridge pulled up smack to the front winders. Fair-haired lady, sir, as pretty as any pictur you ever see.'

'Oh,' murmured Colonel Rowan. But his eye strayed towards Cheviot.

'By your leave, sir!' said Billings, saluting again. 'I hear some horse a-coming up outside. I thinks it's one of the Patrol. I opens the street-door. But 't'an't that at all. It's a footman in livery, on an 'orse. An 'orse!' he added, with much disgust. 'In my time, sir, they made us run. And run like blazes too.'

'Billings!'

'Very good, sir. Oh, ah; well. The lady puts her head out of the kerridge-winder. The footman stops and looks smarmy. She says something to him; can't hear what. He gives her the letter into the kerridge. Presently she gives it out again. He wallops up to me, gives *me* the letter, and wallops off without waiting for a reply. Can't say no more or that, sir.'

('Now what, in God's name,' Cheviot was thinking furiously, 'has Flora to do with this affair? Or, in fact, any affair that concerns the police?')

But he did not speak. The door closed after Billings. In silence Colonel Rowan opened and read the letter. His expression changed and grew more grave. He handed over the letter to Mr. Mayne.

'I greatly fear, Mr. Cheviot,' he said, 'we must postpone our experiment with the pistol. This is a matter of serious import. Someone has again been stealing bird-seed from Lady Cork.'

Pause.

The words were so grotesque, so unexpected, that for the moment Cheviot could not even laugh. He was not sure he had heard aright.

'Bird-seed?' he repeated.

'Bird-seed!' declared Mr. Mayne, who was quivering with excitement. Suddenly an inspiration gleamed in his dark eyes, and he struck the letter. 'By Jove, Rowan! Since our good friend Cheviot fancies his abilities as a detective policeman, here's his opportunity. Mind you, I mean to see he makes good his boast about the pistol. Meanwhile, here's a test to decide whether he gets what he wants!'

'To be honest,' the Colonel admitted, 'I had much the same idea too.'

Both pairs of eyes were fixed on Cheviot, who slowly bent down and fished up his hat from the floor.

'I see,' he remarked with much politeness. 'Then you wish *me* to investigate this abominable crime?'

'Mr. Cheviot, do you find the matter so very amusing?'

'Frankly, Colonel Rowan, I do. But I have been given far more nonsensical assignments in my time.'

'Indeed,' said the Colonel, breathing hard. 'Indeed!' He waited for a moment. 'Are you acquainted with Lady Cork? Or, to give the lady her proper title, with the Countess of Cork and Orrery?'

'No, sir.'

'Lady Cork is one of our leading society hostesses. She keeps many birds in cages, as pets. There is also the famous macaw which draws out, clips, and smokes a cigar. For the second time in a week, someone has stolen the bird-seed from the containers at the side of a number of bird-cages. Nothing was stolen except bird-seed. But Lady Cork is very angry.'

Colonel Mayne, an undemonstrative man, hesitated.

'We — we are a new institution, we Metropolitan Police. I need not tell you how the mob hate and fear us. If we are to succeed at all, we must have the good-will of the gentry. The Duke himself, as Prime Minister, is not too proud to assist us in this. Are you too proud, Mr. Cheviot?'

'No,' Cheviot answered, and lowered his eyes. 'I understand. And I beg your pardon.'

'Not at all. But we must act at once. Tonight Lady Cork gives a ball for the younger people. As a gentleman, your presence will pass unnoticed. You see the virtue of my method, Mayne?'

'Deuce take it, Rowan, never say *I* objected!' cried Mr. Mayne.

'Mr. Henley had better write you a few lines, signed by both Mayne and myself, to serve as your authority. Henley!'

But the chief clerk had already limped back to his writing-desk, and sat down. Flint-and-steel crunched up a brief yellow-blue flame; a lamp-wick, this time in a green shade, burst up with a loud *pop*. Mr. Henley was mending the nib of a pen.

'Henley, I think, had better accompany you should you wish to take notes. We must ring for horses. Stay, though!' Colonel Rowan's face grew blank and detached. 'Am I correct in assuming that the carriage outside is Lady Drayton's?'

There was no sound in the room except the scratching of the chief clerk's pen.

'You are correct,' Cheviot said. 'May I ask where Lady Cork lives?'

'At number six New Burlington Street. — You accompanied Lady Drayton here?'

'I did.'

'Ah! Doubtless she has a card of invitation to the ball; and you would wish to ride there with her in the carriage?'

'With your permission, yes.'

'By all means.' Colonel Rowan looked away. 'You must consult your own conscience as to what questions you ask her about an opened letter. Now, Henley!'

The chief clerk lumbered up with four lines written in a neat round-hand on half a sheet of foolscap. This he put on the table, together with pen and inkstand. Mr. Mayne and Colonel Rowan hastily scratched their signatures. Mr. Henley sanded the document, folded it up, and gave it to Cheviot.

'Now make haste,' advised Colonel Rowan, 'yet not too quickly! Henley must be there before you, on horseback, to explain matters. One moment!'

John Cheviot felt an inexplicable chill at his

heart. Colonel Rowan's large eyes and thin face swam at him with calm but inflexible authority.

'The affair may seem trifling. But I say again that it is of grave import. You won't fail us, Mr. Cheviot? You will do your best?'

'I will do my best,' said Cheviot, 'to solve the mystery of the missing bird-seed.'

And he bowed satirically, his hat over his heart. His last glimpse was of the polished pistol, shining and evil-seeming on the table under the lamp, as he strode out into a worse nightmare than any of which he had ever dreamed.

3

Carnival by Gaslight

Fully a dozen fiddles, animated by the twang of a harp, sang and dipped and raced in the fast tempo of the dance. Open gas-jets, in their flattish glass bowls, jumped and swayed to the music.

As Flora Drayton's carriage turned into New Burlington Street, a very short and rather narrow lane to the left of Regent Steet, they heard the music even at a distance.

Number six New Burlington Street was a large double-fronted house of dark red brick, with a dingy whitish pillar on either side of the street-door, and window-frames picked out in white. The door was uncompromisingly closed. Yet tremulous gaslight, yellow-blue, shone out on the white mist. It shone out through curtains, tasselled and looped, which were only half closed on every window in the house.

Thump, thump went the feet of the dancers, advancing and retreating. Shadows appeared at the windows on the floor above the street: appeared, grew bloated, then faded and dwindled away. The window-frames rattled to the noise.

'Who-o-a!' softly called the coachman, to restive horses creaking in heavy harness. The horses' hooves clopped, swerved badly, and drew up.

'Flora!'

'Y-yes?'

'That music. That dance. What is it?'

'But, J-Jack, it's only a quadrille. What on earth do you think it is?'

To Cheviot it sounded like an old-fashioned square-dance, which in effect it was. But they carried it at a pace which he, for one, would not have cared to try.

Flora, cowering back in a corner after what she had endured even during that short drive, pressed one hand hard against her breast.

She loved him. Seeing him now, the light-grey eyes, the high forehead with the heavy dark-brown hair, the sardonic-humorous lines from nostril to mouth, it came to her with a stab how deeply and passionately she loved him.

Flora was not possessive; or, at least, not very. Being wise, she did not seek to pry into every mood. Soon, she felt, his conscience would be troubling him as usual; then he would turn to that fierce tenderness which had carried her away from the first. But he mustn't quiz or tease her; he mustn't pretend! That frightened her too much.

And Cheviot himself?

Ever since he had left number four Whitehall Place, stepping out again through the mist and dim gas-gleam towards the carriage with the gilt wheels, he had been wondering what he should say to her. As they turned into New Burlington Street, his mind went back to that scene at Great Scotland Yard.

The coachman in red livery had jumped down and held open the carriage-door. Cheviot had hesitated, hat in hand, on the step.

Flora sat back against claret-coloured cushions, breathing emotion though not looking at him. She was still hatless. Her golden hair, exposing the ears and drawn to such a long sweep at the back, did not seem suited to a hat. But she had drawn the red cashmere shawl round her shoulders. Her hands, now white-gloved to the elbows, were thrust into a large muff of fur dyed in yellow-and-white stripes to match her gown.

'Well!' she breathed, still without looking at him. 'Did you obtain this odious and inferior position for which you so horribly longed?'

'Inferior!' exclaimed Cheviot, still hesitating on the step.

Flora tossed her head.

'Is it not?'

'If I obtain the position, I shall command a force of four inspectors and sixteen sergeants, each sergeant in charge of nine constables.'

'*If* you obtain it?' At last she turned to look at him. 'Then you have not?'

'Not yet. First I am being given a test. Flora, would it trouble you too much if we drove to Lady Cork's? I — I suppose you have a card of invitation?'

Had she opened that letter, or hadn't she?

As a rule Cheviot counted himself a reasonably good judge of human character.

But Flora's whole being, the mock-innocent mouth and mock-innocent blue eyes now wide open, disturbed his senses and upset his reason. Besides, what the devil did it matter whether she had opened the letter or not? Her blush, as she lowered her eyes, was vividly real.

'My reputation is not yet so tarnished,' she retorted in a very low voice, 'that all doors are closed to me. Yes! I have my invitation, and yours too.'

From her muff she drew out two engraved cards, square and very large, much too ornate for his conservative taste; and then put them back again.

'But you swore you wouldn't go,' she

whispered reproachfully, 'because you detest bluestockings. I'm not fond of them myself, I allow. And Lady Cork, goodness knows, was the original bluestocking of all. Jack! Please get in!'

'Mr. Cheviot!' called a heavy voice behind him.

Flora shrank back. Cheviot swung round.

On a skittish, eye-rolling black horse sat Mr. Henley, the chief clerk. But his short, stocky figure bestrode the saddle like a centaur, reins gripped in two fingers of his left hand. His glossy beaverskin hat was stuck on rakishly.

The horse clattered and danced. Mr. Henry restrained it. As more suited to an outdoor excursion, his right hand held a thick cane of knobby wood, as well as the flattish shagreen-covered case for his writing-materials.

He bent down towards Cheviot.

'I'm off,' he said. 'But a word in your ear, sir.'

His brown eyes, ordinarily merry in the broad fleshy face, grew very sombre as he glanced left and right in the mist.

'Look very sharp when you talk to Lady Cork. Ay! And to Miss Margaret Renfrew too. That is, if you do talk to her.'

'And all this,' Cheviot thought rather

40

wildly, 'about stolen bird-seed?'

But the chief clerk, he knew, was no fool. Instinctively subservient, Mr. Henley touched two fingers to his hat. Then the black horse clattered away, spurting mud; past the Admiralty, looming dim and unfamiliar at the other side of the street, at a canter and then at a gallop up Whitehall.

'Jack!' Flora pleaded softly. 'Do get in!' She addressed the motionless coachman in red livery. 'Robert. To Lady Cork's, if you please.'

Cheviot got in. The door closed. The carriage lumbered out to the crack of a whip.

Then she even knew his Christian name. Everybody, at least at the Scotland Yard of his own time, had called him Jack. It was all so fantastic that —

' 'Reputation',' Flora said, almost to herself. 'As though it mattered! Oh, as though I cared one farthing for that! My dear . . . '

And again she was in his arms, in an intoxication which blotted out thought.

Yet other thoughts and emotions, always as palpable as the perfume she wore, stirred in Flora. She moved her head back.

'Jack. Who was that man? The man with the despatch-box?'

'His name is Henley. He's the chief clerk to the Commissioners of Police.'

'Margaret Renfrew — ' Flora began.

'Yes?'

'You are not acquainted with Lady Cork,' said Flora. 'I'm *quite* sure you are not acquainted with Lady Cork. But you may have met Margaret Renfrew. Yes; I daresay you know Margaret Renfrew?'

'Flora, I . . . '

'*You do know her, don't you?*'

Suddenly, to his amazement, Cheviot felt he held a tigress in his arms. A soft tigress, but a tigress all the same. Her small fists beat frantically at his chest. She wrenched and writhed, with surprising strength, to draw away from him.

'Flora!' He was more astounded than angry. '*Flora!*' he shouted.

Instantly she was submissive again. He knew, with this power of sympathy which was like a physical touch, that she was near to tears.

'Listen to me, my dear,' he said gently. 'I had never even heard this woman's name, whoever she is, until Henley mentioned it. One day, soon, I may tell you who I am and what I am. I may tell you where, in a sense, I first saw you; and why your image has been with me for so long.'

He felt, rather than saw, the long-lashed eyes stare at him in bewilderment.

'But I won't tell you now, Flora. I won't

42

frighten you; I could not frighten you for worlds. There is only this. In a place I don't know, amid people I don't know, I have been given an idiot's mystery to solve. And I need your help.'

'Dearest, of course I'll help you! What is it?'

Cheviot told her his mission.

'Oh, yes, it's comic enough!' he said, though Flora did not regard it as at all comic because it concerned him. 'But I see why they think it important. Even a character called 'the Duke,' whoever *he* is, thinks — '

Look out!

Cheviot stopped, just in time, as memory opened and showed him the gulf.

'The Duke,' of course, was Prime Minister the Duke of Wellington. Though sixty years old, he was still spry enough to fight a pistol-duel with Lord Winchilsea in March of this year.

('Now, then, Hardinge,' he had said to his second, 'look sharp and step out the ground. I have no time to waste. Damn it! don't stick him up so near the ditch. If I hit him, he'll tumble in.')

Those gruff words seemed to echo in the night. The Duke, frosty-headed and beakier than ever, was very much alive and growling at Apsley House. He loomed into reality, dragging his whole century with him, as the carriage rattled and bumped. Sir George Murray held the Colonial Office; Lord Aberdeen was Secretary for Foreign Affairs. Mr. Robert Peel, above all, was Home Secretary.

John Cheviot's slip had gone unnoticed. Flora was fascinated, deeply fascinated, as is any woman whose aid has been sought in a puzzling question.

'But why . . . ?' she was persisting.

'Why bird-seed? I can't tell. Nothing else was stolen. Are you well acquainted with Lady Cork?'

'Very well. *Awfully* well!'

'H'm. Is she in any way (how shall I say it?) — is she in any way eccentric?'

'No worse than many others. She's very old, to be sure; she must be well past eighty. And she has crotchets. She'll tell you for the hundredth time what Dr. Johnson said to her when she was a girl, and what she said to him. She'll tell you how poor Boswell got fearfully lushy with Lord Graham, and staggered to one of her mother's parties, and made the most indecent remarks about ladies; and afterwards was so ashamed of himself he wrote her a set of verses in apology, and she still keeps them in a sandalwood box.'

'True, true!' exclaimed Cheviot, who was

remembering his Boswell's *Life*. 'Wasn't Lady Cork originally a Miss Maria Monckton?'

'Yes! — Jack!'

'My dear?'

'Why must you pretend you never even heard of her, when you have? And become as tensed and nervous as though — as though you were going to an execution?'

'Your pardon, Flora. Does Lady Cork ever keep large sums of money in the house?'

Flora drew still farther back from him.

'Mercy on us, no! Why should she? Why should anyone, for that matter?'

'Has she jewels?'

'Some few, I think. But they are always kept in a big iron box in her boudoir, the pink boudoir; and she alone has a key to the box. What has this to do with . . . ?'

'Stop, stop! Let me think! Do you know her maid?'

'Really, Jack! One does not know one's friends' maids!'

But Cheviot's gaze remained steadily on her, while he drummed his fingers on his knee; and Flora relented.

'It is true,' she answered, with a lift of her rounded chin, 'I have some acquaintance with Solange. Yes, her maid! Solange, which is often embarrassing, positively adores me.'

'Good, good! That will be useful. Finally,

has Lady Cork relations? Children? Nieces or nephews? Close friends?'

'Her husband,' said Flora, 'has been dead more than thirty years. Her children have grown up and gone.' Impulsively the warm-hearted Flora seized his arm. 'Don't laugh at her,' Flora pleaded gently. 'Most hostesses, I know, make sport of her loud voice and old-fashioned ways. But who else would have the good-nature to give a ball for the younger people, when she prefers tea and conversation about books? They'll only smash her china and stain her carpets and break her furniture. Don't laugh at her, Jack; pray don't.'

'I promise you I won't, Flora. I — '

More than once, on that drive, he had glanced searchingly out of the window. Now, for some time, they had been driving uphill on what seemed a broader road much better paved.

Cheviot bent away from her side. Letting down the offside window with a bang and bump, he thrust out his head. Then he was back again, putting his arm round Flora's shoulder.

'Come!' he said, as though carelessly. 'I knew there wouldn't yet be a Trafalgar Square, or a Nelson Monument, or a National Gallery. But, my God, where are we now? What's this?'

'Darling! It's only Regent Street!'

'Regent Street.' Cheviot pressed his hands to his forehead, and became casual. 'Ah, yes. They've — they've finished it?'

That was the point at which the carriage swung sharply to the left, into New Burlington Street off Upper Regent Street. That was the point at which he saw gaslight streaming out through windows only half-curtained up four floors to the dormers.

He heard fiddle-music sawing and jigging in a rapid whirl. He asked what the dance was. At long last Flora cowered back into the corner, terrified and uncertain. And, as the carriage stopped, Cheviot soundlessly cursed himself.

Before anyone else, he was certain, he could control his speech. But Flora's presence seemed so intimate, so familiar, in some way so right (why?), that he spoke to her and did not stop to think. Without her he was lost.

'Flora,' he said, swallowing hard, 'hear me again. I promised not to frighten you. I seem to have done little else.' Then all the sincerity, all the earnestness of which his dogged nature was capable, rang in his voice. 'But that, so help me, is because you don't yet understand. When I explain, as I've got to, you'll understand and I think you'll sympathize.

Until then, my dear, can you possibly forgive me? Can you?'

Flora's expression altered as she looked at him. Hesitantly her hand stole out. Then he seized her, kissing her mouth hard, while the shadows of dancers grew and dwindled on the mist above them.

'Can you?' he demanded presently. 'Forgive me, I mean?'

'Forgive?' she stammered in astonishment. 'Oh, Jack, what is there to forgive? But don't be a quiz. Please! I can't endure it.'

Then he became aware of the patient coachman, waiting outside to open the door, and he released her.

Flora, too, played her part. She gave little touches to her hair, little touches to her gown, as though she were alone in the carriage. But her cheeks were pink, her eyelids lowered, as Cheviot jumped down and handed her out. Flora slipped the two cards of invitation into his hand.

'You're not in evening-dress,' she murmured, rather reproachfully. 'But — there! Many gentlemen drink so much, before they go to a ball, that they forget to change.'

'Then it won't signify if *I* act a little drunk?'

'Jack!' There was a curious new note in her voice.

'Well, I only wondered.'

Actually, he had been wondering how any intoxicated gentleman could carry a square-dance at that pace without taking a header and landing on his ear. The front door of number six remained uncompromisingly closed, despite the runner of red carpet across the pavement.

But their arrival had not gone unobserved. As he and Flora went up one step, between the dingy pillars and the line of area-railings, the door was opened by a footman in orange-and-green livery. And, stupefying, another blast of noise smote out at them.

They entered a rather narrow foyer, though with eighteenth-century panels painted by some imitator of Watteau or Boucher; a waxed and polished floor; and a rather fine staircase, under ugly carpeting, against the right-hand wall.

Out of the foyer, left and right, doors opened on big empty rooms tonight laid out for a lavish buffet-supper. The noise came not alone from the music and the stamp of dancing, which made the ceiling shake and the gas-jet chandelier rattle. From somewhere invisible, probably a back parlour with a punch-bowl, more than a dozen male voices roared out in song.

A frog he would a-wo-o-o-ing go,
'Heigh-ho!' says Rooow-ley!
Whether his lady would have him or no,
Whether his lady would have him or no,
With a roly-poly, gammon, and spin-
    ach — !
'Heigh-ho!' says Anthony Rowley!

'Ho!' shouted the owners of all the voices at once, and wildly began applauding themselves. A cork popped. Somebody smashed a glass.

Flora handed her cashmere shawl to the impassive footman; though, rather to Cheviot's surprise, she retained the large fur muff. She attempted to say, 'We're awfully late,' but stopped in the uproar. In any case, Cheviot might not have heard her.

He had again, as usual, become the police-officer. He had a job to do. It didn't matter in what strange age this occurred. He had a job to do; he would see it through, though he must make his speech sound like theirs or be betrayed in ten minutes.

To the footman he handed his hat and the invitation-cards.

'I — ' he began.

Abruptly the uproar ceased. With a flourish the fiddles and harp made an end, despite cries of protest. Overhead, footfalls merely shuffled. The singers in the back-parlour were silent. Only a few voices, beginning at a yell and then sinking to normal, set up a vague murmur. You were conscious of the odour of coal-gas; of a damp, stuffy smell even in this rich foyer.

'I am not here,' Cheviot said to the footman, 'altogether for the ball. Be good enough to take me to Lady Cork.'

The footman, in orange-and-green livery, eyed him with very faint insolence.

'I am afraid, sir, that her ladyship . . . '

Cheviot, who had been looking for bird-cages and seeing none, wheeled round.

'Take me to Lady Cork,' he said.

To do him justice, he had no notion of the air of power and authority he carried as he stared the footman in the eyes. The footman moistened his lips.

'Very good, sir. I will tell — '

Then, simultaneously, two things happened.

Out from under the staircase, where he had been put away to sit on a chair away from notice, emerged Alan Henley, with his knobbed cane in one hand and his case of writing-materials in the other.

And, at the same time, a slender woman in a white gown came slowly down the stairs.

'The matter has been arranged,' said the

woman in a husky contralto voice. 'Good evening, Mr. Cheviot.'

Flora, who had been pulling and adjusting her elbow-length gloves so as to take only one hand at a time out of her muff, did not turn round. An expression of utter indifference went over her face. She spoke without moving her lips, in a whisper which Cheviot only just heard.

Yet Flora, who in his estimation could conceal so little, did not try to conceal her bitter, intense scorn and dislike.

'There's your precious Miss Renfrew,' she said.

4

The Woman on the Stairs

Yes, Margaret Renfrew was beautiful. Or almost so.

She was a dark brunette, in contrast to a very fair complexion. There were half a dozen hair-styles fashionable in this year, as Cheviot was to learn. Miss Renfrew wore her hair in thick, glossy ringlets, just below ear-length, and parted in the middle. The fair complexion was perfect, with a tinge of red colour in the cheeks. Her eyebrows were straight and dark, above eyes almost too vivid a dark grey; the nose a trifle long, with wide nostrils, but redeemed by the chin and mouth, whose lips gleamed dark and glossy red.

She smiled, a very little. Straight-backed she moved down the stairs, one white-gloved hand on the banister-rail. Her white, low-cut gown, tight at the waist but wide of skirt like Flora's, carried across its bodice a design of vivid red roses edged out with black.

That almost-beauty shone with its own power in the hot foyer, under fluttery gas-jets. And yet — Cheviot couldn't for the life of him understand or analyze why — there was about it something wrong, something inharmonious or savage, almost repulsive.

Margaret Renfrew reached the foot of the stairs. Her husky voice rang out again.

'Ah. Lady Drayton.' And she dropped Flora a deep curtsey.

Even Cheviot could see it was too deep a curtsey. It was sarcastic, defiant. Flora, who had turned round, inclined her head coldly.

Observed close at hand, Miss Renfrew's gown was an old one, though carefully cleaned and mended. But she flaunted it, seemed proud of the fact, taunted you with it.

'Forgive my boldness,' she said to Cheviot, with an edge of satire on the final word, 'in presenting myself to you. But I have seen you ride in the park; I am not unaware of your accomplishments, sir. Permit me: I am Margaret Renfrew.'

This time she made a real curtsey. Under the straight dark brows her vivid eyes studied Cheviot and found him favourable. In the next second the eyes hardened and grew opaque.

Cheviot bowed in reply.

That word 'accomplishments' brushed his mind with dread. Back flashed Colonel Rowan's words, 'Noted as a pistol-shot, wrestler, and singlestick-player.'

He had a silver cup to prove he had been the best revolver-shot in the Metropolitan Police. How he might fare with an unrifled muzzle-loader, whose bullets were seldom perfectly moulded, might be another matter. He knew nothing of wrestling, except insofar as they had taught him judo. He was not even sure what a singlestick might be. No matter, no matter!

'Your servant, Miss Renfrew. I have had the pleasure of seeing you too,' he lied with the best possible grace. 'You are related to Lady Cork, I take it?'

Margaret Renfrew's voice went high.

'Related? Alas! I am only the daughter of one of her old friends. I am merely a courtesy poor-relation, sir. I exist by Lady Cork's bounty.'

'As a companion, no doubt.'

'What is a companion?' asked the woman, with extraordinary intensity. 'I have never learned. You must define it for me, one day.'

The rose-painted bodice of her gown rose and fell. Confound the woman! What *was* the meaning in that air of lurking mystery, of fierce repression, of mingled shame and pride? Miss Renfrew dragged away her eyes from him, and glanced at Mr. Henley.

'This — this gentleman,' she added with a flick of the glossy dark curls, 'has told us to expect you as Colonel Rowan's representative. Very well; so be it! Follow me, if you will.'

Her skirts swirled as she turned towards the stairs. Whereupon, with a combined whoop, the foyer was invaded.

Half a dozen young men in evening dress, together with a scarlet-coated young Guards officer moustached as well as side-whiskered, raced and reeled out from the back-parlour in a fuming aroma of brandy-punch. Their tight-fitting black tail-coats, and very tight-fitting black trousers, against the white of frilled shirt or waistcoat, made them all appear horribly thin, spindly, unreal, like caricatures.

But they were not caricatures at all.

'Jack, old fellow!' cried a hearty voice Cheviot had never before heard.

His hand was wrung, in an equally hearty grip, by a flushed young man who could not have been more than twenty-one or twenty-two. The newcomer's snub nose, wide mouth, and blurred eyes were encircled in bright-brown hair and whiskers, rather like those of Mr. Richard Mayne.

'Freddie!' exclaimed Flora with real pleasure, and extended her left hand.

'Flora! D'lighted!' cried the young man called Freddie. He bent over her hand, making passionate gobbling noises like 'M-mm-m!' as he kissed her glove, and straightened up with a graceful stagger.

'By Jove!' he added with enthusiasm. 'Must be — what? Fortnight? Yes! Fortnight at least, b'Jove, since I saw either of you.' He waggled a white-gloved finger at Cheviot, and laughed uproariously. 'Sly dog, sly dog! Nem'mind. Envy you. I say,' he pointed upwards. 'Dance?'

'Not at the moment, Freddie.' Cheviot forced out the name. 'The fact is — '

'The fact is,' he was thinking, 'that a man who begins asking himself 'Who am I? What am I?' is already on his way to a strait-jacket.'

Fortunately or unfortunately, such morbidities were swept away. The young Guards officer, with the single epaulette of a captain, and a red stripe down his thin black trousers, lifted his chin to intervene.

'Weally!' he said in a languid, bored, high-pitched voice, with a definite lisp. 'I twust one *can* weach the ballwoom to dance?'

The languid one was thin, but tall and powerful. Suddenly seizing one of his companions by the frilled shirt-front, he flung him aside and sauntered forward.

Cheviot saw him coming, and all his hackles rose. He set his shoulders and braced himself. The Guards officer, who could not be troubled to alter his course for anyone, cannoned straight into him — and bounced off as though he had struck a rock.

Freddie yelled with delight. The Guards officer did not.

'Weally?' he said again, in a loud but even more bored voice. 'Why don't you look where you're going, fellow? Who are you, fellow?'

Cheviot ignored him.

Margaret Renfrew had now gone four steps up the stairs, and was studying Cheviot sideways past her curls. He addressed her.

'If you will lead the way, Miss Renfrew?'

'I spoke to you, fellow!' snapped the Guards officer, and seized Cheviot's left arm.

'I didn't speak to you,' said Cheviot, whirling round and flinging off the other's hand. 'I hope it won't be necessary.'

Captain Hogben's long face, behind the black feathery moustache and whiskers, went as scarlet as his coat. Then it grew mottled-pale.

'By God!' he whispered, beginning to swing back a white-gloved right hand. 'By God!'

Immediately, with a shout of laughter, four of his friends fastened on him and dragged him, writhing and struggling, up the stairs.

'Keep your temper, Hogben!'

'Wouldn't call out the best shot in town. Now would you, Hogben?'

'Isabelle's waiting for you, Hogben! She's pinin' and dyin' for you, Hell-fire!'

The scrimmage bumped the wall past Miss Renfrew, who shrank back in fury; it staggered again, and pushed on up the stairs. Cheviot caught one glimpse of the Guards officer's face, long and malevolent, with the feathery black hair waving above, as the face was thrust out.

'I'll wemember this,' it said.

The young man called Freddie, after a broad beaming wink at Flora and Cheviot, scrambled after them. The tails of their tight-waisted coats flew out as they whooped after their quarry. In an instant they were gone.

Margaret Renfrew lifted one shoulder.

'What puppies they are,' she said without inflection. Then, with great intensity: 'How little amusement they provide! Give me an older man, with experience.'

Now she would not look at Cheviot. Her gaze, curious and cryptic, appeared to be fixed at a point past his shoulder. Afterwards she turned round, and delicately marched up the stairs.

Flora, if she felt any anger at all, did not show it. Flora was only disturbed, nervous, even frightened, as she went up with Cheviot at her side.

'You'll never be warned,' she said in a low voice. 'But I beg you to be warned of one thing!'

'Oh?'

'Don't quarrel with Captain Hogben; pray don't!'

'Indeed.'

'Don't vex him or trifle with him. He's notorious for not playing fair; I abhor to say it, but you'll be hurt!'

'How you terrify me.'

'Jack!'

'I said nothing except, 'how you terrify me.' '

Flora wrung her hands inside the fur muff. 'And — and you weren't very cordial to poor Freddie Debbitt, either.'

Cheviot stopped nearly at the top of the stairs. Once more he pressed his hands hard to his forehead. But his voice was little louder than hers.

'Flora, how many times must I ask your pardon? I am not myself this night.'

'And do you imagine I don't know that? I am trying but to help you!' She was silent again, timid after that soft outburst. Her thoughts seemed to dart away.

'Freddie hasn't a penny, poor fellow, even if he is Lord Lowestoft's son. But he admires you tremendously; that's why I like him. He may upset Lady Cork with his mimicking and his tales . . . '

'Tales? What tales?'

'Oh, only vapourings! About thieves, since you're so concerned with this wretched bird-seed.'

'What about thieves, Flora? Tell me!'

'Oh, that someone might steal Lady Cork's adored macaw, the macaw that smokes cigars, and carry it away perch and all. Or that he wouldn't trouble to break the lock of her strongbox; he'd fetch away the whole strong-box.'

'So!' muttered Cheviot, and snapped his fingers. 'So!'

They had come to the top of the stairs; they were in a broad passage, well illuminated. He broke off to study it with interest.

It was decorated after the Chinese fashion, much admired forty years before, now a trifle musty. The wall panels, of black lacquer thinly patterned in gold dragons, glistened under the light of oil-lamps with fringed silk shades and painted but hollow porcelain bases. These lamps stood on small, low, black teakwood tables, with a carved teakwood chair between each, down both sides of the walls.

Midway down the wall on his left, as Cheviot faced the rear of the passage, he saw closed double-doors painted a brilliant orange with gold arabesques. These led to the ballroom; beyond he could hear a murmur of voices, the *plunk* of tuning fiddles.

All the doors, in fact, were painted orange with gold twinings. They stood out against the black-lacquer walls. A second set of double-doors, also closed, was at the end of the passage. In the right-hand wall were two more single doors set wide apart. The modern, dull-flowered carpet was stained with footmarks in mud and dust.

'Mr. Cheviot!'

But Cheviot was examining the bird-cages.

'Mr. Cheviot!' repeated Miss Renfrew, who had reached the double-doors at the end of the passage facing him.

There were eight bird-cages, four hanging from the ceiling on each side above the teakwood chairs against the walls. Each cage contained a canary, all restless, sometimes trilling song. Each case, gilded, was very large. He had hoped for that.

He reached up and detached the white china seed-container from one cage. It was correspondingly large. The cage swung; the canary squawked and fluttered up; and Cheviot, as he gently replaced the seed-container, saw out of the corner of his eye that Margaret Renfrew was gripping her hands together hard.

'Is it quite kind,' she called, 'to keep Lady Cork waiting?'

Then, unexpectedly, Flora spoke out.

'I'm sure, Miss Renfrew,' she said in a clear voice, 'Lady Cork won't mind if *I* detain Mr. Cheviot for one moment more?'

'You usually detain him, don't you? Still! On this occasion?'

'Oh, most particularly on this occasion!'

'Lady Cork's affairs, you know, are *rather* important.'

'I'm sure they are,' Flora agreed sweetly. 'So are mine. Exactly one minute, then?'

Cheviot, about to protest, swung round and for the first time saw Flora in a bright light.

She was taller than he had imagined; taller, more fully developed of figure. Perhaps he had imagined her as very small, in the carriage, because of her soft voice and small hands. The light shone on the smooth, glowing skin of her face and shoulders. There was a provocative smile on her mouth. Her appearance took his breath away.

At the same moment the double-doors behind Miss Renfrew, doors plainly leading to Lady Cork's boudoir, opened and closed softly.

Out slipped an olive-skinned girl of

eighteen or nineteen. Her lace cap covered her ears; her long apron was of lace. She was pretty, with those shining brown eyes which often seem black, and are at all times expressive.

To Margaret Renfrew the girl murmured, 'Beg-pardon-miss.' Then she hastened towards the stairs at the front of the passage. On the way she dipped a curtsey to Flora, with a furtive and sidelong glance of sheer adoration.

'Mr. Cheviot!' said Miss Renfrew. 'Don't you think, after all — ?'

'Madam!' interrupted a portentous voice.

Cheviot had completely forgotten Mr. Henley, who had followed them upstairs. But he was glad of that stocky, sturdy presence.

'By your leave, madam,' the chief clerk went on, addressing Miss Renfrew and hobbling towards her, '*I'll* take the liberty of going in first. Mr. Cheviot won't be long, I promise.'

'As you please, then.'

She opened one side of the door and marched in. Mr. Henley, after a brief, appealing glare from between his red side-whiskers, followed her and closed the door. Cheviot was alone with Flora in the gaudy, painted passage.

'What is it?' he asked. 'Have you something to tell me?'

Flora tossed her head, shrugged her shoulders, and would not meet his eyes.

'We-el!' she murmured. 'If it isn't asking too much, and you could spare me one dance . . . ?'

'Dance? Is that all?'

'All?' echoed Flora, opening her eyes wide. 'All?'

'I can't, Flora! I'm on duty!'

He said this. But he couldn't resist her, and very well she knew it. And, because of this very reason, it seemed that her heart melted and she would not press him too far.

'No,' she said, yielding with a wry-mouthed smile, 'I suppose this dreadful police business must come first. Anyway the next dance will be a waltz, and some people still think the waltz is improper. Very well! In that event I shall sit down here,' and she did so, gracefully and languorously, in one of the black chairs, 'to wait until you've had done.'

'But you can't wait here!'

'Why ever not? I daren't go into the ballroom; they'd think me unescorted! Why mustn't I wait here?'

'Because . . . well, I don't know! But you mustn't!' With a violent effort Cheviot regained his emotional balance. 'However! If you still wish to help me — ?'

Instantly Flora straightened up eagerly.

65

'Yes, yes! Anything!'

'That dark-eyed girl in the lace cap. The one who passed through here a moment ago. Am I right in thinking she's Lady Cork's maid? What did you call her? Solange?'

'Yes. What of her?'

'This is what I want you to do.'

He gave brief, concise instructions. Flora leaped to her feet.

'Oh, I'll do it,' she agreed, after biting at her lip. 'Though it's so — so embarrassing!'

'Why on earth should it be embarrassing?'

'No matter.' Her eyes, dark-blue and with a luminous quality under the lamp-glow, searched his face. 'You seek something, don't you? You find it suspect, don't you?'

'Yes.'

'What is it? Who is it?'

'I can't tell. Not yet. I'm not even sure I've grasped the right thread. I must get round this dragon of a hostess; and there's little time.' His memory brought back the image of the cold supper set out downstairs. 'Flora! Does Lady Cork customarily join her guests at supper?'

'Yes, of course. Always!'

'At what time will they take supper?'

'At midnight, to be sure.' She was regarding him curiously. 'Then (as surely you know?) they'll dance until one or two in the morning. We're — awfully late, as I said. They did not even offer me a dance-programme, which I thought most ill-mannered. What's the time now?'

Automatically, without thinking, Cheviot thrust out his left arm, pulling back the sleeve to consult his wrist-watch. No wrist-watch was there. Flora stared at him still more strangely.

He dived down for the heavy weight in his left-hand waistcoat pocket. The watch was a thick gold repeater, double-cased. However his finger-tips pried and probed, the case wouldn't open to show the dial.

'Jack!' She spoke in a low voice, but with sudden terror. 'Can't you even open your own watch?'

If it had not been for her disturbing presence, he would never have made that blunder at all. He pressed down the watch-stem; the lid flew open.

'It's twenty-five minutes to midnight,' he said, and cleared his throat.

'Oh, God,' Flora whispered, as though praying.

She had shrunk away from him, both in body and spirit. Mentally he touched mist.

'At first,' said Flora, breathing hard, 'I thought you joked. You haven't been — it can't be — after all you promised — !'

Then she fled from him. She ran lightly down the passage, over the dull-flowered carpet, between the black-lacquer walls and gold dragons, towards the staircase Solange had descended.

'Flora! What have I done?'

There was no reply. She had gone.

Cheviot shut up the watch with a snap, conscious of the weight of watch-chain and seals as he put it into his pocket. He was sweating badly.

He wished, even prayed, he could understand the emotional undercurrents which accompanied every word spoken tonight in this house. They were there; he could feel if not interpret them. They might be an undertow to sweep him away. And yet —

'This won't do!' he said aloud, and straightened up.

He knocked sharply at the double-doors. He could not foresee that, partly because of his own words and actions that night, within twenty minutes there would be murder.

5

The Waltz Played Murder

'Come in!' called a gruff voice.

Cheviot turned the knob and pushed open one side of the door.

He was greeted by so appalling and inhuman a screech, a screech like 'Ha-ha-ha,' that for a second he thought it must have been uttered by the very old woman who sat by a fireplace at the opposite side of the room, her hand on a crutch-headed stick.

She was short, thick-bodied rather than fat, with almost no neck. Her white cap, whose frills stuck straight up above a big head, crowned straggling grey-white hair. Her gown was white too. And yet, despite age, her skin was fair and retained some outline of a face which had once been pretty. Her little eyes were fixed on Cheviot with cunning and expectancy.

'Well, well, shut the door,' she said in a loud voice.

Cheviot closed it behind him.

Just across the fireplace from her, like the beloved companion it was, a large red-and-green macaw stood on a wooden perch. The macaw was not caged; it was held to the perch by a thin chain round one leg. In its head, a colour between mauve and white, rolled a wicked eye. It fluttered its feathers, scraped its claws on the perch like a man cleaning his shoes on a doormat, and threw back its beak to utter the same inhuman screech Cheviot had already heard.

The latter felt his flesh crawl.

'Lady Cork, I imagine?'

'Imagine? God's body! Don't ye *know*?'

'I am a police-officer, Lady Cork — '

'Hey? What's a p'leece-officer?'

' — and I am here to ask a few — '

'What's this?' demanded Lady Cork. 'And from George Cheviot's son too? No pretty compliments? Not a word of how well or handsome I am for my years? Where's manners these days?'

Cheviot pulled himself together, controlling his temper.

Lady Cork might sit in a room crammed with tables and consoles of tortoise-shell or ormolu, with spindly chairs and china vases. The pink walls might be covered with the paintings, the miniatures in gold or silver frames, of the year 1829. But she herself was as much of the eighteenth century as though her thick white gown smelled of it.

He must find not only the proper attack,

but precisely the right words too.

'And yet, madam,' he smiled, 'I had never heard that the late Dr. Sam Johnson paid you pretty compliments at your first meeting.'

Lady Cork, who had opened her mouth, kept it open without speaking.

'Indeed, as I have read, he named you a dunce. But he also called you 'dearest'; and, some time afterwards, made handsome apology for calling you dunce. May I, madam, offer both compliment and apology at our first meeting rather than our second?'

There was a pause. Lady Cork was startled, but not at all displeased. She stared at him, mouth open. Then, instantly, her whole speech and manner changed.

'It gives me much pleasure, sir,' she intoned, rearing up with real dignity, 'to entertain a gentleman who at times beguiles his leisure with books rather than at cards or dice. You speak a compliment the better for speaking it backwards, like a wizard.'

'No wizard, madam, I beg! To the contrary, I would quote Mr. Boswell's lines to you, 'While I invoke the powers above, that I may better live'.'

'Ecod!' cried Lady Cork. 'Ecod!'

('Oh, lord,' Cheviot thought desperately, 'what a ruddy fool of myself I'm making!')

He thought so the more because Margaret

71

Renfrew, who was standing at the left of the marble mantelpiece, her elbow leaning on the edge of it, watched him with ironic eyes.

Some distance back, as befitted a clerk, Mr. Henley sat unhappily at his writing-case, pen poised above a sheet on which he had written no word. But Cheviot's tactics had been admirable.

'My dear young man,' Lady Cork said cordially, 'sit down! Pray sit down! Do sit down, there's a dear!'

She was beaming all over her face, as lively and animated as a girl.

With her crutch-headed stick she pointed to a broad-backed, padded chair not far from the macaw's perch. The macaw, alive with evil, scraped its claws on the perch and made bubbling noises. Cheviot eyed it with as little favour as the macaw eyed him.

'Tush, have no fear!' scoffed Lady Cork. '*He* won't fly at you, poor fellow, since I've had him chained. He has committed but one crime in his whole life.'

'I rejoice to hear it.'

'It is true he made a bit of an assault on the King's stocking. But that was an *offence* merely,' Lady Cork pointed out with severity. 'The crime was running away with a piece of Lady Darlington's leg.'

Nobody smiled, though she seemed to

expect it. Evidently her words reminded her of Cheviot's errand. Though the short, squat figure reared up with immense dignity in the chair, Lady Cork looked uncertain and even uneasy.

'H'm. You've been told, I apprehend, of our — trifling problem here?'

Cheviot sat down.

'It may not be so trifling as you think,' he said.

A queer, cold little stir went through the room. Lady Cork poked with her stick at the very small fire in the grate.

'I have heard everything,' Cheviot went on, 'except of the place from which the bird-seed was taken. From the kitchen, perhaps? The pantry? The scullery?'

'No, no, no!' said Lady Cork. Beginning to point, she found no bird-cage in the boudoir. 'From the thingumbobs. You know. The things that hold the seed on the side of the cages.'

'Yes. I had supposed so. But we must make certain and not guess. Madam, how many bird-cages are there in the house?'

'Well, there's four parrots in me bedroom there.'

Lady Cork pointed towards another door in the boudoir, well apart from the double-doors. If Cheviot had been just entering by the double-doors, this second door would have been on his right. Therefore her bedroom was one of the rooms opening on the passage outside.

'Four parrots!' she said with emphasis. 'There's six more cages, birds all different but almighty exotic and wonderful, in the dining room beyond me bedroom. And eight canaries, as you must ha' seen, in the passage. That's all.'

Twice more the stick jabbed. That, then, accounted for every room on this floor; the ballroom contained none.

'Sir!' hissed Mr. Henley's sibilant whisper from behind. 'Do you want me to put this down in shorthand?'

Cheviot nodded with decision, seeming only to nod at Lady Cork.

'The seed-containers, I understand, were — were attacked twice?'

'Ay! Once on Tuesday, that's three nights ago; again on Thursday, that's last night. Emptied out as clean as a hound's tooth, not a bit o' seed dropped on the floor, and in the middle of the night too.'

'Thank you, madam. Then all eighteen bird-cages were robbed?'

'No, no, no, no!' Lady Cork eyed him with a slight change of manner. 'Only five in all. Four on Tuesday night, in me very bedroom

74

where I was sleeping. One canary cage last night, in the passage out there. That's not much, you say? But it made me mad. God's body, it made me mad!'

'Aunt Maria — !' began Miss Renfrew as though in protest.

'You be silent, m'gel!'

Cheviot remained unruffled.

'May I ask, madam, whether any person in particular attends on the cages? Cleans them, and so on?'

Lady Cork looked pleased and proud, her white frilled cap waggling.

'You may, and there is. Ay! Jubilo!'

'I beg your pardon?'

'Jubilo! Black boy,' explained Lady Cork, holding her hand about four feet up from the floor. 'Me personal servant, special green livery, and cap with black plumes. Lady Holland, or Lady Charleville either,' she added, with a majestic sneer as she mentioned London's other two leading society hostesses, 'can't match him, I'll be bound!'

'No doubt, madam. I believe you never keep money in the house?'

'Money? Money? Down with the Rich!' shouted the wealthy Lady Cork, who was a radical Whig. She hammered her stick on the floor. 'If they put up a Reform Bill, I'll hang flags out of the windows to cheer 'em. Ecod I will!'

'But you do keep jewels — Madam, may I see the strong-box?'

Lady Cork, eighty-four years old, did not hesitate.

She rose up from the chair, and bustled across the room with great animation. From inside the neck of her gown she drew out a string on which hung two keys.

With one key she unlocked a Boule cabinet, and opened it. From a shelf inside she took out the strong-box. Though it was not large, and seemed to be made of ivory, it was lined with iron. She lifted it out and plumped it down on the top of the cabinet, pushing a blue vase to one side.

Cheviot hurried after her.

She unlocked the box and opened the lid.

'There!' she announced, and bustled back to her chair as though dusting her hands of an unpleasant duty.

'My most humble thanks, madam.'

Hitherto there had been hardly a sound except the scratching of Mr. Henley's pen, or an occasional click as he dipped the pen too deeply into the ink-pot. Lady Cork was oblivious to this. But Margaret Renfrew glanced at him several times, shaking back her glossy ringlets. Now the pen stopped.

Cheviot could hear his watch ticking in his pocket. Time, time, time!

The box was not filled or even heavily lined. Except for a tiara and a number of bracelets, most of the pieces were small despite their large value in rubies, emeralds, and especially diamonds. There were rings, pendants, a tiny diamond-crusted watch. He counted them, setting out each on the cabinet as he did so.

Then, in the midst of a silence stretching out unendurably, out smote the music of a waltz from the ballroom.

He would never have believed that fiddles and a harp could make so much noise, or that the one-two-three beat of a waltz could go so fast. With joyous cries the dancers flung themselves into it. He could picture them dipping, swaying, whirling like lunatics across a waxed floor.

But Cheviot, as well as his three companions, heard the soft insistent knocking at the double-doors to the passage.

'Forgive me,' he said politely.

He hastened across to the doors, over the thick carpet, and opened one door only a dozen inches.

Outside stood Flora. She would not or at least did not look at him. But her hand (the left hand in a glove, he noted vaguely) thrust out a folded piece of paper.

He took the paper, closed the door, and went back to the cabinet. Jewel colours burnt in a shifting glitter under the low light, reflected back from pink walls crowded with pictures. Opening the paper, he ran his eye slowly down what was written there.

'Well?' demanded Lady Cork from her chair. 'What's to do now?'

Since Mr. Henley was craning round against one high point of his collar, Cheviot made a sign for him to continue the shorthand.

Smiling, he sauntered back towards his chair.

'Lady Cork,' he said, 'I count thirty-five pieces of jewellery there. And yet, according to my information, there should be forty. Where are the other five?'

'Why, as to that — ' She stopped.

'Come, madam!' He spoke in that persuasive manner he had used so often. 'Wouldn't it be better to tell me the truth?'

The loud waltz-music rose and fell.

'Where'd you get that bit o' paper?'

'Information received, madam. The other five jewels have been stolen, have they not?'

'Ha, ha, ha,' screeched the macaw, and danced and rattled and flapped its wings all over the perch. From the corner of his eye

Cheviot saw that Margaret Renfrew had drawn herself up straight. Her shining red mouth (lip-salve?) was open as though in amazement.

'Are you accusing me,' asked Lady Cork, loudly but without inflection, 'of stealing me own gewgaws?'

'Not of stealing them, madam. Merely of hiding them.'

'Freddie Debbitt said — !'

'Yes. Freddie Debbitt seems to have said many things. Among them, doubtless with mimicry and gesture to alarm you, that a thief would spirit away your whole strong-box. In our experience, Lady Cork — '

'Whose experience?'

' — a woman's natural instinct is to hide things of value, and hide them close at hand, if she thinks them in danger. This is especially so if the things have a great sentimental value too.'

Cheviot still spoke gently, softly, persuasively.

'I can hardly think of a better place to hide rings, brooches, any small pieces of jewellery,' he went on, 'than in the seed containers of bird cages. It does credit to your wit. Who will suspect it? Or, if suspected, the detaching of a container from the side of a covered cage at night may set up a flutter and cry to betray the thief. And so you hid your most valued trinkets. Do I speak the truth?'

'Yes!' said Lady Cork.

It was those words 'sentimental value' which had stabbed her. She twisted round her very short neck and stared at the fire. Grotesquely, from under her wrinkled eyelids, two tears squeezed out and ran down her cheeks.

'From me husband,' she said to the fire, choking a little. 'Ay! And from another man, dead these sixty years.'

The swell of the waltz-music seemed to beat against Cheviot's brain.

'I must remind you,' he said softly, 'that these jewels were stolen. The thief has not yet been found.'

Lady Cork nodded without looking round.

'Aunt Maria,' interposed Miss Renfrew, in a voice of deep compassion, 'they will be found. Don't fear. In the meantime, it is near midnight. Your guests must be advised of supper. Have I your leave to go?'

Again Lady Cork nodded, violently, without turning round. The old, squat shoulders were trembling.

Miss Renfrew, in her white gown with the black-edged roses round the bodice, slipped away by the door to the bedroom rather than the double-doors. Cheviot watched her, began to speak, and changed his mind.

'Lady Cork, I can't and I won't distress you too much. But why didn't you say the jewels had been stolen? Why did you conceal it?'

'And have 'em all laugh at me again? As they always do?'

'Yes. I see.'

'The man who can laugh at you, your ladyship,' suddenly interrupted Mr. Henley, with suppressed violence, 'shall answer to me. By God, he shall!'

This roused her. She turned her head, giving Mr. Henley a singularly gracious smile. But, to conceal the fact that she was openly crying, she glared at Cheviot.

'Now, who'd ha' thought,' she almost sneered, with more tears streaming down, 'that George Cheviot's son would have had the wit to fathom *this*?'

'It's my job, madam.'

'Your what?'

'My work, I should have said. May I venture a further question?'

'Ye may.'

'On Tuesday night, as an experiment, you hid four treasures in the seed-containers of the parrots' cages in your own bedroom? Yes. You were struck with horror, amaze, wrath, when you found them gone next morning. On Thursday night you concealed another

81

trinket in a canary's cage in the passage: something of little or no sentimental value, and perhaps to lay a trap for the thief?'

Lady Cork cowered back.

'Yes! True! But man, man, how did you know all that? Aforetime we spoke of wizards. Odd's life. Are you one?'

Cheviot, taken aback at her reception of his commonplace reasoning, made a fussed gesture.

'It's the most likely supposition, madam. No more.'

'Ah! Then tell me this, Signor Cagliostro!' Shrewdness peered out through the blur of tears. 'Why did this curs't knave empty out the containers, into a bowl or whatnot, and leave 'em empty? Why not fish with his fingers? Draw out the pretties? And leave the seed as though untouched?'

'Madam, there are several explanations. Again I can but give you the most likely.'

'Well!'

'Wasn't it certain, Lady Cork, that next morning you would immediately hasten to the cages, and make sure your treasures were safe?'

'God's body!' said Lady Cork. 'So I did!'

'And the thief, he or she, must act very quickly in the night. It's no easy matter to disturb parrots' cages without a great commotion, which might have aroused you. No doubt the thief cared little whether or not the containers were left empty. But you understand what this means?'

'Hey?'

'For instance. Is your house, on the outside, locked up safely at night?'

'Like Newgate! Like the Fleet! Or more so, from what I've heard.'

'Do you lock your bedroom doors at night?'

'No! Where's the need?'

'Then the thief, he or she, must be someone close at hand. On your honour, madam: you have no notion at all who the thief may be?'

'No.' She rounded the syllable carefully, after a pause.

'Did you confide to any person your intent of hiding the jewels?'

'To nobody!' snapped Lady Cork, with more assurance.

'Then but one more question, madam. You are *sure* you heard no noise or movement, saw no glimmer of light, in the long watches of the night?'

'No. It's — it's the laudanum.'

'The laudanum?'

'Old women, boy, sleep very little.' Then she raged at him. 'I drink it every night, to give peace. I can't help it! Even when I laid a snare on Thursday, with a worthless ring in a canary's cage, I yielded and drank. And where's the harm? Don't the King drink laudanum to ease the pain in his bladder? And, when his Ministers go down to talk o' state affairs, an't he so hocussed he can't speak to 'em?'

She brooded, fiercely, clasping and unclasping her hand on the head of the stick. Yet her tone changed.

'The King,' she said. 'They hate him, don't they? Ay! They hate him. But I knew him when he was young, as handsome as a god, and a paying court to poor Perdita Robinson.'

Again the muscles of her face were writhing past control. Despite herself the tears overflowed and trickled down.

'Be off!' she shouted, clearing her throat. 'I've had enough this night. Be off with ye!'

Cheviot made a sign to Mr. Henley.

The chief clerk sealed his ink-well, put away his pens, closed the writing-case, and limped over softly on his own thick cane to yank the tapestry bell-pull beside the fireplace. Then he and Cheviot moved towards the double-doors.

'Stop!' Lady Cork said suddenly.

She rose to her feet with strange dignity, for

all her tear-draggled look.

'A last word to you! I hear everything. I have heard, no matter how or from whom, about my diamond-and-ruby brooch, formed like a ship. It was the first gift I had from my husband after we were wed. And I hear it's been pledged at Vulcan's.'

Even the surge of waltz-music seemed to infuriate her. She hammered her stick on the floor, so hard that the macaw screeched once more.

'My brooch!' she said, swallowing. 'At Vulcan's!'

'Vulcan?' Cheviot thought. 'A pawnbroker? A money-lender?'

He couldn't ask her who Vulcan was. Clearly she expected him to know. But there were others he could ask, and so he merely bowed.

'Good night, Lady Cork.'

He motioned the clerk to precede him, and they both went out.

There, in the long and broad passage with its two lines of Chinese lamps, they stood huddled in muttered conference as Cheviot closed the door with a loud snap.

'Now, what,' asked Mr. Henley, 'did you make of that?'

'The fact is,' Cheviot answered truthfully, 'she's so much of the eighteenth century I could hardly understand her pronunciation, much less try to imitate her speech. It's a relief to speak naturally.'

(To speak naturally. Over ninety years before he had been born!)

'Ah!' muttered Mr. Henley, assuming a wise look. 'I had a bit of trouble myself, once or twice, though I'm a good deal older than you. But what I meant — !'

'She's not telling us the whole truth. She knows, or guesses, who stole those jewels. If it weren't for their sentimental value to her, she might not have spoken at all. It's fairly clear that — '

Cheviot paused, because his companion had swung round from the door. Mr. Henley was staring ahead; his reddish eyebrows drew together; he half-lifted his cane to point. Cheviot swung round too.

About a dozen feet ahead of them, with her back to them, stood Flora Drayton.

There was nothing unusual in her presence there. She stood somewhat to the right, on the dull-flowered carpet, in the direction of the closed double-doors to the ballroom.

It was her rigid, unnatural posture, head held a little back and hands thrust deeply into the fur muff. Though they could not see her face, yet her whole body was instinct with agony and despair.

Cheviot's heart seemed to contract as though squeezed in fingers.

Two seconds later, a door opened. It was one of the single doors, painted brilliant orange, in the wall now on their left as they faced forwards towards the stairs. It was, in fact, the passage-door to Lady Cork's bedroom.

Out walked Margaret Renfrew, closing the door sharply after her. She was turned sideways, showing little more than the line of her cheek. Miss Renfrew passed well ahead of Flora, hurrying diagonally as though towards the doors to the ballroom.

Then she hesitated, seeming to change her mind. Making a gesture of impatience, she turned slightly and walked straight down the middle of the carpet towards the stairs. She was then about ten feet ahead of the agonized Flora.

And at that moment — let it be the chronicler who states it — somebody fired the shot.

They scarcely heard the shot, for reasons to be explained. A dozen fast-sawing fiddles and a harp, the swish and swirl of shoes as dancers whirled and dipped, the giggles of women and the shouts of men, filled the passage with incredible noise.

But the bullet struck Margaret Renfrew

just under the left shoulder-blade.

Cheviot's long eyesight saw its black speck leap up against the back of the white gown. It was as though someone, with hands more than human, had flung her forwards. She pitched two steps, staggered, and fell flat on her face.

For what seemed minutes, and must actually have been two or three seconds, she lay motionless. Then her fingers, frenziedly, clawed and scrabbled at the carpet. She tried to push herself up on both arms, and succeeded in straightening out to the elbows. But a violent spasm shook her body. Margaret Renfrew's shoulders collapsed. Her forehead bumped against the carpet, the glossy black ringlets tumbling forwards. She lay still.

Up and down whirled the waltz-music.

While we glide on summer's tide, to
  what dream's end?
As we ride, our thoughts abide with . . .

Cheviot raced forwards, past a blur of black-lacquer walls and gold dragons. He knelt down by that motionless figure.

The bullet-hole was small; only a little sluggish blood had trickled down. A small pistol, with a light powder-charge, would have made comparatively little noise. It should not have done much damage, even, unless the bullet pierced the heart.

But it had.

Snatching out his watch, he pressed open the lid. Sliding one hand under the woman's forehead, he lifted her head up and held the face of the watch close against painted lips, automatically noting the time as he did so. Not a breath clouded the glass. She had died within twenty seconds.

Cheviot lowered her head. He shut up the watch and put it in his pocket.

Mr. Henley, as pale as paper and with a sagging fleshy mouth, loomed up over him. The chief clerk all but sprawled on his face as he knelt down too.

'What — ?' he began.

Fortunately he was looking at Miss Renfrew's body. Cheviot glanced behind him, and went cold.

Flora's rigidity had changed. She was now facing him, from ten feet away. Her eyes looked at him without seeing him. She began to tremble all over, beyond control of all nerves. As her arms shook, the big fur muff slipped sideways.

Though she still held the muff with her left hand, her right hand — in an elbow-length glove with one seam split wide open along the back of the hand — fell nervelessly out of the muff.

And a smallish pistol, with a golden lozenge-shaped plate let into the wooden handle, fell with it. The pistol dropped on the carpet and gleamed there.

Flora dropped the muff, too, gasped, and pressed both hands over her eyes.

6

Nightmare in the Passage

Cheviot, who had stood up, clamped his hand firmly on the shoulder of the still-kneeling Mr. Henley.

'Turn her over!' he said.

'Eh?'

'Turn her on her back, and make sure she's dead. You've been to the wars; you won't lose your head. Don't let anything distract your attention!'

'Whatever you say, sir.'

If the chief clerk looked round . . .

But he did not look round. His lame foot gave him difficulty when he wrenched at the limp but dead-weight body.

Then Detective-Superintendent John Cheviot did what he would never have believed he could have done.

Silently he ran to Flora. Her eyes, changing, were now fixed on him in mute, irresistible appeal. He picked up the pistol, gripping it hard with forefinger and thumb round the edge of the muzzle.

Only a few feet from her side stood one of

the very low black teakwood tables. Though the lamp with fringed and silk-brocade shade appeared to have a heavy base of dark-painted porcelain, he knew the base was hollow.

He lifted the lamp with his left hand. With his right he put the pistol underneath. The base of the lamp easily fitted over it and concealed it.

But not before he had noted several things. The pistol was still warm. His middle finger, against the muzzle, came away with traces of burnt black powder. The little golden lozenge-shaped plate, inlaid in the wooden handle, was carved with the entwined initials A. D.

To hide the pistol under the lamp, it had been necessary to turn away briefly. He whirled back again, Mr. Henley had not glanced round. But . . .

God Almighty!

He thought that one of the double-doors to the ballroom had opened only two inches or so, and then closed again. He had a wild impression he had seen something black, a coat or perhaps hair, between the brilliant orange oblongs with their arabesques of gold.

But he couldn't be sure. It was only a flash at the edge of the edge of the eye; uncertain, possibly a complete deception. There was no reason for his nerves to jump.

Margaret Renfrew lay on her back, with her eyes wide open and her jaw fallen. She could not hear the music, or would ever hear it again.

Mr. Henley, still pale but beginning to regain his wits, staggered to his feet.

'Mr. Cheviot,' he said, 'who done this?'

Cheviot risked a look at Flora. His eyes pleaded with her as silently they asked the question, 'Flora, Flora, why did you . . . ?'

Just as desperately her own eyes replied, 'I didn't! I didn't! I didn't!'

'Mr. Cheviot,' the chief clerk repeated in his hoarse, heavy voice, 'who done this?'

Mr. Henley had not even observed his slip in grammar.

'*You* didn't do it,' he said. '*I* didn't do it. With all due respects to the lady, and suggesting nothing,' he jerked his head towards Flora, 'she didn't do it either. I was watching her, and she didn't take her hands out of that muff for one instant.'

It was true.

It was so true, striking like a blow, that Cheviot spoke without thinking.

'You saw the wound. It was a small pistol, what they call a pocket pistol. If you or I fired through a pocket, muffling the flash too . . . '

93

Mr. Henley, startled out of his wits, uttered an expletive.

'Look at my clothes!' he said, staring down over himself. 'You're as good as Superintendent of the Home Division. Go on: look at 'em! I'll do the same for you!'

'But . . . '

'By your leave, sir! I insist!'

Cheviot did so. He even opened the writing-case and examined the cane. He found nothing. But he knew he wouldn't, as Mr. Henley examined him. His thoughts were on Flora's muff. There wasn't any —

'Merely as a matter of form?' he suggested, with what must have been a stiff and grotesque smile. And he picked up Flora's muff.

She could not even have fired through the muff, without leaving a black burned rent from the exploded powder. As he turned the muff over in his hands, he found no such rent; and he gave it back to her.

Flora was no longer trembling. Her fear of him, her shrinking back from him, whatever had been its inexplicable cause, was gone. Her lips scarcely moved when she spoke.

'Darling!' she whispered, in so low a voice that he hardly heard. 'Darling, darling, darling! You *know* I never did.'

Whereupon Flora spoke aloud.

'But who did?' she cried. 'There was nobody else in the passage.'

True again; there had been nobody else in the passage.

Eerily the oil-lamps shone on black-lacquered wood. The canaries hopped, defying the surge of music and competing with it. Cheviot looked back at Mr. Henley.

The latter, instinctively subservient, touched two fingers to his forehead.

'It's no business of mine, Mr. Cheviot. *But*,' and he gestured around, 'there's only one way. One of these doors must have opened, and somebody stuck out a barker.'

'I could take my oath,' Cheviot answered quietly, 'that not one of the doors opened when the shot was fired.'

'Certain of that, sir?'

'Dead certain.'

'But — !'

'Stop, stop! Let me think!'

He stared at the carpet. A woman can't be dead of a bullet wound when there is no human hand to fire the bullet; yet it happened. Mainly Cheviot was conscious of the watch ticking in his waistcoat pocket.

This roused him. Snatching at the watch again, he found it was three minutes past midnight. That waltz must stop soon; it had been going on long enough. Miss Renfrew had been on her way, or so she said, to announce supper. In a short time the whole crowd must come pouring out. If they found a dead body in the passage . . .

'Just a moment!' Cheviot said to his two companions.

He went to the ballroom doors, opened the right-hand one, and looked inside.

Nobody noticed him, or seemed to notice him.

A hot gush of air, stuffy yet scented, swirled out at him with the dipping and whirling of the dancers. The dozen fiddlers sawed and sweated like mad on their little platform. Women's gowns, wide-skirted and some with puffed sleeves like day-dresses, wove a flying pattern of pink, blue, green, white, and primrose-yellow.

He saw the half-dozen hair-styles; many girls had flowers threaded in their hair, some wore feathers. From each slender wrist, a dance programme hung on a thin thread. All the ladies were gloved to the elbow, as the black-coated men wore white kid gloves.

Some people, Flora had said, still considered the waltz improper. Cheviot couldn't understand this. Each man held his partner almost at arm's length. And yet . . .

And yet, in that dream scene under dim fluttery gaslight, there pulsed underneath a queer, repressed excitement. Cheviot himself could feel it. The women's faces were flushed with exercise; the men's with exertion or drink. On a floor waxed to glassiness, past windows with very heavy green curtains looped back, emotions were unloosed and uncovered.

'What accompanies all this?' he wondered. 'Yes, the first thought is easy. But the second is something just as primitive; it could lead to murder.'

On the inside of the door, he saw, there was a large brass key in the lock. Cheviot stepped a pace inside the ballroom. Unobtrusively he put his hand over the key, worked it out of the lock, and slipped it into his pocket.

'On the surface,' ran his racing thoughts, 'it's as proper and decorous as a nursery school. But underneath the surface?'

Look out!

A circling couple, unseeing in the colour-whirl and uncertain light, bore down on him. He had no time to dodge.

There was a soft, flesh-thudding shock. The dancers lurched, but did not lose their footing. Instantly Cheviot was all apologies to the young lady.

'Madam, I entreat you to forgive me. The fault was entirely mine. I had ventured out too far.'

The young lady, a pretty and breathless girl with light-brown hair and wide-set hazel eyes, in a blue silk gown and with forget-me-nots in her hair, breathed fast from the tempo of the dance.

But she did not forget to curtsey prettily, raise her large eyes, smile, and lower her eyes.

And at last Cheviot understood the quality common to all these women, especially Flora herself. It was their intense femininity, the strongest weapon a woman can possess and the one which makes most trouble among men.

'I beg you won't mention it, sir,' smiled the girl, gasping at him as though the matter were of earth-shaking importance. 'Pray don't mention it! Such accidents are quite usual. I am sure my partner agrees?'

She turned. Cheviot found himself looking straight into the eyes of the Guards officer, Captain Hogben, with whom he had already exchanged words on the stairs.

For a few seconds Captain Hogben, exuding wrath and brandy-punch, spoke no word. Yet he did not seem angry; only tall and languid. He stroked his moustache and side-whiskers.

'You again, fellow?' he drawled. 'Well! I must chastise you pwopewly, fellow; at the pwopew time and place. Meanwhile, fellow, be off with you!'

His long right arm darted out to give Cheviot a contemptuous shove in the chest.

It was still more strange a thing. Wrath, which Cheviot seldom felt and never showed, none the less boiled up inside him. By inches and half a second he beat the companion to the shove. His open left hand, with weight behind it, struck like a battering-ram against the Guards officer's padded chest.

Captain Hogben's heels twitched and twitched on the waxcd floor. He sat down with a crash which shook the gas-jets. Immediately he was up again, sure-footed in his pointed military boots under the thin black trousers, but with furious eyes.

It would not be true to say that the brown-haired girl fastened on him. Yet she seized his hands in a position for the dance, pouring out low-murmured, soothing, indistinguishable words.

Cheviot waited, looking Captain Hogben in the eyes.

But decorum prevailed. Captain Hogben bore his partner away. Nobody else, deeply absorbed, had so much as glanced at the incident. A girl in lilac giggled loudly. Round-faced Freddie Debbitt, entranced, sailed past holding at less than arm's length a queenly brunette in a pink gown.

Cheviot backed out of the ballroom. Closing the door, he took the key out of his pocket and locked both doors on the outside. The key he left in the lock.

But a bead of sweat ran down his forehead.

What the devil was wrong with him? Had he too been affected by the atmosphere of the ballroom? Or was it, more deeply buried in his mind, some scratching and nagging doubt about Flora — and Flora's innocence, after all?

Flora herself, moving farther and farther away from that dead body, cried out at him in the quieter passage.

'Jack! What in mercy's name were you doing in the ballroom? At a time like this?'

Cheviot was himself again.

'Locking them in.' He spoke lightly. All the time he studied the limpid sincerity of Flora's eyes and mouth. 'We can't have the place overrun, can we? Gently, now! There's no need for haste.'

'But this is horrible.' She nodded her golden-haired head towards Margaret Renfrew without looking there, and wrung her hands. 'What's to be done?'

'I'll show you.'

Flora nearly screamed when he left them again. He hastened to Lady Cork's boudoir. After knocking, he twisted the knob — which always opened or closed with a loud snap — and went in.

Lady Cork drowsed in the armchair, by the dying fire, her frilled cap sagging, her hand on her stick. Even the macaw's eye was closed. But, at the snap of the lock, she reared up and rolled round her head.

She was a sharp-witted old lady. Something of Cheviot's errand must have showed in his face.

'What's amiss, lad?' she demanded, getting to her feet. 'Come; I've eyes in me head! What's amiss?'

'I regret to tell you that your niece, Miss Renfrew — '

'She's no niece o' mine!' said Lady Cork, her face hardening. 'Or kin either, for that matter. What's she done now?'

'Nothing. She has met with an accident. To be quite blunt, she is dead.'

'Dead,' Lady Cork repeated after a pause, and seemed to go white under the eyes. Then her eyes narrowed. 'Accident, ye say?'

'No. That's only a police formula for softening a blow. She was shot through the heart from the back, and is lying out in that passage. That, madam,' Cheviot caught and held her gaze, 'is where I ask your assistance. As a police-officer, I must not have a great number of people trampling over that passage until I have properly examined it. Will you be kind enough to assist me by detaining your guests in the ballroom, with a speech or the suggestion of another dance or what you like? Detaining them for ten or fifteen minutes, without telling them (as yet!) that anything is amiss? Can you, will you, do this?'

'Ay!' retorted Lady Cork, striking her stick on the floor. 'I can and I will. And there's ten dowagers in there, as chaperones, who'll help me!'

She bustled forward. Then she stopped, lips pursed up.

'Shot,' she said flatly. 'Who did it? Her lover?'

This time Cheviot's face betrayed nothing.

'Then Miss Renfrew had a lover, Lady Cork?'

'Pah! Don't tell me! To be sure she had!'

'His name?'

'How should I know? The jade was too close-mouthed. But couldn't ye see it in her eyes?'

'I saw something, yes.'

'Pride and shame, at the same time? Tetchy and savage, for fear somebody'd read it in her face? When it was printed there for all to read, with rouge and lip-salve? And where was the need for that, at thirty-one?

Pah! These nowadays non-conformist con-
sciences!'

Anger moved across her old face, like
dough with water bubbling underneath.

'That's what I misliked, and I don't deny it.
Sly, curs't sly! Lawks! Did she think I'd
mind?' Lady Cork suddenly cackled, either
with laughter or something else. 'In my time,
lad, a gel wasn't a gel unless she'd had half a
dozen before she was twenty. If ye want to
find Peg's macaroni, he's in the ballroom
there. But *she* denied she had one. — And
now she's dead.'

'Lady Cork!'

The latter had bustled past him and was
almost at the door.

'Hey?'

'Am I correct in assuming, as I have
assumed for some time, that it was Miss
Renfrew who stole your jewellery? Or, at
least, you believe she stole it?'

The music stopped.

It left a great void in the old, musty house.
There was a spattering of applause from the
ballroom, but this sounded merely polite. It
was evident that momentarily exhausted
guests, male and female, desired large
quantities of food and drink.

'Yes, Lady Cork? Did you suspect Miss
Renfrew?'

103

'Lad, lad, make haste! Can't ye hear what I hear? Whether supper's announced or not, they'll gallop downstairs like horses for a trough. Come!'

'They can't gallop yet. I locked the doors on the outside.'

'Lawks!' screeched Lady Cork, rather like her macaw. Her bearing altered. She regarded him with formal, drawn-up sarcasm. 'Now that will quench their curiosity, I daresay, when you desire to keep all things dark? That will discover them rejoicing, when they find locked doors?'

'Will you answer my question, Lady Cork?'

'Young man, are you bullyin' me?'

'No, madam. Nevertheless, if you don't reply, I must assume you do suspect Miss Renfrew. And act accordingly.'

She stared at him.

From her expression he was sure he had found the truth. He could have sworn she was within a hair line of barking out, 'Yes,' but her strange mind altered again. She sniffed, opened the door handle with a snap, and marched out.

Cheviot, in despair, could only follow.

Lady Cork paid no attention either to Flora or to Mr. Henley, who stood as they had stood before. For an instant the short, squat little figure stood blinking down at

Margaret Renfrew's body.

'Poor gel,' Lady Cork said gruffly.

Without another word she bustled to the ballroom doors, unlocked them, marched inside, and closed the doors. The murmur of voices changed to a ripple and then a burst of applause.

'Now!' Cheviot said to Flora. 'Let's see what can be done.'

He should not have allowed the body to be disturbed, of course. It was necessary to disturb it so that he, he of all people, could distract the chief clerk's attention and hide a recently fired, still-warm pistol.

But that was a minor matter. Margaret Renfrew had fallen hard. An outline of her fall, including the position of arms and legs, was printed in the dust of the carpet. Rolling her over again, he set every finger and shoe-tip into line.

Even as he did so, the full helplessness of his position swept over him.

He could not take photographs. He had no chalk, no magnifying lens, no tape-measure. But these were still small matters; he could find rough substitutes for them.

Not a modern ballistics expert on earth could identify a bullet fired from a smooth-bore barrel. Even granting Flora's innocence, and some plausible explanation of the weapon in the muff, he could never prove from what pistol the shot was fired.

Fingerprints, on which he had staked so much in his proposed experiment for Colonel Rowan and Mr. Mayne, were worse than useless here. Aside from servants like Solange, aside from himself and Mr. Henley and Lady Cork, every person in the house was wearing gloves.

His fine advantages had crumbled to ruin. He was left alone to his own wits.

'Mr. Henley!' he said, looking round and measuring distances with his eye. 'In that writing-case of yours, have you by any chance a piece of chalk?'

'Chalk, Mr. Cheviot?' the other blurted, and backed a step away. 'Egad, sir, what do you want with chalk?'

'To draw an outline round the body. We can't keep her there forever.'

'Ah!' breathed Mr. Henley, relieved to hear sanity. 'I have a stick of charcoal, if that's of use?'

'Yes! Thank you! I think the carpet is light-coloured enough for that. If you don't mind, you had better give me the writing-case. I must take sketches and measurements for myself.'

For fully ten minutes, while they watched him, and Flora neared the verge of hysterics, he worked swiftly. For measuring distances he used his own big silk handkerchief. He prowled back and forth, from the body to the walls, and then to the rear of the passage.

Louder and louder grew the clamour of voices from the ballroom. Again Cheviot feared invasion. His pen scratched on bad paper; ink flew wide. There was no damned blotting paper; he forgot the sand.

'That's all, I think,' he concluded, handing back the writing-case and waving the paper in the air to dry it. 'Mr. Henley, I dislike making this request. But you have a horse here. Will you go and fetch a surgeon? Any surgeon, but by preference a good one.'

'Mr. Cheviot! The lady's dead! A surgeon can't bring her back to life.'

'No. But he can probe for the bullet, and tell me the direction of impact.'

'S-sir?'

'Now listen to me!' said Cheviot, fixing the chief clerk's rather large and cow-like brown eyes with his own. 'We agree, don't we, that Lady Drayton fired no shot?'

'Ay! That there I do!'

'You will further observe,' Cheviot insisted gently, 'that Lady Drayton carries no firearms of any kind?'

'Ay again!'

'Very well.' He did not dare look at Flora.

'But there's no weapon in the passage. I've just finished searching. Next remark the position of Miss Renfrew's body. She was shot in the back. We all saw that; we all know it. She lies, as you see, in the middle of the carpet, facing the stairs, and well ahead of any door opening on this passage.'

'Ah! Then it means — '

'It means, as a possibility, that one of those doors might briefly have opened and closed.'

'But you said — !'

'I know I said it. I still believe no door was opened. Nevertheless, unless we accept this possibility, we are left with a belief in miracles or devilry or witchcraft.'

'Here, sir! Steady! Pull up! There may be witches, for all they say it's lies!'

Cheviot ignored this. He took another step forward.

'You ask me what a surgeon can do. In extracting the bullet, he can say whether it was fired in a straight line or diagonally. If diagonally, was the direction from left or right? You understand the vital nature of this? You see it will show where a murderer, visible or invisible, was standing at the time?'

'Ah-ah-ah!' breathed Mr. Henley, and stood up straight.

'Sir,' he added rather huskily, 'I asks your pardon. I see now there's much more to this

108

detective-police business than handling your fives, or beating the truth out of a house-breaker just because you think he may 'a' done it. I've been wasting your time, Mr. Cheviot; but I won't waste any more of it. I'll be off, now, to fetch that surgeon.'

With much dignity he inclined his half-bald head. He turned round, hobbled towards the stairs, and was gone.

For a moment Cheviot stared after him.

'Handling your fives,' he knew, was current slang for using your fists. Despite all his heavy reading in political and social history, so that he might interpret the meaning of the new Metropolitan Police, he could not hope to understand every catch-or-cant phrase.

He could only lurch along as best he could, as in this crime, under the bitter load which time had burdened him with.

Bending down, with one arm under Margaret Renfrew's shoulders and another under her knees, he lifted up that dead, heavy weight.

'Flora!' he said sharply. 'We have to move her somewhere.'

Flora, about to speak, changed her mind. With the muff dangling from her right hand, she ran over and opened the single door nearer the stairs.

Cheviot, in the act of carrying the body

there, hesitated and swung round.

He could hear the babble from the ballroom. Lady Cork couldn't hold them back much longer. It was unlikely, when they came pouring out, that anyone would look under a hollow-based lamp to find a pistol concealed there. All the same —

With a violent effort, the woman's body across his forearms as he bent down, he lifted the lamp with one hand and with his other hand he caught up the small pistol whose lozenge-shaped gold plate in the handle bore the initials A.D.

He couldn't put the pistol in his pocket, or he would have dropped the woman's body. He nearly dropped her as it was; her cheek rolled up, grisly, against his own.

Flora moistened her lips. She was as pale as dead Miss Renfrew. Though Flora's heavy, smooth, silky hair was not at all disarranged, she made a wild gesture with both hands to her exposed ears.

Cheviot followed her quickly through the open door, which led to the dining-room. At each end of a long Chippendale dining-table, cleared and polished, stood a massive silver candelabrum of seven branches. They lit the candles, which had burnt far down, in stiffened drippings of white wax. The flames sputtered, throwing dim and fluttery cross-lights in the big room.

'Jack! What are you doing?'

'Putting her body on the table. They're not making use of this room tonight. Lock the door.'

Even as he deposited that burden face-up on the table, between the sets of dim and unsteady flames, he heard another brass key chatter and tremble at a keyhole. The lock snapped shut as Flora turned it — not one second too soon.

He could hear the double-doors of the ballroom burst open. Though it was a trifle muffled in the locked dining-room, the babble rose so loudly that he could make out no distinguishable word. Afterwards it seemed to swirl down the passage towards the stairs.

Cheviot went to the far and narrow side of the table. There he faced Flora, whose back was pressed against the door. The sight of a corpse in that dim-lit place seemed to wrench her further towards a snapping point of nerves. Yet she was drawn forward, irresistibly and in spite of herself.

He did what had to be done. Facing her across the table, weighing the pistol in his hand, he raised his head and looked her in the eyes.

'Now, Flora,' he said quietly.

7

'For Too Much Love Doth Lead — '

Flora shrank back.

'Now . . . what?' she asked.

'There are certain questions to ask you, my dear. Wait!'

He held up his hand before she could speak. His head had begun to ache, and there was a dull nausea in his throat.

'Please remember that I shielded you. I would never have reminded you of this, Flora, never once thought of reminding you, if it weren't to show you can trust me. — In the past, Flora, you and I have been lovers.'

'Jack! For heaven's sake! Don't say it! What if someone should overhear?'

'Very well. But wait again!' he insisted. 'And for God's sake don't think me mad or drunk' — here her eyes flickered briefly — 'in what I do say. When I first met you tonight, in the carriage at Great Scotland Yard, what did I do?'

'Jack!'

'*What did I do?*'

Flora tossed her head and turned partly away.

'You — you put your arms around me, and your head in my lap, and talked a vast d-deal of nonsense. And you said I was a picture out of a book.'

'Yes. So I thought, at the time.'

'You — thought?' said Flora, and backed away.

Through his brain, in a flash, loomed the vivid colours of face and gown in the folio at the Victoria and Albert Museum. 'Lady (Flora) Drayton, widow of Sir Arthur Drayton, K.C.B. H. Fourquier, 1827.'

'Flora, I'm no ladies' man. I could never even have touched a strange woman unless actually, somewhere at the back of my mind, I knew she was no stranger at all.'

'You and I? Strangers?'

'I didn't say that. All this evening I have had a belief growing to a certainty. Somewhere, maybe in another existence, you and I have been just as intimate as we are today.'

Then Cheviot made a short, sharp gesture.

'That's all,' he said curtly. 'I tell you only to explain to myself, as well as you, why I act as I do. But don't lie to me. This pistol.' He held it up. 'How did you come by it?'

Flora, it was evident, had been through too

many changes of mood that night. His new and abrupt tone, striking like a whip, carried her past exhaustion. It held her rigid, hardly trembling at all.

'How did you come by it, Flora?'

'It — it belonged to my husband.'

'Hence the initials, A.D., carved in the gold lozenge?'

'Y-yes!'

'Why did you bring it here tonight?'

Her utter amazement, he decided, could not have been feigned.

'Bring it here? But I didn't! I never did!'

'Listen, my dear.' He spoke gently. 'Other women may have brought fur muffs to this dance. But not a woman is carrying one in the house. Why do you carry yours?'

It was as though he had asked a question to which the answer was so plain, so blatantly obvious, that she could find no words for a reply.

Instead Flora threw the muff on a Chippendale seat. She thrust out her right arm, pointing and pointing again at the gaping rent in the glove where a seam had burst across the top of the hand. Her mouth worked before she could attain speech.

'When I was waiting for you in the carriage, and you were with Colonel Rowan and Mr. Mayne, I put on these gloves. The

— the seam split then. So I hid my right hand. When you said we were going to Lady Cork's, I was *obliged* to wear the muff. Did you not see how I held out my left hand to Freddie Debbitt? Or gave you the list of jewels with my left hand? Or kept the other hand hidden whenever I could?'

Cheviot stared at her.

'And that's all?' he demanded.

'All?' echoed Flora, as once before that night. 'All?'

'You didn't, for instance, use the muff to conceal this pistol?'

'Oh, God, no!'

'All this, Flora, about a split seam in a glove? Couldn't you have worn the glove as it was? Or simply taken off both gloves in the house?'

Flora was regarding him with something like horror.

'Wear a burst glove in the ballroom? Or, worse still, appear there with no gloves at all?'

'But — !'

'To be sure, had you danced with me as I wished, your left hand would have hidden it and not a soul would have seen. But otherwise?' Her voice rose in a despairing cry. 'Oh, my dear, what's come over you?'

Pause. Cheviot turned away.

The dying candle-flames fluttered with a

watery hiss. Their broken gleams showed the cages, covered and silent, containing what Lady Cork had called birds 'almighty exotic and wonderful.' He could discern only outlines of the dining-room, with its big portraits and its glimmer of silver.

He hated that dim, quivery light. It made even Flora seem ghost-like. But he remembered, with a shiver, that he spoke to a woman out of another age; an age with a code of special social customs as inflexible as once were the laws of Rome.

As he turned back, they regarded each other for an instant without comprehension on either side.

'You don't believe me?' Flora asked incredulously.

'Yes! Yes, I believe you!' he answered honestly. 'But how did this pistol get into the house?'

'She borrowed it.' Flora looked briefly at what was on the table, and averted her gaze. 'More than a fortnight ago.'

'Miss Renfrew borrowed it? Why?'

'For Lady Cork, she said. You can't have forgotten that affright of burglars near a month gone? When three houses in this neighbourhood were robbed?'

'I — no.'

'That odious woman said Lady Cork

feared nothing at all. She said there were no men in this house except the manservants; and Lady Cork would defend herself if need be. I know nothing of such things; I hate them! But Miriam found the pistol, among Arthur's possessions, in his own chamber. There was — a pouch of bullets, and a powder-flask, and a little ramrod. That horrible woman went away with them. And now, she's dead.'

'Flora, what I am trying to understand . . . '

'And not believing me!'

'Yes! I believe you. But I want to understand how the pistol came to be concealed in your muff, and dropped out immediately after — '

'Dearest, dearest, it was not the pistol that — that killed her!'

'Why not?'

'Because it had been fired long before she died. It had been fired when I found it.'

'What?'

'I found it in the passage. That's true!'

Whereupon Flora nerved herself for a pleading of effort.

'Jack, don't be vexed with me. I've been awfully patient. I'll tell you what you like.' Her voice was high. 'But I can't endure longer to be questioned with that woman there before me. With her eyes and mouth open, as if she still wanted to bite.'

Half-blinded with tears, Flora ran for the door. She could not see the key. Her fist beat helplessly at the door.

Without a word Cheviot circled round the table and was beside her. Shifting the pistol to his left hand, he put his arm round her. Flora, relenting even when she sobbed, nestled her head against his shoulder.

'I had not thought,' he said. 'The passage should be empty now. We can go to Lady Cork's boudoir. Gently, now.'

He unlocked the door. They slipped out, Flora moving away from him. Cheviot relocked the door from outside and pocketed the key.

And straightway they came face to face with someone else.

Along the passage, from the direction of the stairs, hurried a girl whom he had seen somewhere before, and recently. She was carrying, rather clumsily, a large plate high-piled with cold meats and also a glass of champagne.

The girl's silk gown was of dark blue, the skirts swaying wide as she moved. Forget-me-nots were twined in her thick light-brown hair. When she raised startled eyes, which were hazel in colour and set wide apart above a short nose and wide mouth, he recognized her.

She had been dancing with the arrogant Captain Hogben when the two of them collided with Cheviot in the ballroom. She was the girl who . . .

Clearly she had not expected to find Flora here, and she stopped short. Flora sharply turned her back on both of them.

'You were not downstairs,' the girl in blue blurted out. 'I had thought to bring you . . .'

She glanced down at the plate and the glass, which suddenly clattered together so that the champagne splashed over.

'My papa-says-I-talk-too-much-and-indeed-it's-true-though-I- have-no-wish-to-intrude-my-company-where-it-is-not-desired-oh-dear.'

All this rattled out, naïvely, as though in one breath. The girl in blue thrust plate and glass at him, so that he was compelled to take them whether he liked it or not.

'It was most kind of you, Miss — Miss — ?'

There was no time to return her curtsey with a bow. Blurting out, 'You-have-forgotten-me-oh-dear-Hugo-Hogben-will-be-furious,' she left him and went scurrying away down the stairs, her brown curls flying out.

Cheviot, now laden with a plate of cold

meats and in his other hand a champagne-glass, with a pistol hanging on one finger by its trigger guard, contemplated the stairs in a way the girl might not have understood.

She had been struck with consternation only when she saw Flora. Presumably it was not usual for men to walk about openly carrying firearms at a ball. Yet the girl in blue had first looked straight at the pistol; and she had shown no surprise.

No surprise at all.

His professional instincts, possibly, were overdoing it. He might see meanings where there were no meanings at all. But he would have pondered the matter, when he joined Flora in Lady Cork's boudoir and closed the door, if he had been given any opportunity to ponder at all.

For Flora whirled on him, her beauty heightened and coloured by blazing rage.

'Did you do this most deliberately?' she asked in a suppressed voice.

'Do this? Do what?'

'As if you didn't know!'

'Flora, what in hell are you talking about?'

'Do you try to make me jealous? And sting and hurt me forever and forever?'

'I still don't under — !'

'Not a ladies' man,' she mimicked, flying in. 'No! If you mean you don't ogle and strut and wear scented whiskers like some of them, I grant it. But what's your reputation, pray? Even that horrible Renfrew woman, for one. And now little Louise Tremayne. Her!'

'Louise Tremayne? The girl in blue? Is that her name?'

Flora, at such apparent brazenness, was past speech. Viciously she struck up at him with her open palm. The blow had little force, but it whacked and smarted across his cheek.

Cheviot did not move. In him, born of an obscure yet fierce jealousy of a dead husband about whom he knew nothing at all, there surged up an impulse to whack her across the face in reply. If both his hands had not been laden, he might have done it. Flora saw it in his eyes, and was terrified.

'I told you once before,' he said with outward calmness, 'that I never even set eyes on Miss Renfrew before tonight. Why should you imagine I had?'

Flora flung away the question, ignoring it.

'Damn her!' she cried, stamping her foot. 'Damn and blast her!'

Even these mild expletives, in Flora's sweet voice, sounded as incongruous as though she had uttered a string of obscenities. And she rushed on.

'Jack, how old are you? Yes; I know already. But how old are you?'

'Thirty-eight.'

'And I'm thirty-one!' said Flora, as though this were middle age or even senility. Her tone changed. 'Didn't you see the woman's expression? Tonight? On the stairs? When those dreadful young men ran past her? And she looked straight at you, and said — '

'But she — '

Their voices clashed. Another notion, which might have helped him much, darted through Cheviot's mind but vanished in emotional turmoil.

'I've never been unfaithful to you,' said Flora. 'After all that's happened between us, you know that. You can't help knowing it. No other man has ever . . . '

Her voice trailed away. She could not help taunting him and stabbing him with that provocative, alluring smile.

'Except, of course,' she added, 'my husband.'

'Then damn and blast *him*!'

'Jack!' She spoke out in mock astonishment and concealed pleasure. 'You're not jealous of Arthur?'

'If you must have it, yes.'

'But, darling, that's absurd! He — '

'I don't want to hear anything about him, thanks!'

Above their voices rose an inhuman screech.

'Ha, ha, ha,' screamed the macaw on the perch behind Flora. Its coloured plumage fluttered up, like the devil in a swamp, as it rattled and scraped and tried to fly.

Back on Cheviot rushed the knowledge of where he was: in the pink boudoir, with a problem before him but also with the eternal Eve to put her arms round his neck and distract him. He set down plate and glass on the tortoise-shell table beside Lady Cork's wing-chair.

But he kept the pistol, transferring it to his right hand with his finger round the trigger. The fire in the grate had gone out. The room was growing cold.

'Flora, this must stop.'

'What must?'

'Don't pretend. You know perfectly well. Sit down there.'

Flora sat down in the wing-chair, though her fingers tightened hard on its sides.

'Oh, Jack, must we — ?'

'Yes. We must. You tell me Miss Renfrew borrowed this weapon, on behalf of Lady Cork, over a fortnight ago. Did you see it, or hear anything of it, between that time and tonight?'

'Good heavens, no! Anyway, I've only seen the wretched thing two or three times in my whole life.'

'Tonight, you say, you found it in the passage. When and where did you find it?'

'Well! You sent me,' Flora retorted, with an accusing note on 'you,' 'to procure a list of all Maria Cork's jewels from Solange. Solange is terribly clever; she could remember every one; but she can't read or write, so I wrote the list. Afterwards I returned and gave it to you without coming into this room. Don't you recall?'

'Yes? And then?'

Flora threw out her arms, but again gripped the edges of the chair.

'Afterwards,' she said, 'I sat down in one of those teakwood chairs by the little tables, and awaited you. Just as I said I should do.'

'Which chair? Which table?'

'Oh, how can I remember? Stay, though; I do! It was the same chair by the same table where later you — you hid that pistol under the lamp with the hollow base.'

'Good! Go on!'

'I had nothing to do but worry and perplex my head. You caused it. I'm not stupid and I'm not a rattle, you know. You would speak of nothing but the ridiculous bird-seed; yet all the time you were apprehensive, all of a dither. You asked questions about money, jewels, thieves. You ordered me to get that list of jewellery, but wouldn't say why you wanted it. Darling, I knew something dreadful had happened, or would happen.'

'Go on!'

'Well! Presently I glanced down on the carpet, just under the table. I saw something golden. It was shining. I thought it must be a bit of jewellery, or the like. But, when I bent down to look closely, I saw what it was.'

'You recognized the pistol?'

'Yes! Oh, God, yes! With Arthur's initials on that diamond-shaped plate?'

'What did you do?'

'I daren't touch it. I was afraid it was loaded and might go off. I pushed it out from under the table with my foot.'

'And then?'

'I saw it had been fired. Look at it now! The hammer is down. Look at those burst bits of metal and paper under the hammer. That's what you call the percussion-cap, isn't it? Yes! And I saw it had been fired, and couldn't hurt anyone.'

'What did you do then?'

Flora braced herself and looked up at him.

'I picked it up,' she said clearly, 'and hid it inside the lining of the muff.'

'Why did you do that?'

'I . . .'

Her voice, hitherto so sweet and clear and firm, died behind shaky lips. She looked down at the pink-and-green-flowered carpet, and hesitated.

'Why, Flora? That's the whole crux and point of what happened — No, hold on! When you picked up the pistol, how did you pick it up? Can you show me? If you're afraid to touch it, I won't press you.'

Again she looked up.

'No, of course I'm not afraid to touch it!'

'Then show me.'

He held it level, gripping the trigger-guard underneath. The palm of Flora's hand went over the top, across the fallen hammer and part of the barrel, her fingers gingerly holding the wooden stock underneath. She held it for an instant; then drew back.

'Thank you, Flora. When you held it like that, was the barrel (that's this part) was the barrel warm?'

'Warm? No. At least, it didn't seem so through my glove.' Though she could not read his mind, she could sense his every mood. 'Jack! What's the matter?'

'Nothing at all. Afterwards you put the pistol inside the muff?'

'Yes. And held it with both hands.'

'How long was this before the murder?'

'Oh, how on earth can you except me to tell? I was too distraught. Finding someone had shot a pistol in a house where there was trouble. It may have been minutes and minutes; I can't say. All I know — '

'Yes?'

' — is that I jumped up and stood facing forward. I stood there. It seemed I couldn't move. Presently I heard the lock click (it always does) on the doors of this room. You and that lame man came out, muttering to each other. I didn't look round; I wished no one to see my face. I heard you say something like, 'She's not telling the truth,' or 'the whole truth'; I can't swear to the words. I thought you meant me.'

'You thought . . . what?'

Flora's gesture stopped him.

'My knees began to tremble, all up over me. I couldn't have moved. Then that awful Renfrew woman walked out of Maria Cork's bedroom, up towards the ballroom. But she altered her mind, and went towards the stairs. She was well ahead and to the left of me. I felt a wind, or kind of whistle or the like, past my arm. She went on a little and fell on her face. I can't tell you more.'

'And yet — '

'Please, dear!'

'But I'm bound to ask, Flora, if only between ourselves: *why?* Why did you conceal the weapon to begin with?'

Flora's rounded chin grew firm as she

looked up. Her eyes were deep and steady; the long black lashes did not move.

'Because,' she replied, 'it was bound to be all my fault.'

'I beg your pardon?'

'When Arthur was alive,' she said with passionate intensity, 'everything that went wrong was my fault. Or I was suspected of it. Now that the poor man is dead, and that's over two years, it's worse. I can do nothing, nothing in this world, without all odious people thinking and saying the worst of me.

'It's not vanity, Jack, to know I'm not ugly or a frump. Can I help that? Yet I can't drive round the Ring in my carriage, I can't smile or even nod to any man, without seeing the eyes and hearing them whisper. 'Aha!' they whisper. They think I'm deep when often I don't even think at all.'

Suddenly Flora darted out her arm and again touched the pistol.

'That belongs to me,' she said. 'Or, anyway, it belonged to Arthur and that's the same thing. Before there had been any — any murder, when there were only hints of thieves or jewels and intrigue, someone fired a weapon that was mine. My only instinct was to hide, hide it, hide it, before anyone could suspect me of anything. Perhaps that seems silly. Perhaps it is silly.

But can't you understand?'

There was a silence.

Cheviot nodded. He put his hand on her shoulder, and she pressed her cheek against it, with a warmth of vitality flowing between them. Then he moved away, looking vaguely at the crowding of pictures and miniatures on the pink walls.

Yes: every word of Flora's story could well be true.

Cold reason told him how counsel for the prosecution, in court, would jeer at it. 'Come, gentlemen! Surely this is just a little thin? Can we credit . . . ?' And so on. But Cheviot, whose business was to probe witnesses' minds and touch the pulse of guilt, felt her words ring with the uttermost conviction.

The macaw, silent on its perch, studied them first with one wicked eye; then craned its neck round in an attempt to study them with the other.

If that macaw screeched again, Cheviot decided, he would wring the damned bird's neck. Meanwhile . . .

'You are saying, Flora, that two shots were fired in the passage?'

'Dearest, I am saying nothing except what happened.'

Cheviot shut his teeth.

'I am bound to tell you something. When

I took up the pistol from the carpet, and hid it under the lamp, the barrel was still warm.'

'Warm? Warm?' she repeated after a pause. 'Why, to be sure it was warm! It had been inside the silk lining of a muff, and grasped in both hands, for minutes and minutes and minutes!' She faltered, and spoke incredulously. 'Do you — do you still doubt me?'

'No. I don't doubt you. You are to trouble your head no more.'

Flora closed her eyes.

'And now,' he went on briskly, 'you must go home. You are in a highly nervous state of mind; you must not so much as speak to anyone else. The footman will call your carriage.'

'Yes, yes, yes!' She sprang up eagerly. 'And you shall go with me.' She hesitated. 'You will, won't you?' she asked.

'No! I can't!'

'And why not, pray?'

'This affair can't be kept secret any longer. It mustn't be kept secret. On the contrary, I must question every guest and every servant in this house.'

'Yes, yes, I daresay! But afterwards?'

'Have you any idea how many people there are here? It may take all night.'

'Oh. Yes. So it may.'

'For God's sake, Flora, don't you see I can't?'

As she moved away from him, he reached out to seize her. But Flora, with a motion as quick and graceful as a dancer's, eluded him and went to the door. There she turned, her chin lifted and her shoulders back.

'You don't want me,' she said.

'Flora, you're mad! That's the thing I want most of all on earth!'

'You don't want me,' she repeated in a higher voice. The tears filling her eyes were less of fury than of reproachfulness. 'If you can't be with me at the time I have most need of you, then there's no other explanation. Very well. Take your pleasure with Louise Tremayne. But, if you will not be troubled now, you really need not trouble to see me again. This is good night, Jack; and I suppose it's also goodbye.'

Then she was gone.

8

Certain Whispers in a Coffee-Room

Dawn.

It was far past dawn, hidden behind a grey and chilly October sky, when Superintendent Cheviot at last left number six New Burlington Street, closing the front door of a house already astir with servants cleaning up the mess of last night.

Cheviot had passed the point of being over-tired. He had reached a state of mental second-wind where the brain seems very clear, very alert; and, treacherously, is not. His black depression, his nerves, all showed it.

He tried to put out of his mind what had happened when he tried to question a mob of guests. It was a humiliation he would not soon forget. He would have chucked the business altogether, he thought, if it had not been for the help of Lady Cork, of young Freddie Debbitt, and that Louise Tremayne of whom Flora had been so unreasonably jealous.

Flora . . .

Oh, damn everything!

Flora, surely, had flown into a tantrum only because she was overwrought?

In his pocket, wrapped up, he now had the bullet which had killed Margaret Renfrew. Curious evidence, much of it concerning Flora, had been provided by the surgeon whom Mr. Henley brought not long after Flora had gone.

Cheviot could not forget that scene, anyway. It was in the dining-room, with fresh wax-lights in the silver candelabra, and the dead woman's body rolled over on the table for the surgeon's examination.

Mr. Daniel Slurk, the surgeon, was a little, bustling, middle-aged man, with a professional grave air of wisdom but a knowing eyelid. On the table he put his bag, which was only a small carpet-bag, rattling with instruments inside. Examining the bullet-wound, he pursed up his lips, shook his head, and said, 'H'm, yes. H'm, yes.'

'Before you begin, Mr. Slurk,' Cheviot had said, 'may I ask a quite private and confidential question?'

The little surgeon took out of his bag a probe and a pair of surgical scissors, neither of them very clean.

'You may ask, sir,' he said, with a sinister look.

'I observe, Mr. Slurk, that you are a man of the world?'

The surgeon became more amiable at once.

'Even in our studious profession, sir,' he said portentously, but with a suspicion of a wink in the left eyelid, 'we learn a little of the world. Oh, dear me, yes. A little!'

'Then does the name 'Vulcan' mean anything to you?'

Mr. Slurk put down his instruments, and stroked his black side-whiskers.

'Vulcan.' His voice was without expression. 'Vulcan.'

'Yes! Could he be a pawnbroker? Or perhaps a moneylender?'

'Come, now!' Mr. Slurk spoke dryly, with a hint of suspicion. 'You also, I take it, are a man of the world. And, as Superintendent of our new Law Enforcement, you tell me you don't know Vulcan's?'

'No. I confess it!'

Mr. Slurk eyed him, and cast a quick glance round. They were alone; Cheviot, deciding he must deal with the case on his own, had sent the chief clerk home. Again Mr. Slurk almost winked.

'Ah, well!' he murmured. 'No doubt Law Enforcement can be blind when it likes. I hear (I say I *hear*) that in the neighbourhood of St. James's there are above thirty fashionable gambling-houses — '

'So!'

'And Vulcan's, it may be (eh?), is among them. Should you care for a fling at rouge-et-noir or roly-poly — '

'What's roly-poly?'

'Tut! My dear sir! Officially it is called roulette. A French name; a French game. Need I tell you how it's played?'

'No. I understand how it's played. Then if a man lacked money to play there, he could always find it by pledging or selling a valuable piece of jewellery?'

'It is often done,' replied Mr. Slurk, even more dryly. 'But (excuse me) that's none of my business. My scissors, now. Dear, dear! What have I done with my scissors?'

The scissors snipped and sheared cloth. There were no undergarments or stays. Mr. Slurk probed. He cut, brutally but quickly, with a far-from-clean knife. He extracted the bullet with a forceps, wiped the blood off on a handkerchief from his pocket, and tossed the bullet to Cheviot.

'You wish to keep that? Well, well! I daresay the coroner of the parish won't mind, when I tell him. They'll fetch her away tomorrow. Meanwhile, as to the direction of the wound — '

135

It was over soon enough. By what the surgeon told him, and by comparison of the bullet with Sir Arthur Drayton's pistol, Cheviot could be sure of one fact.

Flora was completely innocent. If necessary, it could be proved. The bullet in the victim's heart, though small, was just too large to fit into the pistol-barrel at all. Evidently its powder-blackening had been wiped away with the blood; it had not struck bone, and was unflattened; a dull leaden ball you could roll on the table.

True, this new evidence only made the problem more baffling. Hitherto there might have been some way in which a woman could be shot to death before the eyes of three witnesses, by a hand nobody saw. Now, apparently, there was no way.

Cheviot raged. He still raged when he sat down, methodically, to write a report which took nearly three hours to compose and occupied nine closely written foolscap pages. A footman, heavily bribed, engaged to deliver it at Great Scotland Yard so that it should be in the hands of Colonel Rowan and Mr. Mayne that morning.

'There's something wrong here,' he told himself as he wrote. 'It's here, in this report, as plain as the nose on Old Hookey's face. And I can't see it.'

But Flora was innocent.

Such was his state of mind, which he believed clear, when he left Lady Cork's house and felt the fresh wind on his eyelids.

His conscience still nagged at him badly, and wouldn't be still. For the first time in his life he had put falsehoods in a police report; or, at least, he had suppressed truths. He had said little of Flora, except naming her as a witness and quoting the parts of her statement which seemed apt or relevant. The pistol, now tucked away in his hip pocket, he had not even mentioned; after all, whoever had fired a shot with it, it had killed nobody. He simply stated he could find no weapon whatever.

The report was done now; it couldn't be recalled.

Cheviot's skin grew clammy, and not from chill morning air, when he thought what would happen to him if anyone had seen him pick up that firearm from the carpet and hide it under the lamp. Fortunately, he told himself, nobody had seen him.

'Forget this business for a while! Look where you're going!'

In New Burlington Street, at a quarter to eight in the morning, the gas-lamps were still burning. Every chimney smoked against the dull sky, sifting soot-drizzle into the mud of the roadway. But the houses, red brick or white stone, looked trim and furbished and clean. Nearly every private house bore, on its front door, a polished brass plate engraved with the name of its occupant.

'I had forgotten that,' he reflected, 'though it's in Wheatley, of course. What I'd give for Wheatley's three volumes of topography! And also — '

Yes. As he turned to the right along New Burlington Street, left into what was then called Savile Street, and right again down Clifford Street, he saw the street signs were also brass plates affixed to the houses at corners.

Still a broad double-line of gas-lamps stretched ahead. If in fact he occupied rooms at the Albany, as Colonel Rowan had said, this was his shortest way home. In Bond Street a full bustle and stir of life burst over him.

Most shop windows were yellow with gas glare. Cheviot saw the crossing-sweepers busy with their thick-bundled brooms in the mud. He saw the red coat of a postman. But mostly he saw the white, horribly shrunken faces of the very poor, who had no work and nothing to do. They shuffled past, or stared unseeingly into windows full of Chinese shawls, of gold brocade, of those many-hued silk turbans, called *turcs*, which placards in French said were the height of fashion for ladies.

Turning down Bond Street towards Piccadilly, Cheviot passed the lights of an hotel. A glass-panelled door, marked 'Coffee-Room,' reminded him of his ravenous hunger.

While he was hesitating, the keeper of a shop next to the hotel — its curly lettered sign proclaimed it that of a gunsmith and arms-maker — unlocked his premises. The gunsmith, an elderly man with clear silvery hair and no side-whiskers, gave him a casual glance; then a quicker, harder glance.

Cheviot hastily opened the coffee-room door.

Inside, in a hush of deep carpet under gilded ceiling cornices, a row of oaken booths, or boxes with bare tables inside them, stretched along either wall. At the rear of the coffee-room, an immense and full-length mirror reflected back his own image.

A side-mirror, over the chimney piece in the left-hand wall towards the back, gave him a sideways glimpse of two gentlemen eating breakfast in a box opposite it, and having a heated if low-voiced argument.

Both men wore their hats as they ate, so Cheviot did not remove his own hat as he slid into a box nearer the door and sat down.

On the table lay a small and stained

newspaper. Beside it were a bill of fare and a small glass of toothpicks. He snatched up the newspaper and looked at its date.

The date was October 30th, 1829.

The gas burned yellow-blue in brass brackets. There was no sound except the low, insistent voices of the two men in the far booth.

One of them said distinctly: 'Get rid of the rotten boroughs, sir! Reform, sir! A vote for every householder, according to a uniform plan.'

The other said: 'No Whiggery, sir! Let us have no Whiggery, if you please.'

Desperately Cheviot wanted to question Flora. But, apart from the fact that he did not even know where she lived, Flora might still be enraged or too horrified about the proprieties if he burst into her house at eight o'clock in the morning.

With powerful, irrational conviction he felt that Flora, if only unconsciously, held the secret of how and why he had been shut into a past century.

Even in time-trickeries there must be a how and a why. He could not have slipped through a chink and appeared here, for instance, as one of his own ancestors. His forefathers were all West Country squires; not one had lived in London for eight or nine generations.

Everybody appeared to recognize and accept him. All night Lady Cork had been referring to him as 'George Cheviot's son.' But his father's name was —

Was — what?

And Cheviot couldn't remember.

He sat very still, holding the newspaper. Here, this was idiotic!

Even last night his memory had been perfect. He could still see, as plainly as the rather smeary type of the newspaper, the pages of one of the text-books they used at Hendon Police College in the old days, and the section devoted to muzzle-loading fire-arms. Some of the candidates jeered at this, didn't trouble to study it, and got themselves pipped in an examination.

In imagination, too, he could see the faces of his father and his mother. Here was a simple test: what was his mother's maiden name?

That had gone, too.

'Yes, sir?' enquired a voice at his elbow.

The voice spoke in an ordinary tone. But it sounded like thunder. Cheviot looked up at an aproned waiter, with an inquisitive nose.

'Yes, sir?' the waiter repeated.

Cheviot ordered fried eggs, broiled ham, toast, and strong black tea. When the waiter had gone, he wiped sweat off his forehead.

His memories seemed to be slipping down and down, as though into water. Was it possible that in hours, or days or weeks, the waters would close over them and leave him submerged too?

He shut his eyes. In his old life he had lived (good!) in a flat off Baker Street. What was the address, the number of the flat? A sharper-piercing recollection went through him. Was he a bachelor, or had he been married? Surely, of all things on earth, he could remember that. Well! He was —

'Jack, old boy. Hal-lo!' cried a hearty if weak voice.

Beside the booth, swaying a little but reasonably sober, stood young Freddie Debbitt.

'Rather thought,' he said, lurching and sitting down on the other side of the table, 'rather thought I should find you here. Usually do come here, don't you?'

Freddie's high bearskin cap, its nap rubbed the wrong way, was stuck sideways on his bright brown hair. His button nose was red, his round face pale, from a long night's carouse. Collar, neckcloth, and frilled shirt were all rumpled and dirty.

Cheviot shut down the lid on panicky thoughts.

'Where have you been, Freddie?' he asked.

Bitterness rose in his voice. 'Didn't you — er — disappear with the others?'

Freddie gulped, as though he wished to bring up some of his liquor and couldn't.

'Some of us,' he said, 'went on to Carrie's, you know. Got some new gels, Carrie has. Mine was r-rather good, too.'

'Oh. I see.'

But Freddie would not meet his companion's gaze.

'I say, though!' he added suddenly. 'It's about last night. That's why I'm here. Wanted to see you, dash it. Had to see you.'

'About what?'

'Well . . . '

This was the point at which the waiter reappeared, sliding platters of food across the table, arranging a silver tea service with immense cup and saucer, and doing a twinkling conjuring trick with silver cutlery.

'Breakfast, Freddie?' suggested Cheviot.

The boy shuddered. 'No, thanks. Stay, though! Pint of claret and a biscuit.'

'Pint of claret, sir. Biscuit, sir. Very good, sir.' The waiter again melted away.

Cheviot poured tea and pitched in, trying to conceal his voracity.

'Jack!'

'Yes?'

'Last night.' Freddie cleared his throat.

'When you said Peg Renfrew was dead, and asked leave to question all of us, and proclaimed slap-out you were a p'leece-officer — '

'Freddie, I must thank you and Lady Cork and Miss Tremayne for what efforts you made to help. But the others? They did not even trouble to refuse answering questions. They ignored me altogether, and marched out of the house as though I were the scum of the earth.'

Freddie writhed.

'Well, old boy; damme, Jack! — no offence, but they were right!'

'Oh?'

'Peelers *are* the scum of the earth, you know.'

'Does this apply to Colonel Rowan? Or Richard Mayne? Or Mr. Peel himself?'

'That's different. Peel's a Cabinet Minister. The other two are Commissioners. But the rank and file?' Freddie meditated, plucking a toothpick from the glass. 'Deuce take it, I was struck all of a heap! Why didn't you say you were a crossing-sweeper? Or a body-snatcher, even? They'd have taken it better. A Peeler! A *Peeler* put questions to an officer of the Guards, like Hogben?'

Cheviot stopped with his knife and fork above the plate.

But he said nothing; he knew his difficulty; he knew this boy, sixteen or seventeen years younger than himself, was trying to aid him. And he went on eating.

'You!' said Freddie, jabbing at the table with a toothpick. 'You! A Peeler! Still! At least (or I hope, old fellow?) it's not too late?'

'Too late?'

'You haven't gone and joined 'em, I hear? Put your fist to a bit of paper, or the like?'

'No.'

A ripple of relief went over Freddie's pale face and small red nose, agitating the bright brown side-whiskers. He put down the toothpick and spoke quietly.

'You must drop it, old boy. Then they'll all see the joke and laugh with you.'

'Joke?'

'It's your own rum notion of a joke, a'n't it? But drop it. Devilish sorry; capital hoax; but you must. If you don't — '

Freddie moistened his lips. It was difficult for him, standing in so much awe of his companion as a sportsman, to stare back. But Cheviot suddenly realized that in Freddie Debbitt there were more force and strength of character than he would ever have suspected.

'Jack! A lot of us — well, dash it, we like you! But if you won't drop this . . . '

'Yes? If I won't drop it?'

'Then, damme, we'll make you drop it!'

Cheviot put down his knife and fork.

'Now just how do you propose to do that?'

Freddie had opened his mouth to retort when two persons arrived together at the table. One was the waiter, with Freddie's claret and a plate of biscuits on a salver. The other was an officer of the Guards, in full parade uniform.

This officer was a fair-haired, fair-complexioned young man in his middle twenties. His high bearskin cap, with its red short plume on the right to mark him as of the Second or Coldstream Regiment of Foot Guards, towered up as he held himself unnaturally straight.

His eyes were sharply intelligent, his manners formal and courteous, though he had the same lofty and languid look as so many of his tribe.

'Your name is Mr. Cheviot, I believe?'

'Yes?' said Cheviot.

He did not rise to his feet, as the officer seemed to expect. He merely eyed the newcomer up and down, without any favour at all.

'You will not be surprised, sir, when I tell you that I am here on behalf of my friend Captain Hogben, of the First Foot Guards.'

'Yes?'

'Captain Hogben begs to express his opinion that your behaviour last night, on at least two occasions, was of such an insulting kind as no gentleman can endure.'

Freddie Debbitt moaned a whispered oath. The waiter bolted away as though devil-pursued.

'Yes?' said Cheviot.

'However,' continued the newcomer, 'Captain Hogben requests me to add, considering your present somewhat inferior position as a member of the so-called police, that he is prepared to accept a written apology.'

Cheviot slid along the oaken bench and rose to his feet.

'Now damn his eyes,' Cheviot said quite pleasantly, 'but what makes him rank the Army above the Metropolitan Police?'

The other man's hard, intelligent face grew expressionless. But a slight flush mounted under his high cheek-bones.

'I bid you take care, sir, or you may have another challenge on your hands. I am Lieutenant Wentworth, of the Second Foot. Here is my card.'

'Thank you.'

'However, sir, I have not yet done.'

'Then have done, sir, by all means.'

'Failing the tender of a written apology,

Captain Hogben begs you to refer me to a friend of yours, that we may arrange a time and place of meeting. What is your answer, sir?'

'The answer is no.'

Amazement flashed briefly in Lieutenant Wentworth's eyes.

'Do I understand, sir, that you refuse this challenge?'

'Certainly I refuse it.'

'You — you prefer to write an apology?'

'Certainly not.'

It was deathly still in the coffee-room, except for the faint whistling of the gas-jets.

'Then what reply am I to take to Captain Hogben?'

'You may tell him,' Cheviot said almost tenderly, 'that I have work to do and that I have no time for adolescent foolery. You may further tender to him my hope that in due course his mind will grow to maturity.'

'Sir!' exclaimed Lieutenant Wentworth in a human and almost likeable tone. This instantly changed to stiff-jawed grimness. 'You understand the alternative? You know what Captain Hogben may do with this?'

'What he may do with it, sir, I trust I need not put into words. Good day, sir.'

Lieutenant Wentworth stared back at him. His left hand dropped to the hilt of his dress-sword. He was too well-mannered to sneer. But the edge of his lip lifted, with very slight contempt, above the chin strap of his bearskin cap. He returned Cheviot's bow, wheeled round, and marched out of the coffee-room.

The two men in the far booth, who had stood up to look, hastily sat down again. Cheviot saw his own disgrace mirrored in Freddie Debbitt's eyes as he continued, with outward quiet and inward boiling rage, to finish the eggs and ham and toast.

'Jack!'

'Yes?'

'You?' blurted Freddie. 'A shuffler? A coward?'

'Is that what you think, Freddie? By the way,' and Cheviot pushed aside his plate, 'you were about to tell me how you would force me to resign from the police.'

'And now this! My God! Hogben'll horsewhip — '

'How, Freddie? How will you force me to resign?'

'I won't,' retorted the other, who had swallowed most of the claret. 'But everybody will. When this news gets about, damme, you won't be received anywhere. You'll have to resign from your clubs. You can't go to Ascot or Newmarket. As a Peeler, they won't even admit you to a gambling-house . . . '

'Not even,' said Cheviot, 'to Vulcan's?'

'Why Vulcan's?' Freddie asked quickly, after a pause.

'No matter. It doesn't signify.'

'Dash it, Jack, you're not the same man I saw a fortnight ago! Is it Flora Drayton? Or her influence? Or what?' Due to that last pint of claret, Freddie had become maudlin and half-tearful. 'But she can't have wanted you to turn into a dashed Peeler. Last night all you'd do was go on about Peg Renfrew and jewellery and what not. Why, I could have told you — !' Abruptly he stopped.

'Yes,' agreed Cheviot. 'I rather thought you could.'

'Eh?'

'A while ago, Freddie, I thanked you for the help you gave me. You, and Lady Cork, and Louise Tremayne. But you didn't in fact give real help. Lady Cork was too stubborn; Miss Tremayne too fearful of Lord knows what; you too overawed by your friends.'

'Not overawed, curse it! Only — '

'Wait! Even before I questioned you downstairs, it was plain from what Flora and Lady Cork said that you knew a deal of the business. Your high spirits, your sense of humour, persuaded Lady Cork to hide her jewels in the seed containers. You were

150

hovering everywhere.'

'Only fun, you know!'

'Granted. But did Margaret Renfrew steal Lady Cork's jewels, as Lady Cork thinks she did?'

'Yes!' answered Freddie, with his eyes on the table.

John Cheviot drew a secret, deep gasp of relief. But his countenance showed nothing.

'Margaret Renfrew,' he muttered.

'What's that, old boy?'

'I see her.' Cheviot made a gesture. 'A vivid brunette, with a high colour and a noble figure. She would have been beautiful, appealing, except for what? Hardness? Defiance? Shame? She's the one person whose character I can't grasp.'

Freddie began to speak, but altered his mind.

'Listen!' urged Cheviot, seeing that gleam in the blurred young eyes. 'She was shot to death, Freddie. She's the centre of the maze. We shall be nowhere unless we understand her.'

Whereupon Freddie Debbitt, his expression far away, muttered words which for him were surprising and even startling.

''Fire burn',' he said, ''and cauldron bubble!''

'What's that?'

'I say!' Freddie emerged from his trance. 'D'ye know Edmund Kean? The actor fellow?'

'I have never met him, no,' Cheviot answered with truth.

'H'm. Just as well. He's finished now. The drink's done for him; lost his memory; all that. Though, mind you, he's shifted to Covent Garden and he still plays.'

'Freddie! I was asking you — '

'Little bit of a fellow, no mor'n a dwarf,' insisted Freddie. 'But with a big chest and a voice to break the window panes. When Kean was a lion in the old days, my father says he'd seldom go into society. 'Damn 'em!' says Kean. Now that he's done, so weak he can't more than stagger from Covent Garden to Offley's, there's no hostess'll receive him except Maria Cork.

'Stop, stop, now!' said Freddie. 'One night, month or so gone, Kean was at Maria's. Saw Peg for the first time, I think. Gives a start like What's-his-name seeing the Ghost. Stares at her. And —

' 'Fire burn and cauldron bubble!' Damme! Out it came, in a voice to make the footmen's hair stand on end. Can't say what he meant. Full of brandy-negus, to be sure.'

Those words, in the gas-lit coffee-room, sent a shiver through Cheviot. Behind Miss

Renfrew's painted face, her curling lip, what went on in her mind and heart and body?

'Freddie! Will you say what you know of her? And especially this mysterious lover of hers?'

The other hesitated.

'If I do,' he said with sudden and youthfully intoxicated cunning, 'will you drop your tomfoolery of being a Peeler? Hey?'

'I can't promise that. But it might affect my conduct in the future.'

Freddie glanced left and right, carefully. Then he beckoned with both hands.

'Listen!' he whispered.

9

The Innocence of Flora Drayton

Colonel Charles Rowan, standing by the table in his office with Mr. Mayne beyond him and Mr. Henley behind the desk in the corner, was rigid with pride and pleasure.

Yet little of this showed in Colonel Rowan's long, undemonstrative face.

'Mr. Cheviot,' he began, 'may I have the honour of making you known to Mr. Robert Peel?'

The fifth man in the office, who had been staring out of a window at the nearly denuded tree and bushes in Great Scotland Yard, with his hands clasped behind his back and his under-lip upthrust, now wheeled round.

Mr. Peel was a big man, shock-headed, imperious of presence. He wore a long brown surtout with a high black-velvet collar and frogged buttonholes. At forty-one he was growing florid of face, though with large and curiously sensitive eyes. Cheviot, from reading of him, had imagined him as cold and pompous; certainly Mr. Peel's speeches in the

House walked on stilts and unreeled yards of Latin quotations.

Nothing could have been more different from his manner now.

'Mr. Cheviot,' he said, smiling broadly as he gripped Cheviot's hand, 'you've won me over. You've got it.'

'Sir?'

'The position, man! Superintendent of the Home Division!'

'Mr. Peel,' interposed Colonel Rowan, tapping the many and well-thumbed sheets of paper on the table, 'has been much impressed by your report.'

'Best report I ever read,' Mr. Peel said briefly. 'They send you out — on what? A theft of bird-seed. You prove (like that!) it was a jewel-robbery. You demonstrate where the jewels were hid. You surmise who stole them, and virtually lure Maria Cork into admitting you're right. That's as neat, concise a bit of mathematical reasoning as anybody could want. — Mathematician, Mr. Cheviot?'

'No, sir. Mathematics was always my poorest subject.'

Up and down went the eyebrows.

'H'm. Pity. You surprise me. Now *I'm* a mathematician. I'll tell you more: I'm a Lancashire man, a practical man. If one thing won't do, use the opposite measure and stay

155

in office: that's practical politics. Never mind what they call you, if you know you're right. They'll call you names in any case, as they call me.'

Mr. Peel began to pace up and down, like a great wind in a small room. Though the office of Colonel Rowan and Mr. Mayne was not in the least small, the Home Secretary's tall presence made it seem so.

Then the florid face and the shock head turned on Cheviot.

'Thus, sir, concerning *you*. You are Superintendent of this division. All the same! We can't run the risk of wits such as yours being knocked out in a street brawl.'

'But, sir — !'

'I am speaking, Mr. Cheviot.'

It was three o'clock in the afternoon, with a nip in the October air. Watery sunlight, streaming past what few yellow leaves remained, poured through the red-curtained windows and hovered above a red Turkey carpet sprinkled grey with tobacco-ash.

Nothing had changed here since last night. Even the medium-weight pistol, with its silver handle and its hammer at half-cock as a sort of primitive safety-catch, lay undisturbed under a lightless red lamp.

To Cheviot — bathed, shaved, and in freshly fashionable new clothes — his position already seemed less strange. It seemed less outlandish that he should occupy chambers at the Albany, where a young and dull-witted manservant assisted him with the hot tub and set out the garments he wore.

If he reflected on these circumstances, they might have been terrifying. But he did not reflect; the Home Secretary kept his eye hypnotized.

'I am speaking, Mr. Cheviot!' the Home Secretary repeated.

'Your pardon, sir.'

'Granted, granted.' Mr. Peel waved his hand. 'Most of your nominal duties, therefore, will be assumed by the senior Inspector. You will not wear a uniform, even with gold lace round the collar to show your authority. You must remain in coloured clothes, as you are now.'

('Now why didn't that occur to me?' Cheviot was thinking. ''Coloured clothes' merely means plain clothes, as I ought to have guessed from what the cabman said.')

'There can't be any 'detective police' as yet,' announced Mr. Peel. 'More than one man in coloured clothes would make the cry of 'Spy!' even worse. But we can have him,' and he nodded towards Cheviot, 'as a whole detective police under one hat. Are you a mathematician, Colonel Rowan?'

'Mr. Peel,' courteously began Colonel Rowan, 'I have some elementary — '

'Are *you* a mathematician, Mr. Mayne?'

The young barrister, his eyes and his round cheeks bulging from the black circle of side-whiskers, was compelled to check the torrent of words he would have poured out. Mr. Mayne writhed, pop-eyed, and shook his head.

Mr. Peel chuckled.

'Ah, well,' he said. 'You needn't be. Merely jot down the rewards we're obliged to pay these cursed Bow Street men. For taking a house-breaker: forty pounds. For taking a highway robber: forty pounds. For taking a murderer: forty pounds.' Again he nodded towards Cheviot. 'You see the amount of money we save with *him*?'

'Oh, doubtless,' Colonel Rowan said gravely.

'Well?' demanded Mr. Peel, and looked full at Cheviot.

There was a brief silence.

'Yes, sir? What?'

'I must be off to the House. I can't stop here. But one thing I must know.'

Here Mr. Peel retreated to the table, where he struck his big knuckles on the sheets of Cheviot's report.

'Who killed Maria Cork's niece, this

woman Margaret Renfrew? And how the devil was it done?'

Now Cheviot understood why four pairs of eyes bored into him.

It was curiosity, a curiosity simmering almost beyond endurance even in Mr. Peel.

The Home Secretary's lips were drawn down. Mr. Mayne openly stared. Behind the desk in the corner, Mr. Henley had propped himself upright on an ebony stick. Colonel Rowan, though better concealing his feelings, slapped and slapped with his white gloves at the white trousers below the scarlet coat.

'Sir,' Cheviot answered, 'as yet I can't tell.'

'You can't *tell*?' echoed Mr. Peel.

'No, sir. Not yet. This morning I obtained very helpful information from Mr. Frederick Debbitt, which is not in the report. But — '

'Here's a man,' exclaimed Mr. Peel, incredulously appealing to the others, 'who takes but one glance at the evidence before him, and tells us nearly all of what has happened. Yet he can't explain a detail like this?'

Cheviot's heart sank.

After his work last night, work which would not even have earned him a word of commendation from the Deputy Commander in his past life, these people were so impressed that they expected miracles. And miracles they meant to have.

There was more. This old house, much enlarged at the back to form a whole police-office, today stirred and was alive despite its unfinished confusion. The four Inspectors of the division, with short silver lace at the neck, and the Sergeants, with metal collar-numerals from one to sixteen, were present and correct. Sixty-five constables, he had been told, awaited his inspection on a small parade-ground at the rear.

They were a hard lot, ready to snarl or grow sullen under a Superintendent who could not handle them. Even when he entered he had sensed hurrying footsteps, smelt a whiff of brandy, heard the *whack-whack* as two humorists struck in vicious mock-battle with wooden truncheons.

In more senses than one, he was on trial.

But Cheviot, who had been compelled to control his temper since early morning, did not fail to control it now.

'Mr. Peel,' he said coldly, 'I ask you to consider the difficulties here. For instance! You have read my report, I understand?'

'Yes. Every word of it.'

'You have also seen my sketch-plan of the upstairs passage where the crime was committed?'

Without a word Mr. Richard Mayne dug among the sheets of the report, found the plan, and held it up.

'All this,' complained Mr. Peel, 'is surely unnecessary? I have many times seen the passage you describe.'

'And I,' said Colonel Rowan, with his gaze on a corner of the ceiling.

'Forgive me,' said Cheviot, 'but it is not at all unnecessary. Finally, I call your attention to the surgeon's findings and the direction of the bullet.'

He paused, surveying each of the auditors in turn.

'The bullet that killed Miss Renfrew,' Cheviot added clearly, 'was fired in a dead straight line. You mark it? A dead straight line.'

It was as though Mr. Peel had retreated a little, merely watching and weighing with those large, sensitive eyes. Both Colonel Rowan and Mr. Mayne, the Commissioners, edged forward.

'I see what you imply, Mr. Cheviot,' replied Colonel Rowan. He took the sketch-plan from his companion and tapped it. 'In this passage, facing the stairs, we have two single doors on the left, and one set of double-doors (to the ballroom) on the right. Therefore none of these doors could have opened. Else,

161

with this — this poor lady's body lying well to the front of them, the bullet would have taken a diagonal course and not a straight.'

'Exactly! And then?'

'Why, damme,' Mr. Mayne burst out at last, 'it's as plain as a pikestaff!'

'Is it?' Cheviot asked.

'The bullet,' said Mr. Mayne, 'was fired from the rear of the passage. Somewhere very near the place where you and Henley were standing. You allow it?'

'Apparently. Yes.'

'We must grant,' continued Mr. Mayne, regaining his barrister's dignity, 'that neither you nor Henley is guilty. You would have seen each other. But what of the double-doors just behind you? Eh? What, I say, of the double-doors to Lady Cork's boudoir?'

'Well?'

'Your backs were turned to those doors. *They* could have opened, I daresay?'

'In theory, yes.'

'In theory, Mr. Cheviot?'

'Yes. But not,' retorted Cheviot, 'without a snap and crack of the lock as loud as a light pistol-shot. As I pointed out in my report, the lock snaps whenever you open or close the door. We should have heard it; but we heard nothing. Second, is it likely that someone fired a pistol behind my shoulder, or

Henley's, without either of us feeling the sting of the powder or the wind of the bullet?'

'Likely, sir?' repeated Mr. Mayne, with rich courtroom politeness. 'Likely? My dear sir, that is what happened.'

'I beg your pardon?'

Despite himself Mr. Mayne shot out a pointing finger.

'Wherever the place from which the bullet was fired, you have acknowledged it must have been close to you? Yes. And yet, you tell us, you heard little and felt little and saw nothing?'

'Are you calling me a liar, Mr. Mayne?'

'Gentlemen!' interposed Colonel Rowan, very stiffly. Mr. Robert Peel, hugely amused, glanced from one to the other and said nothing.

'As for — er — impugning your veracity, Mr. Cheviot,' the barrister told him with dignity, 'I do no such thing. I am a lawyer, sir. I must examine evidence.'

'I am a police-officer, sir. So must I.'

'Then be good enough to do so.' Mr. Mayne snatched the sketch-plan from Colonel Rowan and held it up. 'In this admirable plan of yours, I note, we have the arrangement of all the doors.'

'We have.'

'Good! At some time before the murder,

163

for example, could someone have slipped out of the ballroom unobserved by any of the other dancers?'

'Not while Lady Drayton was waiting in the passage, no.'

'Ah, yes! Lady Drayton,' said Mr. Mayne in a musing tone. His eyes, round and black and shining, rolled up suddenly; Cheviot felt a twinge of fear. 'But we dismiss her, for the moment. Lady Drayton, as I understand it, was not sitting in the passage for the whole time before the murder?'

'No. She had gone downstairs to fetch a list of Lady Cork's jewels.'

'Pre-cisely!' agreed Mr. Mayne, teetering on his heels. 'Precisely! Therefore I repeat: could an assassin, he or she, have slipped out of the ballroom unobserved by any of the other dancers?'

'Yes; quite easily. When I myself glanced into the ballroom, the dancers were so absorbed that none so much as glanced at me.'

'Ah!' said Mr. Mayne, teetering again. 'I put to you, Mr. Cheviot, a feasible supposition. The assassin, let us imagine, slips out of the ballroom. He, or she, crosses diagonally to the door of the dining-room. We have here,' and he held up the plan, 'evidence that there is a door from the dining-room to Lady

Cork's bedroom, and another door from her bedroom into her boudoir.'

Here Mr. Mayne dropped the plan on the table, and stood teetering with his dark eyes shrewdly shining.

'I put it to you, Mr. Cheviot,' he continued, 'that the murderer could have been lurking in Lady Cork's bedroom. As soon as you and Henley leave the boudoir, closing the double-doors, the assassin moves across and opens one leaf of the doors behind you. Under cover of the noise, he fires a shot past you below shoulder-height. He then closes the doors and departs by way of the bedroom. I put it to you' — again Mr. Mayne's finger shot out automatically — 'that this is quite possible?'

'No,' said Cheviot.

'No? And pray why not?'

'Because,' Cheviot retorted, 'Lady Cork was in the boudoir the whole time.'

'I fail to — '

'Do you, Mr. Mayne? Consider! When I entered the boudoir a brief time afterwards, Lady Cork was dozing beside the fire. But one snap of that lock roused her instantly.'

'Well?'

'Well, sir! Do you imagine the murderer could have crept into the boudoir, opened that cracking door, fired a pistol, shut the door again and moved away, all without our notice or Lady Cork's? Or do you suggest Lady Cork as an accomplice in the crime?'

There was a strained, polite silence.

Mr. Peel nursed his chin, fingers hiding a smile. Colonel Rowan's handsome face, the grey-blond hair swept up above the temples, was apparently not there at all. Richard Mayne remained poised, though the dark eyes sparkled with wrath.

'You prefer an impossible situation, Mr. Cheviot?'

'To your solution, sir, I do.'

'There is, to be sure,' the barrister said thoughtfully, 'an alternative and very easy explanation. But I hesitate to suggest it.'

Cheviot merely lifted his shoulders and made a gesture for the other to go on.

Richard Mayne's round face softened. At heart, as he had proved in the past and was to prove in the future, he was a kindly and very efficient man. But his bouncing energy, at thirty-three, sometimes drove him at problems as though with his fists.

Still hesitating, he strolled over to the nearer window. Mr. Mayne drew back one side of the red curtain. He looked out at the soft mud of the yard, churned with wheel-tracks and enmeshed in dead leaves. He glanced at Mr. Peel's sober but luxurious carriage waiting there, at the dead bushes, at the one tall and crooked tree with a few yellow leaves still clinging to its branches.

Then Mr. Mayne's mouth tightened. He stalked back to the table, and tapped the sheets of Cheviot's report.

'Mr. Cheviot,' he said in a hard voice, 'why are you shielding Lady Drayton?'

Behind the desk in the corner, the pen dropped from Mr. Henley's hand and rolled clattering across until the chief clerk seized it.

Cheviot's heart jumped into his throat.

'Is there anything there,' he demanded, 'to say I am shielding Lady Drayton?'

Mr. Mayne made a gesture of impatience.

'It's not what you say. It's what you *don't* say. Come, man! Here is your most important witness, yet you scarcely speak of her. By your own account Lady Drayton was standing only ten or a dozen feet behind the victim. And, a most unusual circumstance, she was carrying a muff indoors. Are you a student of history, Mr. Cheviot?'

'Fortunately for myself, I am.'

'Then you will be aware,' the barrister said dryly, 'that as early as the late seventeenth century, in the so-called and preposterous 'Popish Plot,' ladies were accustomed to defend themselves by carrying a pocket pistol in a muff.'

Here Mr. Mayne drew himself up.

'It would be a pity, Mr. Cheviot,' he continued with bursting politeness, 'if our association began in a quarrel. But (forgive me!) we know so little of you. You are a well-known athlete, they say. Yet can you dominate the hard-bitten crew you purpose to command? Last night you boasted that any of us might take a pistol — yes, that pistol on the table now! — and fire at the stuffed bear by the mantelpiece, and you would tell us who had fired it. Have you fulfilled that boast? I think not. Instead — '

Abruptly he stopped.

He stopped, and turned towards the windows, because no one could have ignored the voice from outside.

The voice clove through October air now turned from watery yellow to dull grey. Cheviot knew whose voice it was. It belonged to Captain Hogben, and had no trace of a lisp. Harsh, strident, it beat at the house in a fury of hatred and triumph.

'*Come out, Cheviot!*' it screamed. '*Come out, shuffler, and take what's coming to you!*'

10

The Battle in the Yard

Cheviot took three strides to the nearer window, and, like Mr. Mayne, flung back the curtain at one side.

There were three of them, not thirty feet away from the house. They stood in the mud, motionless, under the tall and crooked tree with the few yellow leaves.

Captain Hogben and Lieutenant Wentworth were both in full parade uniform. Against their scarlet coats the white cross-belts stood out vividly in the grey air, as did the white duck trousers for daytime wear. From each man's left hip hung the long sabre in the gold scabbard, as straight as the top-heavy bearskin cap on each head. In fact, except for the short white plume on the left of Hogben's tall cap, and the short red plume to the right of Wentworth's, you could not distinguish the First Foot Guards from the Second.

But there were other differences.

Captain Hogben stood crookedly, under the high and crooked tree above him. His face showed red, his mouth split for yelling above the chin-strap. His left shoulder was up and his right humped down, white-gloved right hand gripping the stock of the horsewhip trailing out snakily behind him.

Lieutenant Wentworth remained straight and rigid. Between them, shivering, stood Freddie Debbitt.

Then Hogben's eyes caught Cheviot's through the window-glass.

'*Come out, coward!*' he screamed. '*Come out here now, or —* '

And Cheviot's temper, so long restrained that day, blew to pieces with a crash all the more violent for being inaudible.

He spun round. On his face was a smile so broad and murderous that for a second his four companions did not recognize him as the same man.

'Excuse me for a moment, gentlemen,' he said in a voice he scarcely recognized himself.

And he ran for the door and threw it open.

Just outside, in the passage, there was already a clump and clatter of hurrying footsteps. Down the stairs poured tall hats of reinforced leather, and tight-fitting blue coats with lines of metal buttons. From the rear of the passage stalked a tall Inspector, with short silver lace at his collar, holding back the staring and straining men behind him.

When they saw Cheviot in the doorway, every man stopped dead.

Just in front of Cheviot stood a shortish but very broad man, marked as a sergeant by the metal numeral 13 on either side of his collar. He had a red face and a good-humoured eye, though his hard glance appraised the new Superintendent even when he stiffened to salute.

'Orders, sir?'

Cheviot did not speak loudly. Yet his voice seemed to penetrate to every corner of the house.

'There are no orders. Let every man stay where he is. I deal with this myself.'

The sergeant's eyes gleamed. From under the back skirts of his coat, where it hung hidden, he whipped out the long baton of that very hard wood called lignum vitae.

'Truncheon, sir?'

'Now what need have I for a weapon? Stand aside!'

Cheviot ran for the front door. It was a large, heavy door. When he turned the knob and flung it open, the knob bounced and rebounded against the inner wall.

Every sense strung alert, eyes moving left and right and forward, he jumped down into the mud. Some dozen paces to his left, far out from the brick wall of the house, Mr. Peel's large carriage waited, with two footmen up behind and a sleepy coachman on the box. One of the horses suddenly stirred and whinnied.

Captain Hogben uttered a yell of triumph. Right hand back, he charged forward across the yard.

According to every rule, Cheviot should have stood still and taken his lashing. He should even have cowered, arms protecting his face, as befitted one who had refused a challenge to a duel. This always happened in books; Hogben, Wentworth, Freddie Debbitt firmly believed it happened in real life.

But he did nothing of the kind.

Instead, left arm slightly lifted and right arm a little below, Cheviot raced forward to meet Hogben in the middle of the yard.

Too late Hogben saw they must collide. Too late he recognized he should have stood off and lashed. But he could not stop his charge, and there was still time to use the whip. His right arm swung forward, the thin black whip curling out.

Cheviot stopped short. Hogben did not. As his right arm flew forward, the fingers of Cheviot's left hand gripped hard round the Guardsman's wrist. Cheviot braced himself hard on his right foot, turned slightly sideways, and yanked with all his strength.

Captain Hugo Hogben, nearly six feet tall and weighing eleven-stone-ten, pitched head-long over Cheviot's left shoulder.

His sword-scabbard rattled and flew. He landed head down, his tall bearskin cap squashing and turning under him to spare concussion of the brain. His body landed with a shock and thud which drove the breath from his lungs and the wits from his head.

Cheviot jumped over that motionless figure, sprawled in scarlet and white against the black mud. He tore the horsewhip from Hogben's hand. Coiling it up as best he could, he threw it far away among the bushes.

Then he jumped back again.

'Now get up!' he said.

A carriage-horse whinnied loudly and reared up. The coachman, down off the box, soothed the horse and muttered words nobody heard. A *whush* of chilly wind swept the bushes. A dead leaf spun off the tree, fluttered lazily, and floated down.

Almost instantly Captain Hogben twitched hard and was on his feet.

His gloved left hand ripped the chin-strap upwards. With both hands he slowly lifted the top-heavy cap from his head, and threw it aside. From uniform to face he was one spatter and smear of mud, except the clear patch over the forehead and eyes and round the ears where the cap had protected him, and a mudless space beneath his right eye.

His eyes were bleared. He was none too steady on his feet. But he had guts enough for ten men.

'Swine,' he said.

And his gloved right hand whipped a vicious round-arm blow at his opponent's face.

Cheviot slipped under the blow. He seized Hogben, and spun him round backwards by his own front cross-belts. The dart was so unexpected that Hogben's shoulders and arms momentarily fell loose.

Instantly his right arm was gripped by the wrist, and locked up high behind his back. By instinct Hogben thrashed out towards the man behind him. He was just able to bite back a cry of agony.

'If you do that again,' Cheviot said clearly, 'you'll break your own arm. Now be off with you before I throw you in the cells. And don't make threats about horsewhipping people until you're sure you can carry 'em out.'

Lieutenant Wentworth, still motionless, spoke in a high voice.

'Release him!' said Lieutenant Wentworth, with so superior and commanding an air that Cheviot's rage boiled again. 'Do you hear, Peeler? Release him, I say!'

'With pleasure,' snarled Cheviot.

He dropped Hogben's arms. Both hands flashed down nearly to the small of the Captain's back. Again all his strength went out in one catapult-shove.

Hogben staggered forward for three long paces, reeled, and just saved himself from falling on his face. He bent down, one knee touching the ground, while you might have counted six.

Then he straightened up and turned round, breathing hard. The white mudless patch under his right eye gave that right eye a singular appearance: tip-tilted, distorted, devilish.

'God damn you,' he whispered.

His left hand jerked the sword-scabbard to one side. There was a rasp of steel as he whipped out the straight sabre and charged again.

There could be no foretelling the result if Hogben, all but on top of his adversary, had lunged out for a thrust with the point. A simultaneous yell of warning, rising from many throats of people Cheviot could not see, burst like a war-whoop over the yard.

But it was not necessary. Captain Hogben flung back arm and shoulder for an overhand cut with the edge. In the split-second he was off balance, Cheviot leaped in at him.

Mr. Robert Peel, Colonel Charles Rowan, Mr. Richard Mayne, and Mr. Alan Henley, all unashamedly fighting each other to look out of one window, had long found their view obscured.

Officers as well as constables, disregarding orders, poured out of the house and lined up against the walls to watch.

Mr. Peel, for instance, saw the sword-blade whirl high in the air. It dropped, point downwards, and stuck upright in the mud not four feet in front of Lieutenant Wentworth. Mr. Peel could not see how Cheviot's hands altered their grip.

But Captain Hogben seemed to sail out in the air, feet forward and back parallel with the ground. They saw the soles of Hogben's boots, kicking towards the house, before he landed on his back and head, and lay still.

It was different, very different, in that deadly little circle of emotion round the fallen Hogben.

Cheviot, the breath whistling in his throat and sweat running down his body, strode forward. With his right hand round the hilt, he jerked the sabre out of the ground. His left hand fastened round the blunt edge. There was a sharp *crack* as he broke the blade across his knee. The two pieces he tossed away.

'Oh, God,' whispered Freddie Debbitt.

Lieutenant Wentworth's fair complexion had gone chalk-white. He moistened his lips. Though he spoke clearly, it was with a kind of horror.

'You have broken the sword of a Guards officer,' he said.

'Indeed?' gasped the unimpressed Cheviot. 'Now just who the devil,' he added, almost pleasantly, 'do you Guardsmen think you are?'

Lieutenant Wentworth did not reply. He could not. It was as though Cheviot had asked the King who the devil he thought *he* was, or perhaps put the same question to the Deity Himself. Again Wentworth was merely bewildered.

'Mr. Cheviot, I — '

For the first time Cheviot raised his voice.

'Now look here,' he shouted, dragging out his watch, opening it, and glancing at the fallen Hogben. 'I'll give you just thirty seconds to take that — that specimen away from here. If you don't, I'll collar the lot of you and charge you with assaulting a police-officer. Take your choice.'

'Jack, old boy!' bleated Freddie.

'Ah, my dear Freddie!' Cheviot said with rich politeness. 'You professed to be a friend of mine, I think? What do you do in the camp of the enemy?'

'Dash it, Jack, I *am* your friend! I tried to prevent this! Ask Wentworth if I didn't!' Here Freddie paused in alarm as he looked sideways. 'Hogben! Stop!'

For the indomitable Captain Hogben had again struggled up to his feet.

'No!' Lieutenant Wentworth said curtly.

Stalking towards Hogben, he seized his friend's left arm and held him back. Freddie, with surprising strength and firmness, dived and held Hogben's right arm.

'No!' Wentworth repeated. 'If you use your hands against him, like a ploughboy, he'll make a fool of you every time. Be still!'

'Ten seconds,' murmured Cheviot.

Wentworth drew himself up formally.

'Mr. Cheviot! You don't really mean to arrest — ?'

'Don't I?' asked Cheviot, with a broad smile. 'What do *you* think?'

'I am informed, Mr. Cheviot, that you are a gentleman despite your profession. A while ago, in the excusable heat of the moment, I uttered words of which I am heartily ashamed. Sir, I apologize.' Wentworth slightly ducked his bearskin cap. 'Nevertheless, matters have gone too far. You *must* meet Captain Hogben in the field — '

'With pistols?' Cheviot asked sardonically. 'Fifteen seconds!'

'Yes, with pistols! You must meet him, I say, or he will have the right to shoot you down in the street.'

Cheviot, about to answer contemptuously, caught sight of Freddie Debbitt's face. Inspiration came to him from the sort of moral blackmail Freddie had attempted to use that morning. He saw now what he stood to gain.

'Agreed!' said Cheviot, and shut up his watch.

'You will meet him?'

'I will meet him.'

'You would have done much better,' said Wentworth, drawing a deep breath, 'had you said so earlier today. To whom do you refer me as a friend?'

'To Mr. Debbitt there. He will arrange matters with you, at any time and place you like.' Cheviot replaced his watch. 'You will, Freddie, won't you?'

'I . . . I . . . curse it, yes!'

'Very well. But, before our formal meeting, I shall insist on one condition.'

Lieutenant Wentworth's back stiffened.

Cheviot, staring out at the cool grey air, went hot-and-cold all over. He was trying, in an abstract way, to remember the appearance of the flat in which he had lived (where?) in his old life as Superintendent of C-One.

He could recall nothing. Slowly, relentlessly, his memory was being submerged. Yet he could now remember the appearance, the numbers, even the smell and atmosphere, of places he did not even believe he knew.

'Joe Manton's shooting-gallery,' Cheviot snapped, 'is at number twenty-five Davies Street? Yes, yes, I am aware Manton is dead! But his son still keeps the gallery, and the gunsmith's at number twenty-four next door?'

'Well?'

'Before our formal meeting,' said Cheviot, 'Captain Hogben and I shall try our hands against each other, six shots each at a wafer, and for any wager he cares to name.'

Lieutenant Wentworth was scandalized.

'Two principals,' he cried, 'to practice together before a meeting? That's imposs — !'

'Stop! Wait!' croaked out Hogben.

Hogben was now pretty steady on his feet. He jerked his arms loose. His face, under mud-stains, was paper-white between the black side-whiskers and feathery black hair. Though he drew his breath with difficulty, he bit at mud-caked lips and spoke again.

'*Any* wager, ye say?' And greed moistened his lips.

'Yes!'

'A thousand guineas? Hey?'

'Done!' said Cheviot.

'You fancy yourself, I hear,' sneered Hogben through panting breaths, 'at pistol-shootin' at a wafer. It'll be different when you face fire in the field, I promise you. Still! You do fancy yourself when there's no danger. What odds d'ye give?'

This time Cheviot drew a deep breath.

'All odds,' he retorted in a loud voice. 'If you outshoot me, in the opinion of judges to be agreed upon, I pay you a thousand guineas on the spot. If I outshoot you — '

'Hey? Well?'

'On your word as a British officer, you shall tell all you know about the late Margaret Renfrew. And so shall your friend Lieutenant Wentworth. That is all.'

Once more the wind went stirring and rustling in the bushes. Mr. Peel's carriage, with its still-restive horses soothed by the coachman, had clopped up to a point almost behind them and towards their left.

'Wait!' said Wentworth, with an indecipherable expression on his face. 'I again protest against — '

Hogben silenced him, still holding himself upright without swaying.

Captain Hogben was not an articulate or an intelligent man, as Lieutenant Wentworth clearly was. For Hogben, at all times, courage alone sufficed. And yet, as he rolled round that one vivid tip-tilted eye, it held a look of such malicious and delighted cunning that Cheviot ought to have been warned. He should have sensed fanged dangers in ambush, an unseen stroke to crush him forever.

'Done!' Hogben said softly.

'I tell you, the code — ' began Wentworth.

'Damn the code. Be quiet, Adrian, and fetch my cap!'

Lieutenant Wentworth hurried to pick up the muddied bearskin cap, slapped at it to clean it, and fitted it slowly down on his friend's head as he adjusted the chin-piece. Hogben winced slightly with pain, but held himself straight. He did not even glance at the pieces of the broken sword.

Freddie Debbitt ran out into Whitehall. Putting two fingers into his mouth, he whistled shrilly. A large and wide open carriage, drawn by two black horses and with its rather grimy silk upholstery in white as though to match the plume of the Grenadier Guards, came spanking into view.

Behind it, almost too close, rattled another open carriage: more severe, but better kept from its red wheels to its glossy dapple-grey mares.

In this latter carriage sat a fat and

to avoid embarrassment.

So he marched straight up, and stopped before the cleared path to the door. There he ran his eye slowly to the left along those motionless lines, and then slowly to the right, as though in careful inspection.

'Which of you,' he asked curtly, 'is the senior Inspector?'

The tall and lean man, whom he had seen before and who had a nose like the as-yet-uncreated Mr. Punch of the magazine-cover, took two stiff paces forward and saluted.

'Sir!' he said. 'Inspector Seagrave, sir.'

'A good parade, Inspector Seagrave. I congratulate you.'

'Sir!'

Cheviot glanced down at the two pieces of the sword in his left hand.

'I have here,' he added, 'a small trophy for our first trophy-room. It belongs to all of you. Take it.'

Abruptly he threw the pieces to Inspector Seagrave, who caught them neatly in one hand with a sharp clash of steel. The short, slight gesture of the Inspector's other hand indicated, 'No cheering!' to the men behind him, though the lines of tall hats wavered and an explosion hovered close.

Once again Cheviot glanced slowly left and right.

purplish-faced gentleman with a velvet-collared surtout over his coat, and a majestic hat. Beside him, on the near side, Louise Tremayne leaned out and looked straight at Cheviot.

Young Louise wore one of the fashionable turbans in blue silk; a white cloak, with blue-striped cape to it, was clasped round her neck. Her hazel eyes, very intense in the pretty, immature face, conveyed a message as plainly as her wide mouth moved without sound.

'I must see you immediately at — '

The fat gentleman, observing the turn of her head, touched her shoulder. While Louise shrank meekly inside her cape, the fat gentleman — obviously father or uncle or close relative — raised his thick black eyebrows so outrageously high that it might have been a gesture of pained astonishment on the stage.

'You, fellow!' sneered Captain Hogben.

Cheviot shifted his eyes back. All hatred rose again.

'Manton's?' asked Captain Hogben. 'Nine o'clock tomorrow morning?'

Cheviot nodded curtly.

'And afterwards, hey, the meetin'?'

Again Cheviot nodded.

Ignoring him, Captain Hogben swung

round and moved towards the first carriage. His step faltered; Wentworth and Freddie Debbitt held his arms on either side. But he had gone only two steps when he whirled round again.

The venom of the one eye had a tint and taint of the demoniac.

'May Christ help you,' Hogben said, not loudly, 'when I get you at the end of a duellin' pistol!'

Lieutenant Wentworth jerked at his arm. He and Freddie hurried Hogben forward, assisting him into the first carriage between them. The driver's whip cracked; the black horses swept the carriage away up Whitehall. A lighter flick danced over the dapple-grey mares of the second carriage. While Louise kept her eyelashes demurely lowered, and the purplish-faced gentleman took a pinch of snuff from an ivory box, the carriage rattled after Hogben's past the grey courtyard of the Admiralty across the road.

Superintendent John Cheviot stood motionless, his head down.

His high collar had wilted; its points ceased to stab him under the chin. He was cooling off, both in mind and body.

He had beaten Hogben hands down. But he was far from sure he had not made a fool of himself. There, in the mud, lay the two pieces of the broken sword. Cheviot, a little ashamed, bent down, picked them up, and weighed them in his hand.

Still with his gaze on the ground, he walked slowly and heavily towards the house.

Then he raised his head — and stopped short.

For he saw what he had never expected to see.

Every man of the division's sixty-five constables stood motionless, in a double rank on either side of the door. Just in front of them stood the sixteen sergeants, eight on either side to mark the path to the door. And, in front of these, the four Inspectors stood two on either side.

They stood rigidly at attention, their shoulders so far back as to threaten the cloth of the blue coats. Their hands were straight down the trouser-seams. Their eyes were fixed straight ahead, in a sightless and glassy stare, though any observer could have seen that each man's lungs were all but bursting to cheer.

Still silence, while only the wind stirred.

It was the greatest tribute they could have paid him. Cheviot knew it. To his heart it drove the blood of pride and pleasure; it straightened his own back, and made his head sing. But he sensed how he must deal with it,

'Stand easy,' he said.

And, smiling for the first time, he sauntered between the ranks, up the step, and through the open door into the house.

He did not even hear the outburst behind him. Cheviot had the bit in his teeth; Mr. Richard Mayne was attacking, and there was one who must be kept from any danger, if he must outface the Home Secretary too.

Striding to the door of Colonel Rowan's office on the right, Cheviot opened it without the formality of knocking. He closed the door behind him.

Then he looked slowly round at Mr. Robert Peel, at Colonel Rowan, at Mr. Alan Henley again behind the desk, and above all at Mr. Richard Mayne.

'And now, gentlemen,' he began briskly, 'as we were saying before this unseemly interruption? Mr. Mayne, I believe, was accusing Flora Drayton of having committed murder?'

11

Louise Tremayne — and Dear Papa

'But, damme, man,' exclaimed Mr. Mayne, removing his hands from under his coat-tails, 'I never said any such thing! I only said — '

Colonel Rowan held up a hand for silence.

The Colonel, who had clipped and lighted a cigar, was pacing restlessly. He stopped in front of Cheviot, with his large nostrils distended.

'Superintendent,' he said, taking the cigar out of his mouth, 'the First or Grenadier Foot Guards are the oldest regiment in the British Army. Your conduct was infamous; I must rebuke you severely. Er — consider yourself rebuked,' added Colonel Rowan, and put the cigar back in his mouth.

'Yes, sir,' said Cheviot.

Mr. Peel, not a man much addicted to mirth, uttered a great gust of laughter. Then his large eyes narrowed with cold shrewdness.

'For myself, Mr. Cheviot,' he said, 'I should give much to know whether you merely lost your temper, or whether you did that deliberately to impress your men. Well, you impressed 'em. And by gad, sir, you impressed me! But you've landed yourself in trouble all the same.'

'With Captain Hogben, sir?'

'Hogben? That lout? The other officers of the First Foot won't even speak to him; that's why he needed a Coldstreamer for support. No! I meant the Duke. The Guards are the Duke's pets. To talk to him, you'd think no other regiments were even present at Waterloo — '

Here Colonel Rowan grew rigid.

' — and there'll be a fine mess if *he* hears of this. Further,' mused Mr. Peel, with his chin in his big hand, 'I wonder what you and Hogben were discussing so formally just before he left?'

'A purely private matter, sir. It does not concern us.'

'H'm,' Mr. Peel said thoughtfully.

Cheviot advanced to the table.

'But what does concern us,' he drove at them, 'is Mr. Mayne's statement that I failed in my duty and that I shielded Lady Drayton.'

'I said as much. Yes!' Mr. Mayne retorted with drawn-up dignity.

'On what grounds?' Cheviot struck the table. 'With your permission, sir, *I* will repeat the argument. You are suspicious, you state, on the grounds of what I 'do not say.' I have never heard, in law, of a man being condemned for perjury because of what he does not say.'

'You are twisting — !'

'I am stating. Your only so-called evidence, which you term an 'unusual circumstance,' is that Lady Drayton carried a muff indoors. Had you read this report, however,' and Cheviot lifted the sheets and dropped them, 'you would have seen it was not at all unusual. Lady Drayton had split her right-hand glove wide open, as everyone can testify; and, like other ladies, she wished to conceal it. Where is your evidence that any pistol was in the muff or existed at all?'

Mr. Mayne's dark eyes glittered.

'Evidence? I mentioned none. I but suggested a line of inquiry which you seem to have neglected.'

'Sir!' blurted out a hoarse, heavy voice behind him.

Alan Henley leaned out with his thick hands on the desk. Though it was only five o'clock, the grey sky had grown so dark that these people loomed up like the ghosts they might have been.

A grease-soaked wick flared up; again, with a loud pop, Mr. Henley kindled the broad green-shaded lamp on his desk, as opposed to the red-shaded one on the table. His big head, with the reddish side-whiskers, was thrust out with great earnestness.

'Sir,' he continued, addressing Colonel Rowan, 'she didn't!'

'Oh? Didn't what?' Colonel Rowan spoke mildly, removing the cigar from his mouth.

'The lady,' insisted Mr. Henley, 'hadn't got a pistol. I was there, sir. I saw. As for the Superintendent being negligent — why, sir, it was the first thing he thought on.'

'Ah?'

'He thought (begging your pardon, Colonel) the lady might have fired a shot. I knew she hadn't; I watched her. She no more had a weapon than me and the Superintendent had. But he asked her to show and turn out her muff, case she might have fired through it. And she hadn't.'

Mr. Henley's honesty, since he really believed every word he was saying, carried conviction.

And all the time, in imagination, Cheviot had been seeing Flora: Flora's jealousies or rages lasted only for a moment, though why could she have been jealous of Margaret Renfrew? All day she would have been waiting for him at her house in Cavendish Square; and he had not called there. He would only have to mutter that it was his fault, and she would pour out frantic cries that it was all her fault, and run into his arms . . .

Here Cheviot checked his thoughts, with a clammy shock over his body.

How did he know Flora lived in Cavendish Square, if she did? How did he know how she always behaved after a quarrel or misunderstanding?

But he must wrench back his mind. Mr. Henley was still doggedly speaking.

' — so you see, sir, *I* didn't read the Superintendent's report. Or hear about it till a while ago. All the same, this surgeon says the bullet was fired in a dead straight line. Well! Anybody can tell you Lady Drayton was standing behind the poor woman a good two or three feet to the right of her. So she'd have had to fire a shot diagonal-like, now wouldn't she?'

Mr. Richard Mayne lifted his shoulders.

'Then you are all against me, it seems,' he said.

'No, sir, Mr. Mayne, we're not!' Again the chief clerk, with heat, appealed to Colonel Rowan. 'One word more, Colonel?'

Colonel Rowan smiled and gestured assent with his cigar.

'*I* think,' said Mr. Henley, 'Mr. Mayne's right about a shot from inside them double-doors behind us. Noise!' he scoffed, with puffed cheeks. 'You're not put off by snapping locks or even light shots. Me and the Superintendent (eh, sir?) were too preoccupied by what Lady Cork had just said. That's what puts you off. If you ask me, somebody could have let off a blunderbuss behind us and we shouldn't have heard. There!'

' "For this relief",' murmured Richard Mayne, ' "much thanks".'

'Mayne!' Colonel Rowan called softly.

'Eh?'

'You and I,' smiled the Colonel, 'have been joint Commissioners without any disagreement so far. Let's hope there will never be one. Still! You are engaged to be married, I believe, to a very charming young lady?'

'Indeed and I am!' declared the other, adjusting his cuffs with pride.

'But a lady who, quite rightly, has strong moral and religious views?'

'We all know, Rowan, your own loose views concerning — '

'Tut!' said the Colonel, waving away cigar-smoke. 'Now confess it, Mayne! Confess it! In your heart haven't you been suspicious from the first of Cheviot and Lady Drayton merely because Lady Drayton is (how shall I put this delicately?) his *belle amie*?'

Mr. Mayne was too honest a man to deny this completely. He took a turn back and forth from the table, flapping his coat-tails behind him.

'You may be right,' he said. Then he struck the table. 'But come now! To business! We have heard what the Superintendent does not say. What *does* he say? Mr. Cheviot, who killed Margaret Renfrew?'

Cheviot moistened his lips.

A wind was getting up and prowling round the house, tugging at the window-frames. In this red, weapon-hung room, lighted by a green lamp, there was a hush more tense than seemed to befit mere investigators.

'In my opinion, sir, she was killed by her lover.'

'Ah!' Mr. Mayne touched the report. 'This mysterious lover at whom you hint so much? What is his name?'

'I can't yet tell you his name,' Cheviot answered with honesty. 'Even Freddie Debbitt, who knows every bit of gossip in London, couldn't tell me that. But I can describe him.'

'Then pray do so.'

'He is a man,' said Cheviot, weighing facts, 'of good birth and presence, though not wealthy and chronically hard up. He is physically attractive to women, though rather older than Miss Renfrew. He is a heavy gambler. He — ' Cheviot paused. 'Tell me, gentlemen. Has either of you ever met Margaret Renfrew?'

Colonel Rowan nodded, his blue eyes regarding a corner of the mantelpiece. Mr. Mayne inclined his head without enthusiasm.

'Very well,' said Cheviot. ''Fire burn and cauldron bubble!''

'I beg your pardon?' murmured the barrister.

Cheviot threw out his hands.

'Here is a beautiful woman,' he said, 'of thirty-one years. Outwardly she is cold and imperious, though of the fierce inward temper she displayed. She rages against her position as a poor-relation, but attempts not to show it.'

'Yes?' prompted Colonel Rowan, slowly blowing out cigar-smoke.

'When a woman like that falls in love, she is apt to explode like a cannon. According to Lady Cork, she *does* fall in love. Fiercely she denies, of course, that this man even exists. She is so passionately in love with him (or in lust, if you prefer the term), that she lies for him, steals jewels for him so that he may gamble at Vulcan's . . . '

'Did Lady Cork,' smoothly asked Mr. Mayne, 'give evidence that Miss Renfrew stole the jewellery?'

'Not quite to me, as you know. But to Freddie Debbitt — '

'Hearsay evidence, my dear sir.'

Cheviot looked at him.

He was not deceived by the barrister's courteous expression, his round face and interested dark eyes. Mr. Mayne was more than an honest man; he was clever, subtle-minded, if more through instinct than through reason. Firmly he had got into his head the notion that Flora Drayton was guilty of something, of anything. The whole powder-barrel would blow up if Cheviot's hand slipped, or Mr. Mayne learned of the facts about Flora which his Superintendent had concealed.

So Mr. Mayne waited, his arms folded. And, metaphorically, Cheviot hit him again.

'Hearsay evidence?' he demanded. 'Good God, what else can I use? I remind you, sir, that we are not yet in court.'

'There is no need for heat, Mr. Cheviot. What do you propose to do?'

'Tonight I visit Vulcan's gaming-house,' said Cheviot, 'at number twelve Bennet Street, off St. James's Street. If necessary, I shall play high at the tables — '

'With whose money?' suddenly demanded Mr. Robert Peel, towering up. 'Not with the

Government's, I warrant you! Not with the Government's!'

Cheviot bowed, touching his pockets.

'No, sir. With my own. That, I regret to say, is why I was late in arriving here today. I was obliged to visit my bankers in Lombard Street.'

'Your own money?' breathed Mr. Peel, much impressed. 'Egad, man, but you're a razor at your work!' He mused. 'I've heard much of this Vulcan's, I'm bound to say. It is one of the few houses in St. James's where ladies are admitted.'

Mr. Mayne raised his eyebrows.

'Ladies?' he repeated. 'Oh! I see. You mean prostitutes.'

Mr. Peel loomed up with the cold arrogance he assumed in the House of Commons.

'No, young man, I do not mean prostitutes. I refer to ladies, and ladies of quality. They are protected by male servants, and never molested. The worst rake in town, when he sits down to cards or roulette, has no eye for anything save his winnings. At least,' Mr. Peel added hastily, catching Colonel Rowan's eye, 'so I have been told.' He turned to Cheviot. 'But what's your scheme, man?'

Colonel Rowan was as deeply fascinated as the Home Secretary.

'Yes! What's the plan?'

'Well — '

'Not a raid, I hope? That's difficult. There's always an iron door at the top of the stairs.'

'No, not a raid. I mean to go in alone — '

'Damned dangerous,' said the Colonel, shaking his head. 'If they've learned you're a police-officer — '

'I must risk that. Besides, with your permission, I shall in some sense be protected.'

'But what'll you *do*?'

It was Cheviot's turn to pace the smoky, dusky room.

'This morning, at the coffee-room of a hotel,' he went on, peering out of the window, 'Freddie Debbitt drew me a sketch of Vulcan's house, including his private office.'

'Well?'

'By Lady Cork's testimony, a very valuable piece of jewellery was pledged, that's to say pawned, at Vulcan's office. This is easily distinguishable: a diamond-and-ruby brooch shaped like a square-rigger ship. Since it was pawned and not sold, it will still be there. It's unlikely the brooch was pledged by Miss Renfrew; her hatred of gaming was well known, and she would never have been so indiscreet. No! It was done by the man. Let me lay my hands on that brooch, and we can force Vulcan to disclose his name.'

'And this,' Mr. Mayne asked rather sarcastically, 'will prove he killed Miss Renfrew?'

Cheviot turned from the window, went to the table, and looked down into the barrister's eyes.

'Legally, no,' he admitted. 'But if you are resolved to have proof of a man's guilt before we even know who is guilty, then all investigation stops forthwith. I have only a strong belief, based on more experience than I care to tell.'

'In short, a guess at hazard?'

'A belief, I say! That this man will be trapped when we know his name.'

'You — you may be right. But, whatever your private beliefs, are you sure of your conclusions?'

'No! No! No!' Cheviot's face was rather pale. 'Is any man, except a star-led maniac like the late General Bonaparte, ever sure? Are you? Is Colonel Rowan or Mr. Peel? I can swear only that it's the likeliest thing. This matter is too perplexed. For all I am sure of, the murderer may even be a woman.'

'A woman?' echoed Mr. Peel.

This was the point at which there was a sharp rapping on the door to the passage.

It was opened by the short, but very broad

and burly, sergeant with the collar-numeral 13, whose red face and expression Cheviot had liked very much. The Sergeant addressed Colonel Rowan, but his stiff salute was directed toward Cheviot alone.

'A lady to see the Superintendent, sir.'

'A lady?' Colonel Rowan, distressed, considered the tobacco-spattered disorder of the office. 'That's impossible, Sergeant Bulmer! We have no place to receive her!'

Sergeant Bulmer remained stolid.

'Name of Miss Louise Tremayne, sir. Says she has important information about a Miss Renfrew. But won't speak to anybody except the Superintendent, and speak to him alone.'

Colonel Rowan extinguished his cigar on the edge of the table, amid a shower of sparks, and threw the cigar into the china spittoon underneath.

'Mr. Peel,' he said to the Home Secretary, 'you have matters of great moment on your mind. We — we cannot entertain this young lady in my living-quarters upstairs. But Mr. Mayne and I can withdraw there, while Mr. Cheviot sees her here. Doubtless, sir, you would wish to leave us?'

Carefully, like a Roman emperor, Mr. Peel placed his tall beaverskin hat on his head.

'Doubtless, Colonel Rowan, I should wish to withdraw,' he intoned. 'But I am hanged if

I will. This accursed drawing-room game, of who-killed-who-and-how, has made me forget my duties to the nation. I account you responsible; but I accompany you.'

In three seconds the Colonel had led them away. In the dim passage still lurked Sergeant Bulmer and the long figure and Punch-like nose of Inspector Seagrave. Holding the door slightly ajar, Cheviot whispered to them.

'Inspector! Sergeant! Are your duties free enough so that you can assist me tonight, say between ten-thirty and one o'clock, for a small mission among the blacklegs?'

It was not merely that the men agreed; eager assent radiated from them.

'Good. Can you also free six constables from their duties too? Good!'

'Any special sort of men, sir?' whispered Inspector Seagrave.

'Yes. I want climbers. Men who can go up over a roof or among chimney-pots as quickly and quietly as house-breakers.'

'Got 'em, sir,' whispered Inspector, after casting up his eyes as though counting. 'Just the men you want. Between ourselves, I shouldn't like to say they haven't *been* house-breakers, at one time or another.'

'Better still. A word in your ear later. Now admit the lady.'

With his arms Cheviot fanned ineffectually

at the air, to dispel tobacco-smoke. He raised one window; but, since there was no window-stick to prop it up, he had to lower it again. Then Louise came in.

Her age he had already put at about nineteen or twenty. In her blue turban, with the white cloak with the blue-bordered short cape outlining the puffed sleeves of her dress as well as its wide skirt about three inches from the floor, the hazel-eyed girl was so charming that she might have turned Cheviot's head if he had been a dozen years younger.

As it was, since he preferred more mature women with skill at conversation as well as other skills, he at first treated her with an avuncular air which she instantly sensed and resented. He sensed it in turn and became very gallant, which vastly pleased her.

'It is the greatest of pleasures to see you, Miss Tremayne,' he said, slapping with his immense handkerchief at a purplish-padded armchair, and only raising more dust. 'Will you have the kindness to be seated?'

'Oh, thank you!'

'Er — the room, I fear . . . '

Louise did not in the least mind the dirt or disorder; indeed, it appeared, this was only what she expected to find. But she kept her eyelashes lowered from him, and cast frightened glances at the window.

'Pray do forgive my boldness, Mr. Cheviot. But it was most imperative to see you. I was even obliged to deceive Papa. Mr. Cheviot, *why* is one's papa always in such a fearful wax about something?'

Cheviot restrained the impulse to say it was because they ate and drank too much at that age, and had it all their own way in the home.

'I have never discovered, Miss Tremayne. But they always are, aren't they?'

'Indeed mine is. As we were driving through Westminster, dear Papa went on awfully about a tailor — '

'About a what?'

'A tailor in Westminster. Dear Papa says the tailor will fire a house, or begin a riot or something, about Reform. We were — well! We were following Captain Hogben's carriage, because Captain Hogben wished us to see him horsewhip you. It didn't happen quite like that, did it?'

Here Louise turned her head, lifted her clear hazel gaze, and looked him straight and unashamedly in the eyes.

'*I* think it was wonderful,' she said.

Cheviot, feeling as though he had been struck by an amorous bullet, swallowed hard. He was not yet used to the way of women in this age. But he liked it very much.

'Er — thank you.'

Louise instantly blushed and looked away. But, now that she felt more confidence, she was going on in her usual rush of speech.

'Dear Papa was furious. But, in his way, I own he was just. 'G.d. the fellow,' he said; wicked words, you understand, about you; 'I've seen wrestling all me life, but I never saw a wrestler like that, and g.d. me,' he said, 'if I can tell how the b.h. that fellow did it.' You see, Papa was cross because he wishes me to marry Captain Hogben — '

'And will you marry him, dear Miss Tremayne?'

'Not if *I* know it!' cried Louise, flinging up her small chin in defiance. 'But I was saying. Dear Papa was so vexed he must stop at his club, and leave me sitting outside. I ran away in the carriage, and told Job to drive me here.'

'You had something to tell me, I believe?'

'Yes, yes, yes! Oh, dear. I must tell you two dreadful things. I desired to tell you last night, but at one time Flora Drayton was there — ' She stopped.

'Yes,' said Cheviot, looking at the floor.

What he felt now, flowing from the slender girl in the blue turban and white cape, were fear and uncertainty. Worst of all, which he could not understand, the fear and uncertainty were about him.

'What I wished to tell you,' she continued, trembling but speaking in a clear voice, 'was about — about *the man.*'

'Man? What man?'

'Peg Renfrew's man,' answered Louise. 'They say she positively adored him. She adored him so much that sometimes she hated him. Can you understand that?'

'I think so.'

'Well, I vow I can't. But they say,' Louise went on with shattering frankness, 'Peg stole money for this man, stole jewels so that he could gamble. But she was in a terribly difficult position: a poor-relation, dependent on Lady Cork. If Lady Cork ever discovered it, she thought, she'd be turned from the house. So, a few days ago, she changed.'

Cheviot nodded without looking up.

Louise's slender ankles, in their French-silk stockings, trembled too. Her shoes, of blue Moroccan leather, were muddy from walking across the yard.

'Peg was hard, hard, awfully hard! She told him, they say, that she'd never steal another penny or another jewel. If he used force, she said, she'd tell of him to Lady Cork and everyone else. And this man (oh, dear, I'm only repeating gossip!) has a most abominable temper.'

Louise was rising in spite of herself.

'And he said, if she ever spoke a word to anyone, he'd kill her. He'd shoot her. And that's what happened. Isn't it?'

Again Cheviot nodded without looking up. He felt she was casting him quick and furtive looks, her broad innocent mouth open.

'Again last night, you see, I t-tried to tell you when you were putting questions at people. But there were so *many*, all listening! I could do no more than hint.'

A sweat of excitement stood out on Cheviot's forehead. He might be closer to finding the murderer than he thought. He stood facing Louise, head down, his left hand gripped round the burned edge of the table.

'Yes, I know,' he said. 'So did Lady Cork. But your hints were so mysterious, all of a jumble, that I could read no meaning into them until Freddie Debbitt explained it this morning in a coffee-room. Louise! All this has been common gossip. Yet I never knew it?'

'Well! Papa and Mama have spoken of it. I always listen, though they think I don't.'

'But listen to me. *Someone* must know the name of this lover who threatened her! Have you heard it?'

'Haven't — haven't you?'

'No; how should I, with all mouths closed? Who do they say he is?'

'C-can't you guess?'

'No, no! Who do they say it is?'

'Well!' murmured Louise, keeping her eyes lowered. 'Some say it was *you*.'

There are some shocks so unexpected and fantastic that they take a little time to seep into every corner of the brain before they are understood.

Seconds passed. Cheviot, resting his whole weight with the left hand on the table, suddenly found his palm growing moist. He slipped, and nearly stumbled forward.

'To be sure,' flattered Louise, '*I* knew it couldn't be truth!'

But she wasn't quite sure; she was terrified of him, despite all the trouble to warn him; her voice pleaded for a denial.

'Although, to be sure,' she went on in a rush, 'you are sometimes a *very* heavy gambler. But that is only when you have been drinking quite heavily, and you are never seen the worse for drink in public.'

They were almost the same words Colonel Rowan had used last night.

Louise stopped. She saw his face as he looked up.

'Louise,' he said hoarsely, 'do you imagine *I* would take money from a woman? Or that I should need to? I'm not hard up!'

'No, no, no! But — but often people say they're not, don't they, when they are? And some wonder, if you had so much money, why you should take this odious place as a police-officer.'

Cheviot controlled himself. He could see the dangers opening all round him, amid dumb-faced people who would neither affirm nor denounce. And *he* had tried to question *them* about the murder!

Did Flora know all this? She must know some of it, at any rate. And that would explain . . .

'Will you believe me,' he asked, 'if I tell you I never met Margaret Renfrew before last night? In fact, she said as much herself before other persons!'

'But — but she would say that, wouldn't she? And Peg always declared she could fall in love only with an older man, who had,' Louise shied away from some word as being improper, 'who had been in the world. Once *I* can recall how she remarked (oh, so very negligently, touching her bonnet) how well you carried yourself on horseback.'

'Listen! The first time I ever heard that woman's name — !'

Cheviot stopped abruptly.

As shocks can stun the emotions, so they can open the brain to facts hitherto observed yet never properly understood. He saw his own words printed in his mind, and the fact they represented. Another fact followed, then another and another.

He could not see them before. He had been blinded by his feelings. Standing beside the table, his gaze wandered down. There, beneath the unlighted red lamp and beside his own report, he saw Colonel Rowan's medium-bore pistol with the polished silver handle.

If only, last night, he had performed that simple fingerprint test to see who fired a pistol, he would have seen through to the heart of truth. Instead —

'Smoke!' he said aloud. 'Smoke, smoke!'

Louise Tremayne jumped up from the chair and backed away.

'Mr. Cheviot!' she breathed, extending lilac-gloved hands and then hastily dropping them.

'I have not told you,' she rushed on, 'the most dreadful circumstance of it all. It concerns both you and — and Lady Drayton.'

Cheviot flung away speculation. 'Yes?' he demanded, rather too roughly. 'Yes?'

Louise moved still farther towards the window. Evidently she was torn between fear and tenderness; a hatred of being hurt, yet an obscure desire to be hurt by him.

'Hugo Hogben and I,' she said, 'were

dancing together. That must have been just after . . . after . . . '

'After Miss Renfrew was shot. Yes?'

'Well! We — ' Now it was Louise who paused, twitching her head round.

She was more alert than he. Cheviot had not heard heavy, fat footsteps squelching towards the house, or a port-winy voice upraised in addressing the door.

'It's Papa,' said Louise. Her short nose and wide mouth seemed to crumple up, like a child's. 'He'll beat me. He's a dear, good, kind man; but he'll beat me if I don't think of some fib. I can't stay; I can't!'

She flew to the door, which opened and slammed behind her.

Cheviot was after her in a moment, but he was too late. Except for a constable examining a number of dark lanterns under a hanging petroleum-oil lamp, the passage was empty and the front door closed.

He could hear the domineering male voice upraised above the creak of hooves and carriage-wheels as the vehicle drove round. He and Flora walked amid still taller dangers; Louise could tell him. But she and her dear, good, kind papa were gone.

Cheviot went to fetch his hat. He did not communicate with those waiting upstairs, in Colonel Rowan's living-quarters. Instead, after brief orders to Inspector Seagrave and Sergeant Bulmer, he hastened out.

At the top of Whitehall he found a hackney cabriolet. After what seemed an interminable drive, through muddy streets beginning to glimmer with gas-lamps, he got down at number eighteen Cavendish Square.

Flora's house was of whitish stone, untainted by smoke. But it was without light or sound, every window closely shuttered. Though he hammered at the door, and nearly broke the bell-wire in pulling at its brass knob, there was no reply.

At half-past ten that night, after dinner and after dressing himself carefully, Cheviot stood back waiting in a dark doorway of Bennet Street, off St. James's Street — looking across towards Vulcan's gaming-house, and what awaited him there.

12

The Black Thirteen

Two faces, one lower down and the other higher up, shone in the gloom of the doorway on either side of him.

Cheviot, in full evening-dress, wearing over it an ankle-length black cloak with a short cape whose collar was trimmed with astrakhan, and the most glossy of heavy hats, stood between them.

'Got yer rattle, sir?' whispered Sergeant Bulmer, on his right.

'Yes.' Cheviot felt in the small of his back. 'The tails of my coat hide it. You can't see it even with the cloak off.'

'*And* yer truncheon?'

'No.'

'No truncheon, sir?' demanded Inspector Seagrave, from his right side. 'But a pistol, surely?'

'Pistol?' Cheviot rounded on him. 'Since when have the C.I.D. been permitted to carry firearms?'

'The — the what, sir?'

Cheviot pulled himself up. He kept

swallowing and swallowing, because he was nervous.

'Pardon me. A slip of the tongue. Now listen, I don't think it'll be necessary for either of you, or any of the others, to enter the house. But if it should be necessary, and any man-jack of you is carrying a pistol, get rid of it. Do you understand me?'

Sergeant Bulmer, he had discovered, was stout-hearted but happy-go-lucky. Inspector Seagrave, though hard and capable, was a constant worrier.

'Sir!' said the latter, his long figure formally drawn up. 'Begging your pardon, Superintendent, but there's a great store of pistols and cutlasses at number four. On special occasions, Mr. Peel says, we're allowed to use 'em.'

'This isn't one of the occasions. Look there!'

It was a fine, cool night; no moon, but a bright crowding of stars.

Bennet Street, a short and narrow lane lighted by only one feeble gas-lamp, was the first street on the right as you turned down St. James's Street from Piccadilly. Cheviot, with his companions, stood in the doorway beside the dark premises of Messrs. Hooper, the coach-builders. Bennet Street was as deserted as a byway in Pompeii. But, through the thick and unsavoury mud in St. James's Street, a stream of gigs, curricles, berlines, hackney coaches or cabs went with a rattle and clop-clop up and down the hill.

Cheviot nodded towards them.

'The time will come,' he said, 'when those people — all people! — will regard you as their friends, their protectors, their guardians in peace and war. It is a high honour. Remember it!'

Sergeant Bulmer was silent. Inspector Seagrave grunted a short laugh.

'Reckon it won't be in *our* time, sir.'

'No. It will not be in your time. But it will come,' and Cheviot gripped his arm, 'if you behave as I tell you. No swords or firearms; your hands and your truncheons if need be.'

'I'm with you, sir,' said Sergeant Bulmer. 'I can't pitch away the barker in the street. But I can unload it.'

'Sir!' said Inspector Seagrave. 'You've been at Vulcan's before this?'

'Yes,' lied Cheviot.

'You know what to expect, then, if they twig it you're an officer?'

'Yes.'

'Very good, sir!' said the Inspector, saluting and then folding his arms.

Fumbling through the cloak with a white-gloved hand, Cheviot drew out the double-cased silver watch, with the silver chain, as befitted evening-wear.

'Just ten-thirty,' he said. 'Time to go in. Oh! One question I forgot to ask. This 'Vulcan.' What does he look like?'

Sergeant Bulmer's astonishment breathed out of the gloom.

'You've been to the place, sir? But you never saw him?'

'Not beknown to me, at least.'

'He's a big cove, sir,' muttered Sergeant Bulmer, shaking his head. 'Taller than you, and broader-like. Got a bald head without a single hair on it, and one glass eye: I disremember whether it's the left eye or the right. Got the airs and speech of a gentleman, too, though I can't say where he picked 'em up. If you mean to talk to him — '

'I mean to talk to him. You already know that.'

'Then look sharp, sir! You can't hear his step, and he moves like lightning. If he tumbles to anything, don't let him get behind you!'

'Why do they call him Vulcan? It can't be his real name?'

'Dunno his real name.' The Sergeant brooded. 'But a gentleman, a eddicated gentleman it was, he tells me the story. It's in the Bible, I think.'

'Oh?'

'Yessir. Vulcan, he's the god of the underworld; and his wife's the goddess Wenus. One day she's up to her games with Mars, who's the god of war, and Vulcan catches 'em at it. Well! It happened the same with *this* Vulcan, across the road.'

'Oh? How?'

'Well! He's got a wife, or a mort, maybe: a handsome piece but a spittin' firebrand. One day he catches her in what you might call an embarrassin' position, no clothes there weren't, with a Army officer. *This* Vulcan pitches *this* Mars out of a two-pairs-o'-stairs window. — He's a hard nail, sir! Look sharp!'

'Yes. Well, you have your instructions. Good luck.'

And Cheviot stepped down and sauntered across the dim street.

Everywhere, all over London, trembled that shaky noise of hooves and wheels: vast, unfamiliar, yet one he could never get out of his ears.

Vulcan's was a trim brick house three floors high, the top storey smaller than the others. Not a chink of light gleamed anywhere, except that the front door was set a little way open, and a tiny glow shone inside the entry. This was common to all gambling-houses, he had been told, as a sign and

216

invitation of what they were.

Cheviot put his foot on the first of the stone steps leading to the front door, and looked up.

Yes; he could admit he was nervous.

But that, he knew in his heart, was because he could not find Flora. During those desperate hours when he searched and inquired after her, he had come to recognize one truth. Flora was more than a woman with whom he believed himself to be in love. She was necessary to him, entwined in his life and soul; and, though he would never have dared to say aloud such hideously banal words, he could not live without her.

Well, you think that. But live you must. And he must live in this lost London, so strange and yet so vaguely familiar, which was Flora's.

If —

Cheviot woke up, his foot on the stone step.

A smart gig with bright lamps, driven by just as smart a manservant, came bowling along from the direction of Arlington Street. It swerved across the street and drew up at Vulcan's door.

Down from the gig, swiftly assisted by the manservant, alighted a gentleman of about Cheviot's own height and dressed exactly as he was. But the newcomer was younger, with a dissipated eye, long red nose, and luxuriant brown side-whiskers.

Together he and Cheviot mounted the few stone steps, silently assessing each other, until they reached the partly open door.

'After you, sir,' said Cheviot, politely standing aside.

'Not at all, sir!' declared the newcomer, who was slightly drunk and elaborately courteous. 'Come, come! Shouldn't dream of it! After *you*.'

This sort of exchange might have gone on forever if Cheviot had not pushed the door wide open, and with mutual bows and smiles they both went into the small, den-like entry. Facing them was another door: heavy, very thick despite its black paint and gilt-work, with an oblong closed spy-hole at eye-level.

With another elaborate bow of excuse, the amiable stranger with the luxuriant side-whiskers leaned past Cheviot and dragged at a brass bell-pull. Immediately the panel of the spy-hole was shot back. First the stranger, then Cheviot, were given careful scrutiny from a pair of sharp, rather disturbing eyes.

A heavy key turned. Two bolts thumped back. The door was opened by a footman in sombre red-and-black livery, lightened by white at neck and wrists and (seemingly) gold shoe-buckles. Like other footmen he wore hair-powder, though otherwise hair-powder had been a dead fashion for thirty years.

Any experienced policeman, after one look at that footman's seamed and shut-up face, would have seen his quality and been on the alert.

'Good evening, my lord,' the footman said very deferentially to the amiable one. Then, only a slight shade less deferentially: 'Good evening, Mr. Cheviot.'

Cheviot murmured something inaudible. His nerves, twitching momentarily at a smell of danger, quietened again as he realized he must be well known here.

Deftly the footman removed the cloak of my lord, whoever he was. But, since my lord made no move to take off his hat, Cheviot left his own hat on his head when the footman twitched off his cloak.

'Ha ha ha!' suddenly chuckled my lord. His eyes gleamed, and he rubbed his white-gloved hands together as though in anticipation. 'Play good tonight, Skimpson?'

'As always, my lord. Will it trouble you, gentlemen, to walk upstairs?'

The marble foyer at Vulcan's was large and high, though of a sour and stuffy atmosphere thickening through a faint scent of flowers. A journalist, describing the foyer, had written

219

that it was 'full of tubs containing the choicest blooms and exotic plants.'

A red-carpeted staircase ascended to a closed door above. Though its hand-rail was of rather fine wrought-iron scrollwork, it was spoiled by being brightly gilded. My lord grew even more affable as he went up beside Cheviot.

'New to Vulcan's, sir?' he inquired.

'*Rather* new, I confess.'

'Ah, well! That don't signify.' My lord's face momentarily darkened. 'I've dropped two thou here, I'll acknowledge it, in a few days. But the play's fair, and that's the thing.' His amiability brightened again. 'And my luck's in tonight. I feel it; I always feel it. What's your fancy? Rouge-et-noir? Hazard? Roly-poly?'

'I fear I have little knowledge of rouge-et-noir.'

Abruptly my lord stopped, and swung round unsteadily with his back supported by the iron hand-rail.

'Not know rouge-et-noir?' he exclaimed, his eyes opening wide in amazement. 'Come! Damme! What a Johnny Newcome you must be! Simplest game there is. Here, I'll show you!'

My lord threw out his white-gloved hands.

'Here's the table,' he explained, indicating

a long one. 'Here's black, that's the noir, on my left. Here's red, that's the rouge, on my right. In the middle sits the croupie — '

He broke off to utter his neighing chuckle; then became very solemn.

'Apologize,' said my lord, with a bow. 'Been so long with these sportin' blades (good fellers, very!) I begin to talk like 'em. I mean the croupier, of course.'

'Yes. I think I understand.'

'All right. The croupie, with six packs of shuffled cards, deals first to the left for black. The idea is to make the pips of the cards reach thirty-one, or as close to it as you can. Suppose the croupie deals thirty-one. He says, 'One!' Then he deals to the right, for the red. Got it so far?'

'Yes.'

'All right. This time suppose he deals an ace (that's one), a court-card (that counts ten), a nine, another court-card, a five, a deuce — ' My lord stopped, puzzling and pursing up his lips. 'I say! How many does that make for the red?'

'Thirty-five.'

'Ah, that's bad! The croupie cries, 'Four! Black wins.' Simple: you lay your wager on black or red, that's all.' My lord hesitated. 'True, there's always the chance of an _après_.'

'And what, if I may ask, is an _après_?'

'Ah! That's when both red and black make the same number. Thirty-one, thirty-four, what you like. Fortunately, it don't happen often.' My lord frowned a little. 'In that case, the bank rakes in all the money.'

'*The bank rakes in* . . . ' Cheviot was beginning, astounded in his turn, when he caught himself, coughed, and nodded.

'Simple, ain't it?' inquired my lord.

'Very. Shall we go on up?'

On the landing they faced a door which clearly was of thick iron, without any peep-hole. Cheviot, who was reflecting, hardly saw it.

Rouge-et-noir was not only simple; it was simple-minded. With six packs of cards being dealt, the same number for red and black would come up more often than the punters, obtuse in their lust for play, seemed to imagine; and then the bank won all. The bank, in fact, took no risk whatever: the punters were merely betting against each other.

'Now *my* game,' exulted my lord, 'is roly-poly. I'll break 'em tonight; you see if I don't. Besides, there's always an attraction at the roulette-table. Kate de Bourke.'

'Oh, yes,' Cheviot agreed, as though the name were well known to him. 'Kate de Bourke.'

My lord winked.

'She's Vulcan's property,' he said, 'but she's anybody's woman. Always at the roulette-table, you'll have remarked. If her name wasn't first Katy Burke, then mine's not — well, never mind. Hair like a raven! Plump as a partridge! Dusky as — '

He paused. Some signal by bell-wire must have been sent by the footman below.

Without noise, without any sound of its felt-covered bars inside, the four-inch-thick iron door swung open. Another footman stood there: Cheviot found himself looking at dead eyes and a face-scar covered with powder.

Out of the broad, high gaming-room stirred a breath of thick, stuffy, almost unbreathable air, heat-laden and foul. The room must occupy the full width of the house.

There were no windows. Curtains of yellow velvet, with looped pelmets in scarlet, muffled most of the wall-space down to a deep-piled scarlet carpet with yellow rings for its pattern. In the wall towards his left, Cheviot saw a marble fireplace where a too-large fire roared and shimmered. Against the other wall, towards his right, white-draped tables bore silver platters of sandwiches or lobster-salad, bowls of fruit, and long ranks of bottles.

But, most of all, he was conscious of the fever pulsing here, as high crowns of wax-lights shone down on the gaming-tables.

Two tables — each one eighteen feet long, rounded at the ends, and covered in green baize with bright markings for the stakes — were set with their long sides longways towards the iron door.

The nearer table they had marked out for rouge-et-noir, with large red triangles at one end and large black triangles at the other. A little obscured from Cheviot's view, the far table resembled an ordinary modern roulette-bank except that the wheel appeared of cruder design.

At each table, facing him, one croupier sat in the centre. Beside each stood a second croupier, holding a long-handled wooden rake.

'By-by!' said my lord, waving to Cheviot and moving soundlessly away on the thick carpet. His voice seemed to ring loudly.

For there was silence here except for the mutter of a croupier's voice, the slap of cards upturned, the skitter of the ball in the wheel, or the rattle of the rake drawing in ivory counters.

Cheviot, his eyes moving to spot Vulcan's blacklegs and bruisers, approached the table. It was pretty well patronized, mostly by men in flawless evening-clothes, wearing their hats, and sitting close to the table in flimsy imitation-Chippendale chairs.

The croupier, sweeping his glance along to see that both red and black were covered in white ivory counters stamped from five pounds to a hundred, dealt rapidly for black.

Cheviot moved close to the table as the cards flicked over.

'Six!' muttered the croupier. 'Deal to red.'

A young-old man, who looked about forty but was more probably twenty-one or -two, breathed hard and drew his chair closer.

'Got it already!' he whispered. 'Red's bound to get under that! Bound to! I'll wager another — '

'Sh-h!'

The croupier dealt to the other side. His wrist turned quickly, but not so quickly that anyone failed to see the pips of the cards.

He dealt the queen of diamonds, the knave of clubs, and the ten of hearts, each counting ten. He hesitated, and then turned up the eight of clubs.

'Seven!' he said. 'Black wins.'

The young-old man, his face sagging as though pulled down from under the eyelids, muttered something and started up from his chair. Beside him a stoutish, bluff-looking man, with the air of a retired naval officer and the whitest of linen shirt-frills, reached up gently and pulled him down again.

Cheviot circled round the table and approached the roulette-bank. The fire popped and spat, its shifting light reflected in the rows of bottles across the room.

There was a little cry from someone at the roulette-table as one play ended. The counters rattled under the rake. This table was crowded. Footmen moved soundlessly over the carpet, carrying salvers and offering claret, brandy, or champagne.

As he neared the roulette-table, Cheviot stopped and glanced up. All along the back wall, about fourteen feet up and a little back from the roulette-bank, ran a narrow gallery whose hand-rail also resembled gilded iron scroll-work, but was more probably gilded wood. This gallery, with its own set of yellow-velvet curtains and scarlet pelmets, had a narrow staircase curving down at each end to the gaming-room floor.

'That's it,' he thought.

The yellow curtains did not conceal three doors facing out on the gallery. The middle one was of heavy polished mahogany, bearing the gilt initial V.

'Vulcan's private office. If he's thrifty, and Freddie's description was accurate, and my plan has any value . . . '

He looked down again at the thronged roulette-table. Two women sat there.

One of them, from my lord's description, must be that Kate de Bourke who belonged to Vulcan.

She sat at the right-hand end of the table, her back towards the white-draped ledges of sandwiches and lobster-salad. Kate was smallish, handsome, and surly. Her shining black hair was drawn back, exposing the ears and terminating in a long coil. No flash lit up her vivid eyes, of strong whites against dark-brown iris and dead-black pupil. In her right hand she held a pile of counters, absent-mindedly dropping them one atop another on the table. She dreamed sullen dreams, her thick lips compressed.

The other woman . . .

Cheviot's glance ran along the far side of the table, to a chair just to the right of the first croupier.

The other woman was Flora.

'Lay your wagers, ladies and gentlemen.' Thin, automatic, sing-song: the croupier. 'Lay-your-wagers; lay-your-wagers; lay-your-wagers.'

Flora had been conscious of his presence long before he was conscious of hers; perhaps from the time he entered. She sat with eyelashes lowered, in a dark-blue velvet gown bordered with gold: low-cut, but with shoulder-straps and, as with most evening-gowns, having at the shoulders short blue-and-gold cloth projections like narrow epaulettes.

A little pile of ivory counters stood on the green-covered table before her. Flora's heavy yellow hair was dressed as it had been the night before, and as Kate's was now. Just behind her chair, watching, on guard every second, stood her liveried and muscular coachman.

Briefly, she raised her eyes towards Cheviot.

Contrition, apology, appeal were in that glance. As soon as they looked at each other, it was with an intimacy as great as though they were in each other's arms.

'What are you doing here?' her glance said, with a little of apprehension.

'What are *you* doing here?'

Flora looked down again, disturbed, touching the counters. The coachman recognized Cheviot and drew a breath of relief.

Carelessly Cheviot strolled round the side of the roulette-table, where many persons were snatching glasses from the footmen before placing their bets.

The gambling-fever, rising all about him, did not touch him at all. He could never understand the strange minds of those who, of an evening, would occupy themselves with cards when there were books to be read. True, there were other temptations. Except for his self-discipline, he could easily have gone to the devil with drink and women.

In fact, as a very young man during another life now gone, he very nearly had done so. When he came down from Cambridge, some girl raved and refused to marry him because of his determination to enter the police instead of reading law. He was too stubborn to yield, but he had gone on a drinking-bout of dangerous duration. The girl had said —

Cheviot's mind wavered and grew dark.

Memory submerged; he could not even remember her name or what she looked like.

The foul air, the roaring fire, the movement of guests who did not even play but strolled slowly round the yellow-hung room, darkened his eyesight and made his head spin.

He counted to ten, and his sight grew clear. So long as he could remember police-work, it didn't matter. If that failed him too —

He found himself on the other side of the roulette-table, sauntering past it. There was the board, in yellow squares with black or red numbers on either side of the clumsy wheel. It had —

His wits jumped to complete alertness.

When the roulette-ball fell into the number marked zero, the bank won every stake on the board. This wheel had not only a zero, but a double-zero. There was something else too.

'Lay your wagers, ladies and gentlemen! Lay-your-wagers; lay-your-wagers-lay-your-wagers!'

Cheviot edged into the group, his thigh against the table, between Flora and the first croupier. The coachman bowed respectfully and stood aside.

Cheviot did not speak to Flora. Gently he put his hand on her shoulder. The flesh was warm and damp, and the shoulder trembled slightly. Again she gave him only the quickest of backward looks. Flora's face was a little flushed and moist where the rice-powder had run beneath the heat of melting wax-lights.

'Good evening,' Cheviot said loudly, to the nearer of the two croupiers, and to draw attention to himself.

The croupier looked up to nod and smile, showing decayed teeth. He said, 'Good evening, Mr. Cheviot,' and returned to his sing-song whisper as punters thrust out counters on the table.

Cheviot leaned past to address the second croupier.

'To begin with,' he said, even more loudly, 'let me have a modest two hundred. In fifty-pound counters, if you please.'

From his hip-pocket he took out the money he had drawn from Groller's Bank. A thousand pounds, in five-pound notes, makes a sizeable lump of money.

Instantly a dozen pairs of eyes slid round towards him; slid round, then grew opaque or filmed.

At the rouge-et-noir table he had already spotted nine of Vulcan's blacklegs or bruisers. There were at least four among those who lounged in the room and watched. With the twelve at the roulette-bank, on both sides of an eighteen-foot-long table with the wheel in the middle, that brought the number up to twenty-five.

There were probably more, say four or five: thirty among a hundred and twenty guests.

The second croupier, who had before him an immense heap of notes and gold as well as piles of counters, merely nodded. Shoving the rest of the money into his hip-pocket, Cheviot proffered forty five-pound notes and received four counters stamped fifty each. He was careless or clumsy in receiving them.

One counter slipped out of his hand. It fell on the carpet beside the first croupier, who presided over the wheel. Bending down to get it, Cheviot took a quick look at the croupier's right foot beside the imitation-Chippendale chair.

Then he straightened up.

'Tonight,' he declared in a ringing voice, 'I am inspired.'

And, remembering Sergeant Bulmer's collar-numerals, he reached out and planked down a hundred pounds on the black thirteen.

This time there was a sharp stir round the whole table.

'Jack — !' Flora began, in instinctive protest.

Again he pressed her shoulder, reassuringly.

It was as he had hoped. Whenever a man shows supreme self-confidence in backing a number against ruinous odds, there is a rush to follow him.

Faces were thrust out, reddened with claret or brandy. Hands scrabbled among ivory counters. The character known to Cheviot only as my lord, his nose fiery with more drink, tossed a twenty-pound counter on the black thirteen. So did a stout young man with yellow side-whiskers, at the far side of the table, whom Cheviot vaguely remembered seeing at Lady Cork's ball.

Others, more cautious, backed red or black, odds or evens, above the line or below

232

it. At most they quartered four numbers, with the exception of a very tall, lean young gentleman who stood up with the black-browed air of a man playing Hamlet and dropped counters totalling sixty pounds on the red six. Then, his hat jammed over his eyes, he sat down again.

The board was laden, the game heavy; and the croupier's drone changed.

'The game is finished!' he said, standing up and speaking almost clearly. 'Nothing-more-goes; nothing-more-goes; nothing-more-goes.'

With one hand he spun the red-and-black wheel in one direction. With the other he tossed the little ivory ball in the direction opposite.

Dead silence, except for the skittering noise of the ball.

It fell into the wheel, bounced out again, and swirled round the outer ebony rim. It hesitated, running backwards and forwards on the rim. It began to slow down.

As it did so, Detective Superintendent Cheviot was again apparently careless with his two remaining counters. One dropped on the carpet. He bent to retrieve it; looked quickly at the croupier's right foot; and straightened up.

The ball stopped, as the wheel slowed down to a shade of motion. The ball swayed a little, and then bounced with a click into zero.

Round the table ran a hiss of indrawn breath, a murmur like one stifled groan, the intense swallowing of oaths and curses.

That was the point at which Cheviot sensed the presence, behind him, of someone watching.

Just under the shadow of the high gallery above, against yellow curtains with red pelmets, stood Vulcan himself.

13

The Gathering of the Damned

But he dared show no curiosity. He did not even turn his head round. Only a blur, at the corner of his eye, gave him the impression of a very big and broad man, with a shining bald head, and in immaculate black and white.

Smiling, self-assured, Cheviot faced the table.

As the long-handled rake darted out to sweep in all the counters, there were many persons who looked daggers at him: concealed daggers, thumb on the blade.

But my lord, his flushed face expressionless, merely shrugged his shoulders and drew out a red-silk purse. Beside him sat an obvious blackleg, a powerfully built man with a piebald wig to hide head-scars, who whispered encouragement in my lord's ear.

Equally expressionless was the stout young man, with the yellow side-whiskers, who had danced last night at Lady Cork's. Beside him, too, a blackleg breathed flattering encouragement; this was a bony middle-aged man with a lined face and false teeth which tended to surge forward when he talked.

'Jack!' whispered Flora, who had loyally staked fifty pounds on the black thirteen. 'Don't you think it time to . . . ?'

'I do indeed, madam.' Cheviot's gallantry was of the heaviest sort. He glanced towards the white-draped ledges of food and wine, well beyond the far end of the table, and threw his two remaining counters on the green cloth. 'Some refreshment, I think?'

'Yes, yes, yes!' Flora rose up, and he drew back her chair.

'Our luck will be better afterwards,' Cheviot added, addressing the muscular coachman. 'In the meantime, will you hold Lady Drayton's chair and guard our stakes?'

'Yes, Robert, do!' urged Flora.

'I will,' said the coachman, nodding grimly. 'Depend on it, sir and madam: I will.'

In looking at the far end of the table, Cheviot could not help seeing Kate de Bourke.

Alone, aloof, speaking to nobody, Kate sat with her elbows on the green cloth and toyed with ivory counters. She wore a light-green gown, emphasizing into relief her broad-fleshed charms. Only once, when Cheviot made his bet, had she lifted her eyes for a speculative look at him. Afterwards she toyed with the counters again.

Click, click, click-click, went those same counters, as Cheviot sauntered past under the gallery with Flora on his arm.

Round swung Kate's dark head, for a short, hard appraisal of Flora, before returning to her dream.

Flora's golden head was just above the level of his shoulder. In her dark-blue gown bordered with gold, in elbow-length white gloves and a gold-dusted reticule in one hand, her beauty dimmed the tawdry room.

But she kept her head down, gaze on the carpet, and spoke softly.

'Jack.'

'Yes?'

'Last night,' Flora burst out, still softly, 'you were so patient. And I was so hateful and odious and spiteful. How shamed I was afterwards! Shamed and shamed and shamed!'

'My dear, don't agitate yourself. We are consulting together. But we must have an understanding now. Last night, for instance, I had heard no gossip about — '

' — yet nevertheless,' Flora interposed in exactly the same tone, 'you might have visited me today.'

'Visit you? I did! I nearly broke the bell-wire. But no one answered.'

Flora's tone was almost airy as she lifted her head.

'Oh, as to that! I had gone deliberately to see my aunt at Chelsea, and told the servants not to answer if you rang. But you might at least have put a note through the letter-slot, to show you'd been there.'

Cheviot stopped and studied her.

'Good God, Flora, must you always be so perverse?'

'Perverse?' The blue eyes widened and sparkled; they melted his anger even as she began to be angry. Then Flora herself was stricken. 'Perverse,' she added in a whisper. 'Yes. I own I am. Dearest, dearest, what am I doing *now*?'

'Nothing at all,' he smiled, 'except using women's weapons. In this age — '

'In this age?'

'You have no rights, little freedom, no privileges. What other weapons can you use? But don't, I beg, use them against me. There's no need. Flora! Look at me!'

They were standing by the buffet.

Cheviot, who long ago had doffed his hat and thrust his white gloves into the opening of his waistcoat, set down the hat on a white-draped table. He held out a silver platter of sandwiches, with stale bread and ham cut enormously thick. Flora took one, still without looking at him.

Along the tables stood silvery buckets, cold-wet outside, from whose tops projected the necks of open bottles above melting ice. Drawing out one dripping bottle, of a brand of champagne unknown to him, he filled two glasses. Flora accepted one, still not turning her head.

'Let me repeat,' he said, 'that last night I had never even heard any of this gossip about — about Margaret Renfrew and myself. You had heard it, I imagine?'

'And pray who has not?'

'Have you heard anything else about it?'

'No. Is there so very much else to hear?'

'Flora! Look at me! Look up!'

'I won't!'

'Then had you heard,' he asked sardonically, 'as a part of the same gossip, that she stole money and jewels for me, and I accepted them?'

Up lifted Flora's eyes, filmed with tears, her lips parted in dumbfounded astonishment.

'But that's utterly ridiculous! *You?* Do that? Why, it's the silliest . . . it's . . . I wonder what awful woman *dared* to say it?'

'And yet it's a part of the same gossip, you know. If you believe one, you must believe the other. Do you?'

'I — '

'Aren't you only using women's weapons, Flora? Don't you know, in your heart, this Margaret Renfrew was never anything to me, or I to her? Don't you know that?'

There was a silence. Then Flora nodded quickly.

'Yes,' she said. 'That is, I knew — if you were with me, you couldn't very well have been with her.' She flushed, but regarded him steadily. 'It's my horrid *thoughts*, that's all. I can't help it.'

'Then need there ever be any misunderstanding between us?'

'Never! Never! Never!'

He lifted his champagne-glass. Flora touched the rim of her glass to his. Both gulped down the champagne in quick swallows, set away the glasses, and, with mutual instinct, put aside the sandwiches neither of them could eat.

And Flora held out her hands to him.

He couldn't, physically, couldn't tell her of the worst danger they both faced. He could not tell her of Mr. Richard Mayne's suspicions, hovering and swooping. If anyone had seen the pistol fall from Flora's muff, or seen him hide it under the hollow-based lamp, they might both stand in the dock on a charge of murder.

But of one thing he must warn her quickly. He drew her closer and spoke in a whisper.

'If you trust me, my dear, then you must do as I ask. You must leave here, and leave immediately.'

'Leave?' He felt her start. 'Why?'

'Because of Vulcan's blacklegs. There are too many of them. I can smell trouble.'

'Blacklegs? What are they?'

Once more Cheviot studied the room while not seeming to do so.

'In the vernacular, they're extra-flash-men hired by the house at two or three guineas a night.'

'Yes? Don't stop there!'

'They lure in the pigeons and the Johnny Newcomes to play high, and encourage 'em again when they lose. The blacklegs, of course, only make dummy bets against each other; they must return their winnings to the house before the bank closes about three in the morning. If the pigeons grow suspicious — well! It may be hushed up. If not hushed up, the blackleg is a bruiser or a knife-and-pistol man.'

Again his gaze roved among the men against the yellow curtains.

'I tell you,' he added in a fiercer whisper, 'there are too many of them! There's too much noise and talk; can't you hear it? And the tension's too high; watch the corners of their eyes slide round to each other.'

'*I* can't see anything!'

'Perhaps not. But I can. They're waiting for something to explode.'

'To explode? What?'

'I'm not sure, but . . . Flora! Why did you come here tonight?'

'I — I was hoping to find *you*. I — I thought . . . ' She stopped.

'You thought me again gambling heavily and drinking even more heavily, lost and out of my wits? As you suspected I was last night?'

'I don't mind that! Really and truly I don't! Only — '

'Well, observe that I am in no such condition. All the more reason why you should leave here before the boiler blows up. Go; cash in your counters; Robert will see you home safely enough.'

He was so close to her that he could have bent over and kissed her mouth. He felt emotions through her body rather than saw them in her face; and he felt her mood change in a flash.

'Oh, God,' Flora whispered, 'is this to happen again?'

'Again?'

'As it happened last night. You promised,

on your honour. I awaited and awaited you, with the rush-light burning.' She did not speak in anger, but in desperate curiosity. 'Does it give you pleasure, Jack, that I should tumble, and toss, and weep and bite my pillow, until the dawn comes up and I am drained of tears or any feeling at all?'

Cheviot nodded towards the gaming-room.

'Tonight,' he said, 'you're in danger. And so, in some very small degree, am I. But it is my duty to remain here. My work — '

'Yes.' He felt her shiver of disgust. ''Your work.' I'll be honest with you. That's what I hate.'

('And you, too, Flora?')

'Danger?' she said in a low voice. 'Why, all true men must face danger; so much is natural; as they must drink and gamble and — !' She swallowed. 'If you were an officer of the Army or the Navy, and war came, I should be fearful. But I should be pleased and proud too. Proud!' Her disgust, showing now in her face, trembled through her. 'But these police! Filthy gaol-birds better back in prison! Can you ask me to suffer this? We are not married. Have you the right to ask it?'

'No,' said Cheviot, and dropped her hands.

'Jack! I did not mean — !'

Cheviot picked up his hat from the table.

He was so long-schooled in hiding his thoughts that even Flora, who knew him or believed she knew him, could not read the fury and bitterness behind his placid face.

'Why, then,' he replied almost agreeably, 'to the devil with this police-work! Let us forget it. I accompany you home, and I shall be there for as long as you please.'

'Jack!' A slight pause. 'You mean that?'

And for the time being, in his bitterness, he honestly believed he did mean it.

'What's the good?' he was raging silently to himself. 'Can I, single-handed, conquer prejudices established since Cromwell's time? Why should I batter my wits, and endure only humiliation, to convince fools that one day the police will mean only fairness and law? Better strong love with Flora than a smashed skull in an alley, which most of us will come to. What matter? Who cares?'

He fought down the thoughts.

'You may be sure I mean it,' he declared, with what he swore was sincerity. 'And we must go now.'

'Yes, yes, yes!'

'Have you a cloak or a pelisse?'

'Yes, downstairs. In the foyer!'

'Then we can collect the value of our counters and be off. My arm, Flora?'

And, as they walked along the rear wall,

under the gallery and past the length of the roulette-bank, he could feel Flora's exaltation and pride flowing through her finger-tips. He himself was buoyed up, his senses all too conscious of her presence.

The second croupier at the roulette-table, scarcely taking his eyes from a board on which play now ran very high, changed their counters for notes and gold. The wheel spun again. Intent gamblers, eyes fixed and shining, did not even glance up.

And yet . . .

As he took Flora across to the door, the coachman following, Cheviot had the feeling that many heads were turned and that eyes bored into his back. It was an animal-like sensation; animal-like, he stiffened to it.

The footman, with the dead-looking eyes and the powdered-out face-scar, stood by the iron door with its two felt-covered bars. It seemed he hesitated very slightly before drawing the bars back without sound, and opening the door.

And then, behind Flora and Cheviot, spoke out a soft, deep, cultivated voice.

'Come, Lady Drayton!' it said. 'Come, Mr. Cheviot! Surely you are not leaving us so soon?'

Behind them towered up Vulcan. Beside him stood Kate de Bourke.

Seen close at hand, Vulcan was some two or three inches taller than Cheviot. He was correspondingly broad and thick, though much of this lay concealed under admirably tailored clothes. Some of the bulk might be fat, though Cheviot doubted it.

The man was too cat-footed of step, his neck too thick and firm in carrying the immense bald head. He had scarcely any eyebrows. The glass eye was his right; it gave the only staring, rather sinister touch to a manner of charm and grace. But he kept it as much as possible from the light, using his good left eye. His age might have been forty-five. Vulcan, with infinite toil and patience, had through long years got himself up to resemble someone in the Peerage — and then spoiled everything by wearing one emerald and one ruby ring on his left hand, and a single large diamond ring on his right.

He glanced down at Kate. This charmer, with her broad gipsy allure in the light-green gown, plainly adored him. Vulcan had brought her to the door, Cheviot suspected, only to feed his vanity.

'I believe, Lady Drayton,' Vulcan went on in his big, soft voice, 'this is the first time you have honoured us with a visit?'

'I — I believe so.'

The iron door was wide open. Flora cast a glance towards it over her shoulder. The coachman, Robert, stood behind her with his eyebrows drawn down.

'In that event,' smiled Vulcan, 'may I make you known to my wife? Kate, I present you to Lady Drayton.'

Kate was so obviously a woman of the streets that Cheviot marvelled. Vulcan's tutoring must have been long, careful, even savage. Gone was Kate's sulkiness or fierce brooding. Her inclination of the head matched Flora's in manners; she murmured polite words in a contralto voice whose pronunciation was like Vulcan's own.

'Mr. Cheviot!' said Flora in a formal tone. She indicated the open door. 'Don't you think it's time to . . .'

'Alas!' said Vulcan.

He turned up the palms of his big hands, so that the green, red, and glittering-white rings flashed and sparkled.

'As a good host,' he went on humorously, 'I can but speed the parting guests.' His tone sounded faintly hurt. 'But you, Mr. Cheviot! In you, I confess, I find myself surprised.'

'Oh? How?'

'I have never known you, sir, to fear high play. Or, indeed, to fear anything else.'

To anyone else the words would have

247

sounded like an idle compliment.

But, as he said this, the big man swung down on Cheviot his lifeless, staring glass eye. The stare of the glass eye, even while Vulcan smiled, turned those words into a challenge and even a jeer.

That was the point at which Cheviot knew he couldn't leave here.

He couldn't! He must have been insane, under Flora's spell, even to think of such a thing.

He had a job to do. He could hardly desert Inspector Seagrave, Sergeant Bulmer, and the six constables posted at his instructions. Once before, for Flora's sake, he had betrayed his duty; and it had haunted him ever since. He couldn't do this for her or for any woman on earth. He looked at Vulcan.

'Come!' he said, snapping his fingers. 'I thank you for the reminder. There *was* one small matter of business I wished to discuss with you.'

Vulcan spread out his hands in assent and welcome.

Cheviot turned to Flora.

'I think, madam,' he smiled, 'it would be better if you left us, after all. You will be safe enough in Robert's care.'

Flora had gone very pale, clutching her gold-dusted reticule in both hands.

She was no fool, Cheviot knew. She would guess the reason why he felt he must stay. But would she understand it, or at all sympathize with it? A faint sweat stood out on his forehead.

'Madam, we have an appointment tomorrow,' he said, appealing with his eyes in the intense dumb-show that he meant tonight, tonight, tonight. 'If I am one minute later than one o'clock, you may disown me.'

Flora's answer was without inflection.

''Disown'?' she repeated. 'Can one disown what one has never owned? Good night, Mr. Cheviot. Robert, follow me.'

She swept through the doorway, Robert shambling after her. The iron door closed; its felt-covered bars shot soundlessly into their sockets.

'And now,' thought Cheviot, 'and now, as the ghost said in the story, we're all locked in for the night.'

Vulcan's big face wore a look of faint distress.

'Mr. Cheviot, Mr. Cheviot! This business-matter!' His hand moved towards the inside pocket of his coat; then it dropped, embarrassed. 'Pray forgive me. But if it should be a momentary lack of funds, you can always be accommodated.'

'Oh, it's not money.' Carelessly Cheviot took the wad of banknotes from his pocket, and replaced them. 'No, not at all!' He looked up at Vulcan, at one good eye and one lurking in ambush. 'It is, as I say, a business proposition from which, I think, both you and I can derive profit.'

'Ah?' murmured Vulcan.

'Is there somewhere, perhaps, we can speak in private?'

'Oh, by all means. My office. Kate, my dear, will you accompany us and kindle lights? If you will follow us, my dear sir.'

Cheviot followed them, over the soft carpet, again in the direction of the buffet.

His pulses had jumped at Vulcan's words. Vulcan *was* thrifty. He kept no lights burning in an office when he was not there.

But there was no need for his heart to beat faster than it already did. As soon as he had felt those eyes boring into his back, he had known that all this tension was fastened on him: on him alone.

They knew.

Every blackleg in the room knew he was a police-officer, and waited for the kill.

Again he sauntered past the gamut of eyes. He was conscious, as through the pores of his skin, of all small details: the smell of Macassar oil on the men's hair, the shifting of a chair on the carpet.

Vulcan, with the flary wax-lights polishing

his skull, making broader and thicker his massive figure, bent down to speak to Kate.

'Fond of me, little one?'

'Yes!' Kate said in a low voice. She enlarged on this with a stream of passionate obscenities so picturesque that Cheviot was forced to admire. If it had not been for Vulcan's bishop-like decorum, Cheviot felt, she would have tried to jump up and bite the lobe of his ear.

Vulcan's vanity expanded and purred.

'Ah, here we are!' he said.

They had passed the place at the buffet where Flora and Cheviot had been standing. Only a few feet away was the righthand staircase of the two ascending to the narrow gallery above.

From a saucer on the table Kate snatched a long waxen spill out of a bundle there. But she did not light it. Indeed, except for the fire at the opposite end of the room, there was no place at which she could have lighted it.

Cheviot moved forward, a little too hastily, and stopped. At all costs he must be first up those stairs. But Vulcan, stepping back, made it easy for him.

'After you, my dear sir,' he said, with a stately bow and a beam from his good eye.

As Cheviot mounted the narrow stairs, he found his guess had been right. Stairs and gallery were made of wood. Even the handrail, gilded to resemble iron scrollwork, was of old and flimsy wood. This would be no pleasant place in the event of fire.

There could be no mistaking the centre door to Vulcan's office. A bracket on either side, a little way out from the yellow curtains and holding a candle in a parchment shade, threw light on the deep red mahogany and brightened the gilded letter V.

Vulcan was just behind him, with Kate following. Cheviot glanced over the hand-rail. Below was the long roulette-table. The room had grown eerily silent after too-loud talk. He could feel the blacklegs' unspoken glee.

Cheviot leaned casually against the left-hand frame of the door. Taking from his waistcoat pocket a key-ring with two keys, one short and the other long, Vulcan unlocked the door and swung it inwards to the right.

'Again after you, my dear sir,' Vulcan said.

Kate was already raising the waxen spill to light it at the candle burning on the right.

'Thank you,' said Cheviot.

He entered with the appearance of blundering, as a man does in a dark room. As though to make way, he immediately moved along the wall towards the left.

Then, with blinding swiftness, he made the move which might win or lose his life.

14

Flash-and-Fraud

About four feet along the wall, projecting from it, was the brass knob of a bell-pull communicating with the only bell-wire in the room.

Cheviot's fingers encountered it.

He had about twelve seconds to accomplish what must be accomplished.

If the gleam of the waxen lighting-spill fell into the room before he had finished, he was finished too.

His hat fell softly on the carpet. From his waistcoat pocket he jerked out the object for which Sergeant Bulmer had searched over half the town before finding one at a spectacle-maker's: a very tiny screw-driver, less than an inch long.

Cheviot's forearms no longer trembled. His fingers were cold and quick and rapid. Working in darkness, by a sense of touch alone, he found the microscopic screw on the projection of the knob, which held the knob to the bell-wire as such a screw holds a knob to the spindle of a door. The edge of the screw-driver fitted in . . .

'And pray what takes you so long, my pet?' That was Vulcan's soft bass.

'Ah, ducky, but blast your bloody eyes — !' That was Kate's refined contralto.

'I have warned you before, my pet, against using unseemly language.'

The tiny screw fell into Cheviot's hand, just as the waxen spill flashed into flame from the candle outside the door.

As it did so, Cheviot's heart jumped into his throat for fear the bell-wire would clatter down inside the wall, or the knob fall off inside the room.

But the wire, from long fixture in that position, remained as it was. So did the knob. There was just time for Cheviot to slip both screw and screw-driver into his pocket. He was well out from the wall, bending over to pick up his hat, when the glow of the waxen spill sent a wavering light out across the carpet.

'Now here, Mr. Cheviot,' Vulcan's rich voice went on, 'we have what the newspapers are wont somewhat vulgarly to call my sanctum sanctorum. Kate, be good enough to light both lamps.'

Cheviot could dimly make out the lines of the good-sized if low-ceilinged room. Its walls were papered, after a French Empire fashion long dead, in vertical stripes of orange and green. Two smallish windows, heavily muffled in orange-plush curtains, were in the rear wall opposite the door.

'Observe the table,' Vulcan suggested rather smugly.

There was little furniture. Cheviot had already noted the table.

At first glance, in gloom, it appeared to be a roulette-table. It was eighteen feet long, set longways to the windows, and a roulette-wheel had been let down into the middle.

But this was decorative. The table, on either side of the wheel, had a top of polished mahogany. Some distance out, on either side, stood a solid-looking china figure: each one about a foot high, tinted in natural life-colours and with a high, hard glaze. Beyond these, at both ends of the table, loomed up a lamp in a cut-glass orange-coloured shade.

'Observe again!' said Vulcan, as Kate tilted the shade and lighted the lamp on the right.

An orange glow, dull and rather menacing, filtered through a room whose windows had not been raised in years.

The figure to the right of the roulette-wheel represented the popular notion of Vulcan: black from the forge, stooped and yet broad and powerful, a hammer in one hand

and a net in the other.

'Yes,' agreed Cheviot. 'I see. And the figure on the left — ' He stopped.

Pop went the wick on the other orange cut-glass lamp, as Kate moved quickly to the other end of the table and lighted it.

The other figure, nude, represented Venus rising from the sea. So much power or skill had seldom been breathed out by the potter, the fire-glazer, the painter, in what appeared living sensuality.

'In classical mythology,' pursued Vulcan, 'Venus or Aphrodite is usually represented as being fair-haired. You, Mr. Cheviot, were perhaps thinking of . . . '

He paused, coughing delicately.

'But *this* Venus,' he went on, and even his glass eye seemed to gleam, 'is dark. See how the black hair streams down over her shoulders. Her eyes are half-closed; her arms straight down at her sides, hands turned outwards. You do see?'

'Very well. It is admirable, if unorthodox.'

Vulcan laughed his soft laugh. Kate de Bourke, her thick lips drawn down, had been standing above the second orange-gleaming lamp. She ran along the line of the table to the right of the room.

Against the right-hand wall stood a large and deep cabinet of painted Chinese lacquer, with double-doors. Before this background Kate posed and poised, chin up, eyes half-closed, arms down at her sides with hands turned out.

'It's me,' she said, dropping the refined speech. 'I'm proud it's me! Ah, so-and-so, why pretend?'

'*Kate!*'

Kate ran at Vulcan, greedy-mouthed, and threw her arms round his neck.

'Give us a kiss, ducks. 'Tain't as if — '

With sudden violence Vulcan's shoulders twitched. He flung her off, so that she staggered backwards. Her spine and head banged against the edge of the Chinese-lacquer cabinet on the wall to the right of the open door.

But Kate only laughed, delighted. This time she sidled toward him with a coyness which, despite or perhaps because of her beauty, was almost grisly. It flashed through Cheviot's head that this was a deliberate imitation of Flora Drayton.

'And yet, dearest, may I not remain while you speak with this gentleman?'

'No. This is business. Leave us!'

Vulcan, his hand at her back as he turned her towards the open door, recovered his mantle of benevolence.

'Come, Mr. Cheviot, I neglect you! Pray be seated — there.'

His gesture was so quietly commanding that Cheviot looked round behind him.

Against the wall to the left of the door, not far beyond the brass knob in the wall, stood a large and weighty flat-topped desk of Regency design. Its polished top was inset with green leather; on either side, two tiers of drawers had metal handles with the metal design of a lion's head on each.

At either side of the desk, sideways, stood outwards a wide-backed armchair uphol-stered in green plush, with green buttons to indent its bulges.

Then Cheviot's eye caught something else. Propped against the far edge of the long table were two of Vulcan's famous collection of walking-sticks. One of them, twisted like a corkscrew, was of very heavy black wood with a silver top. The other, its handle curved, appeared to be much lighter.

A remembrance of advice tapped out a warning:

Don't let him get behind you! Don't let —

But Vulcan was some distance away.

The thick mahogany door closed with a slam as Cheviot swung round. Vulcan, using the longer key from his ring, carefully locked the door.

'Merely a precaution,' he explained, 'against intruders on our privacy.'

'Of course,' Cheviot agreed, and sat down in the far armchair his host had indicated.

Vulcan replaced the key-ring in his waistcoat pocket.

His air of self-satisfaction seemed almost to burst his evening clothes. He towered up as he approached, a massive shadow of him spreading out behind on the orange-and-green walls.

'Is it not strange?' he asked in a musing tone. 'Strange, I say, that a man — a man, I again explain, with so few natural advantages — should yet hold a compelling fascination for so many women? Even women (I do not mention Kate, though I am fonder of her than any), even women of high birth and refined tastes?'

Here Vulcan glanced down over his white shirt-front, his immaculate cuffs, the rings a-flash on his fingers.

'Yet I know such a man,' he added, and almost smiled.

'Oh, yes,' said Cheviot, without looking at him. 'So do I.'

Vulcan stood very still, beside the desk and in front of the other armchair.

It was as though an arrow had struck home, with mysterious effect, as Cheviot meant it to strike.

'May I offer you a cigar, Mr. Cheviot?'

'Thank you.'

Most of the cigars he had bought and smoked in this age were the vilest of weeds. This one, offered from a thin deep sandalwood box on the desk, was the finest Havana. With the cigar-cutter in his right-hand waistcoat pocket, at the end of the chain which ran to his heavy silver watch in the other pocket, he snipped off the end.

Vulcan took a cigar, and did the same.

'A glass of brandy, my dear sir?' he beamed. 'Tush, don't hesitate! This is the Napoleon *cru*, of admitted excellence.'

'I can't resist that, I thank you. I have never tasted true Napoleon brandy.'

Vulcan unstoppered a cut-glass decanter, on a silver platter amid glasses. He poured the brandy into two glasses, without moving them. Cheviot rose to his feet and moved across. There, apparently, he stumbled, slipped, and bumped straight into Vulcan with a heavy thud.

'Come, I do beg your pardon!' Cheviot blurted, disengaging himself. 'It was unpardonably clumsy of me!'

'Not at all,' said Vulcan.

Taking the glass of brandy, Cheviot sat down again. Vulcan, still standing, whisked an inch-long metal rod across the base of a gold-and-silver toy pagoda. Oil-soaked flame curled up. Vulcan carefully lighted Cheviot's cigar, moving the flame back and forth.

Next he lit his own cigar, took up the glass of brandy, and settled his weight back comfortably into the green-padded armchair.

'As we were saying — ' Cheviot began, drawing smoke into his lungs.

A brief smile, like a shark opening its jaws, flashed across Vulcan's face and was gone.

'Yes,' he said, 'it really was clumsy when you pretended to stumble against me. It was to test my weight, was it not? And you found me solid enough, I think?'

Cheviot did not reply.

'And now, Mr. Superintendent Cheviot,' said Vulcan, with absolutely no change of tone, 'what do you really want of me?'

Cheviot's voice remained just as detached.

'As I told you,' he answered, blowing out smoke and studying it, 'a fair business-bargain. An exchange . . . '

'Of what?'

'Information. It will benefit both of us, believe me.'

'Forgive my frankness, sir,' Vulcan said dryly, and shook his big head, 'but I think you have very little to offer. However! Speak on.'

'You've heard, I suppose, of the murder of Margaret Renfrew at Lady Cork's house last night?'

Vulcan looked shocked.

'My dear sir! Who has not? The columns of the *Morning Post* were full of it.'

'Well! A diamond-and-ruby brooch, shaped like a full-rigged ship, was pledged here at your establishment by a person we believe to be the murderer. Four other pieces of jewellery, of which I have a list here,' and Cheviot touched his breast-pocket, 'may have been pledged too.'

'It distresses a gentleman to say so. But I have a fully legal pawnbroker's licence.'

'These jewels were stolen.'

'And was I to know that?' inquired Vulcan.

For a moment he sipped brandy and drew at his cigar.

'If they were stolen,' he continued, mighty in virtue, 'they shall be returned. But think of my difficulties! What was it you said? A diamond-and-something brooch, shaped like a ship? Have you any notion how many such trinkets pass through my hands, or those of my chief croupier, in the course of a year? Yet you ask me to remember one of them?'

'Oh, come off it,' Cheviot said vulgarly.

'I beg your pardon?'

'I said come off it,' retorted Cheviot, finishing his brandy and setting down the glass on the desk. 'You don't issue pawn-tickets, I understand. You keep account-books, with a description of the article set down opposite the name of the person who pledged it. Yes or no?'

'Yes.' Vulcan spoke after a pause. 'I keep account-books. What, exactly, do you wish to know?'

'The name of the man who pledged that brooch.'

'And what do you offer in return? — One moment!'

Vulcan lifted the hand which held his glass. He sat up straight. The sheer force of his personality, apart from any size or weight, seemed to dwarf Cheviot and pin the latter in his chair.

'Let *me*,' he suggested, 'tell *you*. Any offer you make must concern my gaming-house here. True, to keep a gaming-house is illegal. But the law is seldom enforced. Why? Because you cannot convince any man that gambling is a crime, provided the play at the tables be fair. As mine, notoriously, *is* fair.

'So I will give you three good reasons,' he continued, 'why you cannot help me; still less hurt me. First, if the new police meditated any attack on my premises, I should be warned beforehand.'

Cheviot nodded.

'Oh, yes,' he said. 'I was aware of that.'

Again it was as though a driven arrow had struck home.

The force of Vulcan's personality did not alter. His tone did not change. But his glass eye, in the orange light, remained dead; his good eye took on a glitter of malice.

'Second,' he said, 'you could never find witnesses to testify against me in the box. The high-born, fearing scandal, would not testify. The — shall we say medium or even base-born? — dare not testify — '

'Because they would be bribed, intimidated, or beaten within a gasp of death by your blacklegs?'

'I don't like your tone, Mr. Cheviot.'

'Nor I yours. May I hear your third reason?'

'Willingly!' said Vulcan, softly putting down his cigar on the edge of the table and his glass beside it. 'Third, your police could not get in. You took note of my iron door, which is four inches thick in a thick wall. By the time your police could force that door, with axes or what tools you like, it would take twenty minutes or even half an hour. You agree?'

'Yes.'

'By that time, dear sir, no evidence of gambling would remain. My guests, or such as wished to do so, would have disappeared. The intruders would surprise only quiet talk in a gentleman's drawing-room.'

Cheviot laughed.

It was a jarring sound, as he meant it to be.

'Vulcan,' he said, 'you disappoint me.'

There was no answer. The cut-glass bowls of the lamps seemed to grow dull and darken their orange light.

'Forgive my frankness,' said Cheviot, in mockery of the other's voice, 'but you are like any other householder, in any other street. You make your front door so strong, so impregnable, that no intelligent bur — housebreaker would think of attacking it. Then, like another householder, you completely neglect your back door.'

Cheviot nodded to the two windows, closely muffled in orange curtains, in the rear wall.

'Outside those windows,' he said, 'two steeply pitched tile roofs slope down to a back wall in a mews. When I visited the mews very late this afternoon, the back door was wide open for air. It gives on a scullery and kitchen. These lead, left and right, to a ground-floor supper-room and dice-hazard room.'

Still Vulcan did not move or speak.

'When I visited the mews late this evening,' Cheviot went on, 'your back door was still on the jar. Vulcan, Vulcan! If I had fifty constables outside that back door at this minute, they could be up into your gaming-room within twenty seconds.'

Then Vulcan moved.

Amazingly, in so vast a man, he bounced to his feet like an india-rubber cat. He darted behind his chair. His right hand shot out towards the brass knob to the bell-wire, seized it, and pulled hard. The knob came away in his hand.

'No,' said Cheviot. 'You can't summon your blacklegs like that.'

The knob dropped on the carpet with a faint thud. Without speaking, without smiling, Vulcan moved across to the mahogany door.

His big fingers fished in his waistcoat pocket, fished again, then flew across to his other pocket . . .

'No,' Cheviot told him, 'that won't do either.'

Reaching into his side pocket, he drew out Vulcan's key-ring with the two keys.

'I greatly fear,' he said, 'that I picked your pocket when I bumped into you. Was *that* so very clumsy, do you think?'

Vulcan's bald head turned slowly round. His good eye gleamed and burned.

'It is true,' Cheviot added, 'you can always hammer on the door and scream for help.

And yet, since you are known to be alone with only one unarmed man two or three stone lighter than yourself, I think you would be ashamed to do it.'

'Yes,' Vulcan agreed, 'you are right. But what need have I,' and at last he smiled, 'when I can always take the keys from you myself?'

Cheviot considered this.

'Now I wonder if you could?' he mused. 'But reassure yourself. There are no constables outside your back door.'

'If this is a lie, or a piece of bounce — !'

The latter term, which in after years would come to mean bluff, stung Cheviot far worse than he had stung Vulcan.

'I never lie,' he said, 'and I never use bounce. I despise those who do.' He controlled his voice. 'Besides, you have talked a great deal. You haven't even heard what I offer in exchange for a murderer's name.'

'Very well. Speak.'

Cheviot leaned across and carefully put down his half-smoked cigar on the silver platter of the decanter. He stood up, bracing himself on his right foot.

'Your roulette-wheel is rigged,' he said. 'And I can prove it. If I do, it will ruin you.'

Only Cheviot's next words, sharp-pierced

with common-sense, stopped Vulcan's charge at him.

'Gambling?' Cheviot said. 'What matter to me if you fleece a thousand young block-heads, provided I can avenge one human life? Human life means little to you? By God, it means all to me! I want no violence, no fight, if we can make terms. Nor do you. Shall I demonstrate how your wheel downstairs is rigged?'

Without waiting for an answer he backed away. He backed past his chair, round the left-hand side of the table where the two walking-sticks were propped up, and behind the roulette-wheel with his back to the curtains.

In the wheel lay a small ivory ball. Cheviot picked it up.

Whereupon, without even glancing at Vulcan, he went down on his knees against the thick green carpet. His fingers explored the carpet to the right of where a croupier's chair would have stood. They ran along the carpet to the left.

Cheviot stood up.

Vulcan was looking at him from just across the table, two and a half feet wide.

'Yes?' prompted Vulcan.

'This table is not rigged. But I can show you the principle. It is so old, so old and primitive, that no one would use it in any modern — ' Cheviot stopped.

'Yes?'

'The croupier's right foot,' returned Cheviot, 'controls four (yes, four) very small buttons under the carpet. These, connected by taut wires, lead to rods up the legs of the table and inside it. A very slight pressure sets in motion three separate coiled springs driven by compressed air. You are acquainted with the principle in your — our time. But the full weight of each spring must never be uncoiled at once. If it did, it would explode mightily.'

Cheviot paused.

All of a sudden, as he spoke, his gaze seemed to fix on the cigar-smoke rising from the desk at the far side.

'No, no, never!' he breathed, as though fighting his own senses. 'A very slight touch; the air must be preserved, in touches, for use all night!'

'And what end, may I ask?'

'Follow this!'

Cheviot gave a whirl to the silvered pivot of the wheel, which flashed into a red-and-black-blur. Next he tossed in the ball.

It bounced down; jumped, and, as always, went whirling and spinning round the outer ebony rim. Presently, while the clicking grew more soft and only Vulcan seemed to breathe, it slowed down.

'And to what end, I repeat?' demanded Vulcan.

'Look at it!'

'I see nothing!'

'As the ball slows down, it is certain at one revolution or other to roll somewhere near the zero or the double-zero, set side by side. A touch of the croupier's foot, heel or toe, can control three of the hidden springs at once. It does not matter where the ball is; the wheel is quartered. A touch tilts up three sides of the wheel: slightly, invisibly. If this wheel could tilt up . . . '

Cheviot leaned forward, his fingers darting out.

'By the Lord, it does tilt up!'

Cheviot's fingers could only flick lightly at the sides, far less effectively than a simultaneous mechanism. The tilting of the wheel, swaying as it rotated towards a stop, could not even be detected. But the ball slid down and dropped with a click into double-zero.

Vulcan's shaven jowls bore not even any side-whiskers. A bright drop of sweat appeared on each cheek-bone.

'*I* tried it only once,' said Cheviot. 'How

many weeks or months has your croupier practised it?'

'I — '

'It's finished,' said Cheviot, looking up straight into his eyes across the table. 'Don't you think your own number's up, Vulcan?'

15

The Rites of Venus

How he wished he could dent the hard expressionless look, the placidity, of Vulcan's face! But he couldn't.

'Don't you think your own number's up?' he repeated. 'If you compel me to expose this — '

'Dear sir, you will never leave this room to expose it.'

'No? I can leave this room,' Cheviot said, 'at any time I please.'

'Lies? Lies again?'

Cheviot moved back to one window, and partly twitched open an orange-plush curtain.

'I told you truthfully,' he said, 'there were no constables at your back door. But outside these windows, on the roof-slope, are six constables and two officers. I have only to raise a window and spring my rattle, or even smash a pane. They will be over the sill and inside before you can even touch the door.' He drew the curtain wider. 'Vulcan, do you challenge me?'

'Drop the curtain! Close it!'

Cheviot complied. The two stood watching each other with deadly wariness from opposite sides of the table. But Vulcan remained agreeable.

'Mr. Cheviot, what are your terms?'

'You've heard them. The diamond-and-ruby brooch, and your account-book with a certain man's name written opposite its description. In return, we let you alone.'

'We-el!' murmured Vulcan in his soft bass. 'After all, I am a law-abiding man. And already you have the key.'

'Key?'

'On the key-ring you were deft enough to steal, the shorter key will open any drawer of my desk. The left-hand tier of drawers contains my collection of jewellery; thrown in higgledy-piggledy, I regret. The two top right-hand drawers contain my account-books. *Voilà tout.*'

Vulcan's cigar was acridly burning the edge of the desk. He went back to take it up in one hand, his unfinished brandy-glass in the other hand. As though to show his entire detachment, he strolled along the side of the table.

Towards the door? Yes; but he did not even glance at the door. Passing the big Chinese-lacquer cabinet, he moved round towards Cheviot's side of the table.

Cheviot slipped away to the right, round the other end of the table, and up to the desk.

One eye peered over his shoulder, keeping watch on Vulcan. Vulcan had stopped about the middle of the table, putting down glass and cigar on what was now the far side, and apparently studying the roulette-wheel.

Compelled to look away, Cheviot slipped the smaller key into the lock of the top drawer in the right-hand tier. The key turned easily. He pulled open the drawer.

Vulcan had not lied about this, at least. Inside lay four account-books. They were big ledgers, bound in thick stippled cardboard, the topmost bearing a pasted white-paper label with the inked figures, *1823 – 1824*.

The ledgers were so big that he must work each ledger sideways out of the drawer before he could find the one he wanted. He must —

Don't let him get behind you! Don't let him . . .

With the sole of his shoe Cheviot pushed back the armchair, to have free play on either side. Unseen, shielded by his body, he slipped out his watch of bright polished silver like a mirror, and propped it up tilted at the back of the drawer.

He could see reflected, over his shoulder, any attack which came close.

Then he eased out the first ledger, and put

274

it on the desk with his eyes on the polished surface of the watch. The second ledger, disconcertingly, was dated 1822 – 1823. He wormed it out and pitched it on the desk.

Underneath lay the account-book for 1828 – 1829.

Got it!

Cheviot could not see Vulcan dart along the left-hand side of the table behind him. He could not see Vulcan snatch up, by its silver head, the very heavy black cane twisted like a corkscrew.

But he saw a black shape loom up in the watch-mirror. He saw the flash of the diamond-ring as Vulcan's arm whipped back. Just before the cane lashed over, in a blow to smash his skull, Cheviot leaped sideways and to the right.

It would have missed his head, missed even his shoulder and arm, if —

The watch, jerked out of the drawer by its chain, lodged under the top edge of the drawer. There was only a breathing-space before the chain yanked loose the cigar-cutter from Cheviot's other pocket.

The blow, meant for the back of his head, caught him glancingly on the side of it over the thick hair, missing arm and shoulder as Cheviot dodged.

But it was bad enough. He felt that flying

weight crack the side of his head. The wave of pain went out in eerie tuning-fork noises to dim his eyesight.

He heard Vulcan grunt as the cane whacked and tore green leather, sending a spasm of agony through Vulcan's wrist. It was all the time Cheviot needed. Though his head felt swollen and throbbed with pain, his arms and legs were steady.

Catching up the light and curved-handled cane — of no earthly use to anybody except as a blind — he ran round the table and stopped beyond the roulette-wheel. There he steadied his swimming eyesight, sweeping from the table an empty glass and a dead cigar.

Vulcan had turned round, showing his teeth. The heavy cane was in his hand as he moved, cat-footed, again with the width of the table between them.

Both spoke only in murderous whispers.

'If you touch that curtain — ' This was Vulcan's whisper.

'I won't. Unless you touch the door.'

'This is between ourselves?'

'Yes!'

Instantly Vulcan lunged and lashed out, across the width of the table, at Cheviot's head.

Cheviot didn't attempt to parry with the

light cane; it would only have smashed to flinders. Instead he jumped to one side. The crooked stick, missing widely, struck with a *crack* against the far side of the table. It gashed and scarred mahogany. It made the orange lamps jump and quiver, the china statues rattle.

But Vulcan, never off balance, was instantly back on his feet. Cheviot could only face him with silent derision. He dared not try for a judo-hold, against such strength and quickness, unless —

Unless he could madden Vulcan into lunging off balance.

Vulcan watched, moving right and left. Cheviot approached and stood against the edge of the table, daring him.

Crack!

Vulcan lashed and missed again, so widely that Cheviot's derision grew broader.

Slowly Vulcan drew back from the table. Slowly he moved towards the left, behind one of the china figures. He had only one eye, Cheviot's look seemed to imply; his measuring of distance would be poor.

Vulcan knew that, and it infuriated him still more. He drew farther back, as though about to turn away. Cheviot, on the contrary, pressed against the edge of the table and leaned partly across it.

Vulcan whirled back, ran in, and struck. Too late he saw where the blow must fall; but he could not stop his arm. The crooked weight smashed full down on the half-smiling Venus, with her black hair over her shoulders. The china figure burst to pieces, all but disappeared, as the cane hit the table.

Still nobody spoke. Vulcan stood motionless, his good eye wide with horror. His pale face grew paler. In a paralysis he whispered the only words of human feeling Cheviot ever heard him use.

'Kate,' he said. 'My poor Kate.'

Whereupon fury caught him. The blood surged up in his cheeks, leaving only his skull white. He raced along the table to the middle, Cheviot following him. Seeing that hated face, Vulcan lunged far and struck — completely off balance.

Cheviot had already thrown away his useless cane. As Vulcan's right arm shot across the table, the fingers of his left hand gripped the wrist as he had gripped Captain Hogben's. He jerked that Leviathan bulk across the table and past the roulette-wheel.

For a second Vulcan's neck rested on the other edge of the table, as in the collar of a guillotine. The edge of Cheviot's right hand, like a hatchet, chopped down across the back of the neck. Then he yanked Vulcan fully over, setting a-spin the pivot of the roulette-wheel.

Vulcan landed sideways, quivering, and rolled over on his back. His eyes were glazed; the eyelids fluttered and closed. He did not seem to breathe.

The roulette-wheel, at first wildly spinning, steadily slowed down and came to a stop.

And Cheviot, sweating with fear at what he might have done, stared down at Vulcan.

A blow like that, in the proper place, could kill and not stun, as he intended. But *had* he intended merely to stun? *Had* he struck in the place to stun and not kill?

That whole battle, except for four whispered words and the crack or thud of Vulcan's stick, had gone in dead silence.

Silent now, horribly silent, Cheviot searched for his watch to see whether breath would cloud the glass. His watch was gone. He bent down and felt for a pulse. He thought he felt one beating, but he could not be sure. Tearing open Vulcan's shirt, ripping down the thin silk undervest beneath, his fingers sought the heart.

And the heart was beating, thinly but steadily. Vulcan was only knocked out.

Cheviot lurched to his feet. The act of bending over threw a dazzle of pain through the left side of his head. He steadied himself against the table. After a moment or two he hurried round to the desk. He took out the account book for 1828–1829, and put it on the desk. He retrieved his watch, chain, and cigar-cutter. He took the shorter key out of the lock, replacing the key-ring in his pocket.

Then, listening for any noise below, he hurried across to the windows. There was much trouble in opening the windows; they were stuck fast. He wrenched one of them up, cracking a pane in the glass. His hands hammered and bumped at the other until that went up too.

To gulp the cold night-air was heartening, soothing. Drawing together the curtains behind him so that no noise could be heard inside, Cheviot took out the rattle from under his coat. Its noise tore and splintered out against the night sky.

He walked back, stepping over a Vulcan now breathing stertorously beside the crooked stick, and went to the far end of the table nearest to the door and the Chinese-lacquer cabinet. Now that the shock of the fight had passed, he was again strung to alertness and anticipation.

Through the drawn curtains, like demons in a pantomime, leaped Inspector Seagrave on one side and Sergeant Bulmer on the other, their truncheons drawn. They moved aside. Six constables, wearing duty-armbands and with truncheons drawn, flowed over the sills and spread out in a line.

'Orders, sir?' demanded Inspector Seagrave.

'First, clap a pair of darbies on that sleeping beauty. He'll wake up at any moment.'

Sergeant Bulmer whipped the handcuffs from under his coat, and clicked them shut on Vulcan's thick wrists. But his eyes bulged out as he did so.

'Gord!' blurted Sergeant Bulmer.

'Quiet!' said Cheviot.

'But what did you do to the cove, sir?' insisted Bulmer. 'We couldn't see or hear a thing, 'cept what sounded like a fight. You've got a nasty lump on the side of your head, too. Couldn't have been easy, downing old Vulcan.'

The always-worried Inspector Seagrave silenced him with a glare and remained wooden.

'Orders, sir?' he repeated.

'The same as our original plan. I was to come into the house and find the device, packed cards or a rigged wheel, Vulcan employed to fleece his guests. If I found it, I was to use it as a weapon to get his account-book and the diamond-and-ruby brooch.'

'And — and you've done that, sir?'

'Yes, by luck. Look for yourself! His account-book for 1828–1829 is over on the desk there. The left-hand tier of drawers, four of them, is packed with his collection of jewellery. Here!'

Cheviot took the key-ring from his pocket and put it on the edge of the table.

'The shorter key,' he said, 'opens any drawer. The only reason why I called you in here is that we must make great haste. Four of you will each take one of the drawers and go through it. Get the brooch alone; that will do as evidence; but get it quickly before we're discovered.'

'And after that, sir?' insisted Inspector Seagrave, who wanted to have every detail right in his head.

'After that, we release Vulcan and go down over the roofs. We don't touch Vulcan or his house. I made a promise, and I'll keep it.'

'Begging your pardon, sir,' spoke up a hoarse and dogged voice from one of the constables, 'but ain't there to be any fight?'

Cheviot, who had moved back almost to the armchair where he had been sitting, wheeled round.

'Fight? Can nine of us meet thirty blacklegs, probably half a dozen more in the footmen down there, and most of 'em armed?'

A stir went through the line along the opposite wall.

'Thirty? Maybe thirty-six?' cried Sergeant Bulmer. 'Sir, that's twice the lot of legs that Captain Whimper and the Black Dwarf used to stuff the house and make sure they cut Billy Hench's throat!'

'Well, Vulcan packed the house against me. He knew I was coming. Somebody warned him beforehand. But never mind that! Hurry! Don't you see, with the evidence we have, we've won the game? We've completely — '

He stopped.

There was a woodeny, rattly kind of flap and crash. Cheviot, staring at Bulmer across the room, saw its effect reflected in his men's eyes before he turned.

The double-doors of the big Chinese-lacquer cabinet had been hurled open as though by the hands of a maniac, which was very nearly true.

Inside the cabinet, crouching, stood Kate de Bourke.

Her glossy black hair was torn down over her shoulders, torn by her own fingernails, just as they had ripped down the bodice of her green gown. The lips were drawn back over her teeth. Her eyes seemed swollen lumps of fury.

'She's been there all the time,' flashed Cheviot's thought. 'I never actually saw her leave the room. Vulcan keeps a witness for everything. She's heard every word, and seen her image smashed, without daring to help. She — '

Then Kate screamed.

The screams went piercing up, and must have been audible to everyone in the big gaming-room downstairs. Kate's wide skirts billowed out of the cabinet. She was nearly blind from being so long in the dark. But even dim eyes saw the gleam of the keys lying at the edge of the table just in front of her.

Kate seized the keys, tottered round, and ran to collide with the mahogany door not three paces away, just as the paralysis lifted from every man.

'*Bulmer! Grab her!*'

Cheviot raced for the door as Bulmer and Seagrave did. They were too late.

In fact, they overshot the mark. Cheviot never knew by what miracle Kate found the lock, instantly unlocked the door, and flung it open.

As he and Bulmer crowded together in the doorway, he threw out his arm and held Bulmer back. After all, he could hardly collar the woman like a felon. She had done nothing.

But Kate, flying out on the narrow balcony, momentarily stopped to look back. He had a glimpse of her face over her shoulder, past the tangled hair. He saw the mouth drawn up at one corner, and the terror in her eyes.

She must many times have peeped out of that cabinet. What she saw, blurred, was the face of the man who had thrown her unbeatable Vulcan across a table and knocked him senseless with a blow across the neck.

In a space only while you might have counted two, Cheviot was conscious of men jumping to their feet in the big yellow-hung room below, of faces upturned, of three great chandeliers, dazzling with candles, about on a level with his eyes.

'Stop!' he said. He tried to speak gently, but his voice seemed to thunder out. 'We mean you no harm. We won't hurt you. But stop, or you'll hurt yourself!'

What Kate heard was the frightening voice of the man who —

She screamed again. She ran blindly to the right. Once more she tried to look over her left shoulder. Her eyes saw only the blaze of yellow candlelight from the chandeliers. And her wits dissolved along with her sight.

She turned and ran straight for the wooden handrail in front of her.

The crack of tearing and splintering wood,

as her body struck gilded and flimsy scrollwork rotted through, was not as loud as the crack of Vulcan's cane on the table. But it seemed to go on longer.

Kate turned in the air and fell face down. She fell fourteen feet, her hair lifting from her shoulders, and her body as limp as a dead woman's because she had fainted. That dead-weight landed on the right-hand side of the long roulette-table just below.

Under such an impact one of the table-legs, underneath the same side, broke off completely. The other, wavering, splintered and broke as well. The opposite end of the table, eighteen feet long and covered with green felt, grotesquely jerked up and tilted into the air.

Ivory counters, banknotes, gold coins rolled over and spilled down to the right. But that was not what drove a stamp of silence on every mouth.

With a ripping and twanging noise, two long taut wires tore the carpet underneath the table. Those wires ran to the two good table-legs on the left. They glistened as they surged up, tearing the carpet still further and exposing a metal plate with four black buttons.

Then it was as though the table, endowed with life, went mad. Machines do go mad, when you smash them. Few understood the exploding hiss of compressed air. But they saw the roulette wheel itself jump up as a coiled spring emerged at one side, crawling and expanding like a metal snake. Another uncoiled spring shot up as though to attack the wheel.

Every man down on the floor there, punter or blackleg, stood up or ran to look. All stayed motionless, hats falling off or eyeballs glistening, when they saw.

Cheviot alone, at the broken handrail, was looking at Kate de Bourke.

She had slid down the table, her skirt dragged above her knees. He could not see her face. But her outspread arms moved. Her fingers clutched at the green baize. Slowly, dazedly, she lifted her head and blinked round.

Nobody heard Cheviot's strangled gasp of relief.

He had given the wrong order — 'Bulmer! Grab her!' — which might have sent a half-crazed woman to her death. It turned him sick when he saw her fall.

And yet, as so often happens, she had fallen as flat and limp as a jockey or a drunken man. Far from being dead or bone-smashed, the woman was not even hurt.

Hardly two seconds had elapsed since she

fell. But every one of his eight men, despite his frantic gesture, had run out into the gallery and lined up on either side of him.

They were trapped here amid thirty-odd blacklegs, whose eyes were beginning to move up to the gallery.

They were trapped here, that is, unless . . .

The bursting hush still held. Vividly Cheviot was conscious of four persons standing up at the far side of the roulette-table. The tall young man addressed by the footman as my lord, he of the luxuriant brown side-whiskers and the red nose, was stricken cold sober. Beside him stood the thick-set bruiser in the piebald wig, hand threateningly half-raised towards him.

Beyond the wheel, staring at it, was the stout man with the yellow side-whiskers, whom Cheviot had seen at Lady Cork's. Beyond *him* loomed the lean, bony blackleg with the lined face and the false teeth.

'Yes!' Cheviot shouted.

A quiver went through them all. All of them looked upwards: seeing uniforms, seeing truncheons, seeing only Cheviot in evening-dress and empty-handed.

His voice rang out again.

'That is how they fleeced you,' he said, pointing down to the roulette-table.

From across the room, at the rouge-et-noir

table, he heard the click as the hammer of a pistol was drawn back to full-cock.

'Yes, we are the police,' Cheviot said. 'But on whose side do you stand: on the side of those who robbed you — or on ours?'

One, two, three, four . . .

'My lord' whirled round to the bruiser in the weird wig. My lord's high, harsh voice rose up.

'You damned cheating leg,' he said, almost in surprise.

His left fist swung and drove into the bruiser's fat stomach. His right came over to the head. Taken completely off-balance, the breath squeezed from his lungs, the bruiser sat down hard on a chair which broke under him.

At the same moment the expression altered on the face of the bony man with the false teeth. A knife slipped out of his sleeve. He had no time to use it on Yellow-whiskers beside him. Snatching the rake from the hand of the second croupier, Yellow-whiskers lunged with the head of the rake and smashed the false teeth down his throat.

At the rouge-et-noir table, two punters ran in together at the croupier, pulling him over backwards by the neckcloth and flinging him on the carpet under a rain of cards from six packs. Somebody threw a bottle. Somebody else raised a war-cry. The battle boiled over.

At each end of the gallery above, a small staircase led down to the floor. Cheviot ran to the head of his men on the right-hand side. Catching sight of Inspector Seagrave on the extreme left end, he raised his hand high, singled out the three behind him, and snapped his fingers.

'Now!' he said.

And empty-handed he led three constables down into the brawl on the right stairs, while Inspector Seagrave led four men down into it from the left.

16

'I Kissed Thee Ere . . . They Killed Me'

The clocks were striking three in the morning when a hackney cab turned into Cavendish Square towards Flora Drayton's house.

The passenger inside, despite his uneasiness, was jubilant. He almost sang.

Outwardly he looked respectable enough. Neither his cloak nor his hat had entered the brawl at Vulcan's. The cloak was worn closed and fastened at the chin, the hat jolted on the seat beside him because the head-bruise ached.

Cheviot's jaw felt very sore on the right, but it did not seem to be swollen. He scarcely felt his body-bruises, though they would be stiff enough next day. On the seat at his right lay two account-books, and Cheviot's handkerchief, tied up in a knot, containing five pieces of jewellery.

'Ta-ti-ta!' sang Superintendent Cheviot, who was not very musical.

If only it were not for Flora's wrath . . .

The cab slowed from a trot and drew up at the door of her house.

Cheviot glanced out of the window. The house would be dark and sealed up; he must, of course, find some way of breaking in. He looked. Astounded, he looked again.

A gleam of gaslight illuminated the fanlight over the front door. Though the shutters were closed inside the windows to the left of the door, they bore tiny star-shaped openings; and the room was lighted too.

Gathering up hat, handkerchief, and account-books in a bundle, Cheviot hastened to jump down and pay the cabman who opened the door. By this time he had discovered that you did not tip cabbies in the way he knew it; the jarvey stated from threepence or sixpence more than his actual fare, and you paid that.

He ran to the door. He had hardly touched the bell-knob when the door was opened by a middle-aged, almost stately woman, rather stout, in a lace cap and long lace apron. She resembled a housekeeper rather than a maid.

'Good evening, sir,' she said as casually as though they were meeting at seven in the evening, and not at three o'clock in the morning.

'Er — good evening.'

'Your hat, sir?'

'Thank you. But not,' he said hastily, 'the cloak or — or these other things.'

'Very good sir,' said the middle-aged woman, who was now beaming at him.

'Er — is she — Lady Drayton — is she — ?'

The woman merely curtseyed gravely, indicating closed double-doors at the left of the marble-floored foyer.

Flora made no pretence that she had not heard wheels stop in the street outside. Still fully dressed in her dark-blue gown bordered with gold, she was sitting up straight at a round table near the fire, her fingers pressed hard on the pages of the leather-covered book she had ceased to read.

A petroleum-oil lamp burned on the table. Gaslight flickered yellow from a bracket on either side of the white-marble mantel-piece, and there was a good blazing fire. All these brought out the delicate hollows under her eyes.

When Cheviot opened and closed the doors behind him, she still sat rigidly: her slender neck upright, her eyes searching him in fear that he had been hurt. When he seemed uninjured, she uttered a little cry.

Hastily Cheviot put down the account-books, the handkerchief-wrapped jewellery, on a chair of cherry-covered velvet. For Flora ran across to him, throwing her arms round him with such violence that he tightened his shoulders against the pain of body-bruises. Flora put her head back. He kissed her so hard and in such a complicated way that after some seconds he thought it better — let us say more delicate — to hold her a little away from him.

His voice was husky. But he tried to assume a light tone.

'May I observe, my dearest, that of all the women on earth you are the most utterly unpredictable?'

'What a pretty compliment!' Flora almost sobbed. She really thought it the highest of compliments. 'You can bandy words fairly, when you like.'

Whereupon she must put on a grand-hostessy and haughty air, drawing back from him even while she clung to him.

'Foh!' said Flora, in pretended disgust. 'You have been smoking again.'

'Certainly I have been smoking. But you needn't make it sound as though I had been smoking opium or hashish. After all, it's only tobacco.'

'Which,' declared Flora, drawn up even with tears in her eyes, 'is a filthy and repulsive habit, not permitted in any wellbred house. If a man must smoke, he goes upstairs and smokes up the chimney.'

'He — *what?*'

'He sits on the hearth,' here she grandly indicated the hearth of the fireplace not far from her, 'and puts his head inside and lets the smoke go up the chimney. Of course,' Flora added hastily, 'there mustn't be any fire.'

Cheviot was in a mood which combined desire, hilarity, and the knowledge that he was beginning to understand her at last.

'I sincerely hope not,' he said with a grave face. 'If I were obliged to stick my head up the flue over a fire, I might find my whiskers a trifle singed before I had finished the cigar.'

'But you haven't got any whis — oh, stop! You're quizzing again! I hate you!'

'Flora, look at me. Do you honestly mind the smoking?'

'No. Of course I don't. Kiss me again.' Then, after an interval: 'I allow I was cross with you tonight — '

'You had cause.'

'No, no! I was furious,' said Flora, dropping her grand airs and becoming natural, 'because I was so frightened. Do you imagine I had heard nothing of Vulcan? Or his reputation? And there he was, daring you to remain. And there you were — oh, no matter! But there *was* trouble, was there not?'

'A little, yes. Nothing to speak of.'

'Thank God,' she said breathlessly. 'Darling! Come and sit down and tell me. Let me have your cloak.'

'No, no! Not the cloak!'

But Flora had already unfastened the catch and slipped off the heavy astrakhan collar. When the cloak fell into her hands, she leaped back and stifled a shriek.

His collar and neckcloth were gone. His shirt was crumpled, dirty, and in two places spotted with dried blood. His trousers, split at both knees, were as dust-patched as the torn coat. In this coat, slewed back round as well as possible when he had washed his hands and face at a pump, the right sleeve showed the black-burned rent of a bullet-hole.

'I — I see.' Flora spoke in a low voice, swallowing. 'I remark it. There was but little trouble; nothing to speak of.'

She began to laugh, and went on laughing.

'Flora! Enough of that! You must not give way so!'

Her laughter ceased as he spoke. Pressing the cloak hard against her breast, she looked up with such intense tenderness that he could not meet her gaze.

'Nay, that was no nerves or megrims, Jack. It was honest laughter for the comical. But it came from the heart, which must hurt a little too. Now I will tell you what I determined, and determined this night.'

She moistened her lips, pressing the cloak more tightly against her breast.

'To be open with you, my dear, there is much I don't understand. Of you. Sometimes you might be a man from another world. I don't understand why you insist so much on 'your work'.' Perplexity made her bite her lip. 'A gentleman does not work, or at least need not. Never, never, my father said! No, don't protest! — For why need I understand?

'Shall I be a silly woman,' she cried, 'as so many are silly? And fancy that affectations are realities? I was stupid last night — yes, I was! — and again tonight. You won't find me stupid another time, if you love me. And, if you are so devoted to this cause of the police — why, then, so am I! That is no merit in me. It is because I love you, and I would not have you other than as you are.'

Still Cheviot looked down at the carpet. He did not raise his head. There was a lump in his throat, and he did not look up because he could not.

Flora had moved closer. He reached out; and, as she shifted the cloak to her left arm, he lifted her right hand and pressed his lips to it.

And then, as complete understanding came to them and wrapped them round in a warmth which seemed never to be broken, there rose up from somewhere at the back of the foyer the clank-jangle-rattle of the front door-bell.

Flora drew back from him and stormed.

'At this hour?' she exclaimed. 'No! I'll tell Miriam to admit no one. They shan't take you away from me tonight!'

'You may be sure of that.' He spoke grimly. 'No power on earth could compel it.'

There was a light, discreet tap at the door; then a long pause; then the door was opened by the stately housekeeper.

'My lady — ' she began in some hesitation, and paused. 'I should not have disturbed you, as well you know, save that . . . it is Lady Cork.'

'Lady Cork?' Flora spoke blankly.

Cheviot's begrimed white gloves, adhering with dried blood to the knuckles inside, cost him pain as his fists clenched.

'We had better see her,' he muttered.

'You — you are sure?'

'Yes. This afternoon, Flora, I began to see the solution of the problem.'

'Of Margaret Renfrew's murder?'

'Yes. I had been blind. But I saw who committed the crime; and tonight, at Vulcan's, I realized how it was done. Barring one detail, and one question which you and Lady Cork alone can answer, my cause is complete.'

Flora drew a deep breath. 'Miriam, please beg Lady Cork to come in.'

As the door closed, Cheviot spoke again in that same rapid mutter.

'You are not to be alarmed at what I say. All is well. But this morning Mr. Richard Mayne, one of the Police Commissioners, did his best to make out a cause that you had killed the Renfrew woman and I had shielded you. No, I beg: don't start or put your hand to your mouth!'

Cheviot glanced at the closed door and spoke still more quickly.

'At any time,' he said, 'I could have cleared you. But only by confessing that both of us had told lies and suppressed evidence, which would have been more dangerous still. My only hope lay in showing how this murder was done. And that I think — I say I *think* — I can now prove to the full.'

He held up his hand for silence. Catching the cloak from Flora's arm, he draped it round himself and fastened the collar as Miriam announced the Countess of Cork and Orrery.

They heard Lady Cork's sniff, and the tap of her crutch-headed stick, before the little, stout-bodied, vigorous old woman stumped in.

Lady Cork did not wear her white frilled cap, but the white poke-bonnet with long sides gave much the same effect as her shrewd eyes probed out of its shadow. Her white gown was the same, under a grey fur pelisse rucked up round her.

The eighteenth century, with all its train of ghosts, crowded in round her and fluttered the gas-jets with their presence.

'Lawks, girl!' she said to Flora, with a hint of apology even in her defiant tone. 'I'd not ha' been so troublesome to you, at this time, if I hadn't seen lights burning on the ground floor.' There was a very slight emphasis on the word 'ground.'

Even two or three days ago, Flora might have been in agitated confusion. But she was all coolness and graciousness, smiling.

'You are most welcome, Lady Cork. But surely you are up late?'

'I'm always up late. I don't sleep.' Lady Cork craned her neck round. 'No, no, wench, I'll keep me hat and coat. Don't fuss me!'

This last remark was addressed to her pretty young maid, Solange, hovering in the doorway. Solange's soft and liquid brown eyes peered out from the hood of a green cape, herself in confusion at seeing Flora.

'Sit down there,' Lady Cork told Solange, pointing with her stick at a far chair, 'and be vanished. My visit's a brief one.'

'As is mine,' murmured Cheviot, touching his cloak.

'Is it, George Cheviot's son?' Lady Cork asked sardonically. Her eyes moved to Flora and back to him. 'Is it? Bah! Tell the truth and shame the devil!'

'A practice, madam, I strongly recommend to yourself.'

'Hey? D'ye say I don't tell the truth?'

'Sometimes, madam. But seldom directly.'

Nor, as he knew, would she approach any subject directly. Lady Cork snorted. She peered round the room, papered in silvery grey, its chairs and sofa and ottoman upholstered in cherry-coloured velvet.

Snorting, she hobbled over and plumped herself down in Flora's armchair, under the lamp and beside the fire, with the little round table at her elbow. On the table lay the book, opened, which Flora had been reading when Cheviot entered.

Lady Cork blinked at the pages. It was as though the very sniff of printer's ink set her off.

'D'ye know where I've been this night? No? Well! I've been a-dining with John Wilson Croker,' Lady Cork said ferociously, 'and a parcel of other red-behinded Tories. Can you imagine what Croker has the impudence to propose?'

'Yes,' returned Cheviot. This was the only way to keep her from flying off at a tangent. 'Mr. Croker proposes to edit and annotate a new edition of Boswell, which may take him two years or more. No doubt he wished for your reminiscences?'

'Ay; so he did. Why, curse his dem — '

'Have no fear, madam.'

'Hey?'

'Young Mr. Macaulay, who writes such admirable articles in the *Edinburgh Review*, hates Mr. Croker worse than cold boiled veal. In due time he will dust Croker's jacket so thoroughly that future generations may remember it.'

'Ay, so Rogers prophesies.' Lady Cork brooded, her hands folded on her crutch-headed stick. 'But what does it matter? I've given 'at homes' for all the cursed literary lions in recent years, from Washington Irving to young Ben Disraeli, when he made the town stare with that novel *Vivian Grey*. But the wit's gone. The light's gone. All's gone.'

'Not the wit, I protest!' exclaimed Flora. 'Is Mr. Disraeli, for instance, in town at the moment?'

'Lawks, now!' sneered Lady Cork, rearing

up her thick neck. 'Who don't know he's tourin' the Continent, and says he'll stand for Parliament when he comes back?'

'He will make his mark, madam.' Cheviot spoke gravely. 'He will make his mark, I promise you that.'

'Ben Disraeli? And what are you grinnin' at?'

'I was only thinking of *Vivian Grey*. One of the imaginary characters is called Lord Beaconsfield. Mr. Disraeli, in his youth, never dreams that one day he himself will be called — '

'Well, lad? Don't stop as though you'd bitten your tongue through! Called what?'

'To another sphere, I was about to say.'

A large sofa was drawn up straight towards the fire, sideways to Lady Cork's armchair. Flora sat on the sofa nearer her guest, and Cheviot beside her.

But a change had deepened wickedly in Lady Cork when he said those words. She leaned over her stick, her jowls flattening, and said abruptly:

'I heerd something else at Croker's, too.'

'Oh?'

'Yes. A footman came up and whispered it in John Wilson's ear, about half-past twelve. I heerd,' said Lady Cork with much deliberation, 'that Superintendent George Cheviot's son, with only eight Peelers, bobbed up like a flash o' magic at Vulcan's. The devil knows how they got in. But they beat the blacklegs, and rolled every one of 'em down the front stairs, in seven minutes by somebody's watch.'

Cheviot sighed.

'That is not quite an accurate account, madam.'

'Then what did happen?' the old woman asked truculently. 'Eh, lad? What did happen?'

Cheviot looked back at her steadily.

'The story,' he answered, 'must wait for some other time. It will suffice to say this: that the swell yokels — '

'The — the what, please?' asked a bewildered Flora.

'I beg your pardon. A swell yokel is a gay or dashing fellow. I referred to the gentlemen, the honest punters. They were enraged by a rigged or false roulette-wheel. They turned on the blacklegs, at least eighty per cent of them, and fought on our side. As a result, we so far outnumbered the blacklegs that it was hardly a fight at all. They were overcome in five minutes, not seven.'

Brushing this aside, he still kept his gaze fixed on Lady Cork.

'But I don't imagine, madam, you came

here at past three in the morning to seek details of a broil at Vulcan's. Could it be some interest in a brooch belonging to you?'

Lady Cork's eyes wavered and fell. All her feigned ferocity dropped away.

'I'll not deny it,' she muttered. ' 'Twas a wedding-gift, ye comprehend. The first ever I had. Four other pieces of jewellery *may* have gone to Vulcan. He may keep 'em, for all I care; they don't signify. But the brooch — !'

Cheviot rose to his feet. He went to the chair near the door. On top of the two account-books lay the bag formed by his tied-up handkerchief.

Returning to Lady Cork, he put the bag into her lap. He untied the knot and opened it. Under the flicker of gaslight, under the glow of the cherry-and-grey-coloured lamp, burned a shifting litter of precious stones.

'Permit me,' he said gently, 'to show you all five.'

Lady Cork looked down. She did not exclaim or even speak for some time. She pressed her withered hands against her lips, palms upwards, and rocked her stout body in the chair.

Presently she seized only one of them, a little ship of diamonds and rubies, pressing her mouth to it, and then her cheek, and

305

crooning a sing-song which was of sixty years gone by.

Flora turned her head away. After a moment Lady Cork cleared her throat and peered up.

'Nowadays, lad,' she said, 'they don't make many men like you.'

'But I did little or nothing!' He told her this sincerely; he believed it. 'If you would praise anyone, praise Seagrave, Bulmer, my six constables. By God, madam, they were magnificent. In my report, already sent to the Commissioners, I have given them the highest possible commendation.'

'While you, I dessay,' Lady Cork sneered, 'stood by and did nothing?'

'I — '

'Enough!' said Lady Cork, in a voice of really impressive dignity. She sat up. 'Mr. Cheviot. I cannot say or express how much I am beholden to you. But I'll write to Bobby Peel. Ecod, I'll write to the Duke!'

'And yet I had rather you didn't.'

'Eh?'

'If you wish to show any gratitude, madam, you have only to tell the truth.'

The dark shadow was back again.

The brooch fell from her hands into the other jewellery. A thin singing of gaslight, a clenching of Flora's hands, reminded them they were still in the presence of a dead woman shot through the back.

'Last night,' continued Cheviot, 'you told me a certain story. You said that four of your best treasures, including the brooch, you hid in the seed-containers of the bird-cages in your own bedroom on Tuesday night.'

'But I did! So I did! You said as much yourself!'

'True; I don't gainsay it. However, what of Thursday night?'

Lady Cork opened her mouth, shut it again, and looked away.

'On Thursday night, madam, you told me you set a snare for the thief.' Cheviot reached down, and picked out the only ring amid the pieces of jewellery. 'You said that you put a ring, which you called 'worthless,' into one of the seed-containers of the canary-cages in the passage? Yes?'

Again Lady Cork began to speak, and hesitated.

'You then stated,' Cheviot went on, 'that you succumbed to temptation and swallowed laudanum. You drank the laudanum, and did not see the thief after all.'

'I — '

'Forgive me, but I found that flatly impossible to believe. You were all in agitation, all aghast. You *must* learn the

307

identity of the thief, even if you only suspected it. This ring you hid, for instance.'

Cheviot held it up. Its single large diamond flashed back malevolently.

'In Vulcan's account-book it is pledged (pawned, not sold) for a hundred guineas. Hardly worthless, as you stated? You must set good bait for your thief. Is it reasonable to think you would drink laudanum before you could possibly see the thief? No.' He paused. 'You saw the thief, did you not? And recognized her as Margaret Renfrew?'

'Yes,' said Lady Cork, after a pause.

'Would you so testify in the witness-box, madam?'

'I could and I would!' retorted Lady Cork, lifting her head.

Then she mused for a time, her old eyes wise and shrewd.

'I saw her,' Lady Cork added suddenly. 'In bare feet, and a thin night-shift, carrying a light. Ecod! Peg was never a prude; I always guessed that, though I well knew,' the eyes twinkled, 'her choice was not *you*. But — egad! Until I saw her there in the night, with her mouth open and her cheeks afire, groping for the ring, I never felt in me bones how much of that gel was the world, the flesh, and the devil.'

' 'Fire burn',' muttered Cheviot, ' 'and

cauldron bubble!''

'Eh, lad? What d'ye say?'

'Forgive me.' Cheviot was contrite. 'Only a quotation I have several times applied to her. The fire burned too high. The cauldron bubbled over. Whereupon she stayed herself; she became again her quiet, shut-in self, with a conscience.'

'Oh?' said Lady Cork in a very curious tone.

He dropped the diamond-ring back among the other jewels in Lady Cork's lap.

'There is but one more question, madam; then I have done. It concerns a letter you wrote on the night of the murder. It even concerns Lady Drayton here.'

'It concerns *me*?' Flora cried.

Cheviot smiled. Above the fireplace, between the gas-jets, hung a full-length portrait of Flora herself, painted three or four years ago by an ageing Sir Thomas Lawrence, who seldom accepted commissions now that he was President of the Royal Academy.

All the time Cheviot could not help glancing from the pictured Flora to the real one, who in more than the pictured sense was more alive. With his gloved hand, openly, he tilted up her chin as she sat on the sofa. Even through the glove he could feel the softness of her chin and cheek.

'You?' he repeated. 'My dear, when Mr. Richard Mayne was driving at me with questions this afternoon, I was in fear lest he remember a certain letter. I should have had no answer for him.'

Standing straight on the hearth-rug, he turned back to Lady Cork.

'Last night, the night of the murder, you wrote a letter to Colonel Charles Rowan at Scotland Yard?'

'Ay; and what of that?'

'You sealed it conspicuously, and in yellow wax? Yes. Why, if I may ask, did you despatch it to Colonel Rowan and not to both Commissioners of Police?'

'Lad, lad, Charles Rowan comes often to my house. He was even acquainted with poor Peg.'

'I see. Flora!' He looked down. 'If you recall, you were waiting outside the police-office in your closed carriage. A footman rode up with the letter. You stopped him, and asked to see the letter.'

'Oh, dear!' Flora sat up straight. 'So I did! I had forgotten.'

'So, fortunately, had Mr. Mayne. Why did you ask to see the letter?'

'As you say, it had a conspicuous seal in yellow wax. I saw it by the light of the carriage lanterns.' Flora paused, her face growing crimson. 'All the world knew,' she added defiantly, 'I should be with you. And all knew where *you* were going that night. I thought the letter might be for me.'

'You took it then. Did you break the seal?'

'Good heavens, no. It was addressed to Colonel Rowan. Besides, the seal was already broken.'

Cheviot stared at her.

'Good!' he exclaimed. 'Better still. And now, Lady Cork, if you please! To whom did you give this letter when you had written it?'

'Why, to Peg Renfrew, of course! I was upstairs in me boudoir, and — '

'To whom did *she* give it?'

'To the footman downstairs. Who else?'

'The seal,' he muttered, staring at the fire, 'was broken when it came into Colonel Rowan's hands. Then the likeliest person to have broken it was Margaret Renfrew herself.' He slapped his hands together. 'Yes! She interpreted (pray forgive me, madam) your customary oblique approach about stolen bird-seed. She knew the police would be there. Lady Cork! Did you remark her manner afterwards?'

'Ay.' The old woman nodded grimly. 'I remarked it.'

'Hard, defiant, ashamed? Yet ashamed mainly because . . . stop! Under all that hard surface, couldn't you discern a clamor of conscience? If I had pressed her sharply with questions at that time, might she not have confessed?'

'She might,' agreed Lady Cork, with a snap. 'I'll say more: I thought she would. Else I might ha' — bah, no matter! Who can say what goes on in the heart of a lonely woman? She might, or she might not. But . . . '

'Yes. The murderer stopped her mouth.'

Still contemplating the fire, its heat fanning his eyelids and its crackle dim in his ears, Cheviot saw the pattern take form.

'He shot her. He shot her in cold blood. And all because he must not be exposed. And all for a handful of jewellery. And all for a wad of flimseys — I beg your pardon: I mean banknotes — '

'Jack!' Flora interrupted. 'Where on earth did you learn all these dreadful terms? 'Extra-flash-men.' 'Swell yokels.' 'Flimseys.' And a dozen more. Where did you learn them?'

Cheviot stood very still. 'I — I am not sure.'

'I ask,' Flora persisted uncertainly, 'because some of them are in that book. The book I was reading when you arrived.'

'Book?' he repeated, jerking his head towards the round table.

To the astonishment of both women, he moved over and snatched up the leather-covered book. He opened it and glanced down the title-page.

'This,' he said, 'was published five years ago. I may well have read it, and partly forgotten or never finished it. But it hardly seems your sort of reading, Flora. *The Fatal Effects of Gambling exemplified in the Murder of Wm. Weare, and the Trial and Fate of John Thurtell, the Murderer, and His Accomplices, with* — '

Flora intervened hastily.

'No, not that part! The second part of the book. Look lower down!'

'*The Gambler's Scourge*,' he read aloud, '*a complete exposé of the Whole System of Gambling in the Metropolis; with . . .* '

There was more print, but he did not read the rest of the title-page. Quickly he turned to the back of the book, flipping over the pages. Again Flora protested.

'No; you've passed the gambling part. That's the appendix. It's about a horrible man named Probert, who was concerned in the murder of Weare, and what he testified after he was reprieved.' She broke off. 'Jack! What's the matter?'

For Cheviot, paler of face than she had ever seen him, was holding the open book under the lamp in hands that trembled.

He had reason to behave as he did. On the four hundred and eightieth page, there had jumped up at him a dozen lines in type which seemed even more heavily leaded than it was. He read the lines slowly. He read the next page, and the following three, without enlightenment. Then, at the top of the next page, six lines stung out like an adder.

'Come!' growled Lady Cork, peering past the side of her poke-bonnet and looking disquieted. 'What sort of behaviour's that, now? What d'ye call it?'

'I call it finality,' said Cheviot.

'Finality?'

'Yes.' He closed the book. 'I did not really need this. Yet it is confirmation. It tells me where to find what I want.' He smiled a little. 'You spoke of the murderer, madam?'

'I didn't, but — '

'I have him,' Cheviot said without expression. 'I have him,' and he closed the fingers of his right hand, 'here.'

'Ecod,' bellowed Lady Cork, hammering her stick on the floor and all but spilling the jewels from her lap, 'but who *is* this murderer? And how was the dem thing done?'

'I am sorry, madam. I must keep my own counsel as yet.'

'You won't tell me?'

'I can't.'

'Well! Here's more fine manners! In that event, I'll take my jewels (thanking you very much) and be off.'

Upset, angry without quite seeming to know why, she began fumblingly to tie together the edges of the handkerchief when Cheviot intervened. Putting down the book on the table, he bent down and finished tying the knot. Then he took the jewels away from her as gently as he could.

'Much though it distresses me, Lady Cork, I cannot allow you to keep the jewels just yet. They must be used in evidence.'

A stricken look crossed Lady Cork's face.

'Not keep 'em? Not even the brooch? Not even the wedding-gift?'

'Madam, I am sorry! They will be returned to you, of course. I will write you a receipt now, if you like.'

'Receipt!' cried Lady Cork, as though this were the greatest outrage of all. 'Receipt!'

She pushed herself to her feet on the crutch-headed stick, jerking the fur pelisse round her shoulders.

'Good night to ye, ma'am,' she said to Flora. And: 'Come with me, girl!' to the olive-skinned Solange, who had been sitting unobtrusively in a corner, ankles crossed, all eyes. Solange hastened across to open the double-doors. Lady Cork marched towards them like a man-o'-war.

'The coachman'll be cold, and so am I,' she snorted. At the open doors she half turned, glaring at Cheviot.

'Hey-dey! I'd not ha' thought to see you so pale. And your hands tremble! You'll find yourself nobly fit, I dessay, when tomorrow you meet — '

Glancing at Flora, she bit at her under-lip and stopped. Into her face, instead of anger, came a certain shame.

Cheviot, staring back at her, wondered how she seemed to know everything. Freddie Debbitt, probably; you could not shut Freddie's mouth. But tomorrow, after shooting against the man for a wager, he was engaged to fight a duel with Captain Hugo Hogben. And he had completely forgotten it.

Lady Cork, upreared in the open doors with her hand on her stick and a glimmer of gaslight behind her, bit her lip and changed again.

'Mr. Cheviot! I — I ask your pardon, sir, for the vapours of a cross-grained, bad-tempered old woman. I have a fondness for you; you know it. I am much your debtor; that you know too.' Tears glimmered in her eyes. 'Good luck, lad. God speed your aim.'

The doors closed behind her. They heard a murmur of voices, then the closing, locking, and bolting of the heavy front door.

Flora, who had risen when Lady Cork did, now sat down on the far end of the sofa, near Cheviot as he stood and looked at the door.

'Jack, what did she mean? About — speeding your aim?'

'Nothing! At nine o'clock tomorrow morning I have a practice-match at Joe Manton's gallery. That's all.'

'Oh.'

Still he looked at the closed doors. He had never practiced with their accursed pistols. He was not even sure of the weight, the balance, the throw of the bullet. He might never see Flora again.

A burning log exploded in the fireplace, showering out sparks. Cheviot turned round. He bent down and gathered Flora quickly, violently, into his arms.

17

Six Shots at a Wafer

The pistol-shots, exploding in that long brick room against a thick iron-back wall, set up a din as loud as cannonading in a battle.

The smoke of black powder had thickened to such a haze that even Joe Manton the younger, who was used to it, could hardly see the face of his customer — critical, without any other expression — as Cheviot threw out his arm for the final shot.

Whack! Lead smote on iron. The flattened bullet rattled down to a stone floor.

So great a stillness crept out in the gallery that you could hear, through an open door to the gunsmith's shop, a big white-faced clock ticking on the wall there. It was ten minutes to nine. Superintendent Cheviot had been practising, alone, since twenty minutes past eight.

Joe Manton the younger moved along behind the grilled iron railing, a little less than waist-high, which separated the visitors from the thirty-six paces to the target-wall. There was a creaking of rope as he tugged at the pulleys of the big skylight, tilting it to let out smoke.

The brick walls were whitewashed; they needed a fresh whitewashing every fortnight or so. In the right-hand wall was a many-paned window, already pushed partway up. Through it the smoke slipped, curling with furtive eddies as it billowed out up the skylight.

Black-powder stings the eyes; it makes the nostrils and lungs ache. But, as the haze lifted, Cheviot's face emerged. Both their faces were powder-smudged.

'You can do it, sir,' said Joe, coughing. 'You can do it.' Inside himself, a protest squirmed and struggled. 'But, begging your pardon, Mr. Cheviot, you do it all *wrong*.'

'I know.'

'But, sir — '

On the shelf above the iron-grill partition lay one medium-bore duelling-pistol.

Cheviot had tried as many as a dozen pistols: from the murderous twelve-bore, all but useless because its jump threw the bullet too high, to a small pocket-weapon not unlike the one belonging to Flora's late husband.

Each time, after he had fired, Joe the younger would deftly slip the pistol aside, flick off the burst percussion-cap, rapidly clean the barrel with rod and greased rag, and

319

hang it back again in the long racks of pistols along the left-hand wall.

Cheviot still remained motionless, studying the effect of his last shot. There seemed nothing to study. The iron wall was powder-dark, in some places scarred or uneven, spotted over with what looked like bits of white paper.

Joe the younger fidgeted down to his toes. He was a thick-set, sandy-haired young man, with high cheekbones and earnest eyes. His face was as powder-black as a goblin's. He wore a dark coat, a brown waistcoat, and mulberry-coloured breeches with dark gaiters. He had not yet attained the polite manners yet the shatteringly frank speech of his famous father, gunsmith since 1793.

'Here!' Joe was thinking. 'Here, now!'

He wished this new gentleman, with the broad shoulders and the light-grey eyes, would smile or laugh or crack a joke as the others did.

This Mr. Cheviot, except for spotless white linen, was dressed all in black: even a black waistcoat.

'Why?' thought Joe. 'There isn't going to be a duel, is there? He says it's only a match. Besides, they'd fight a duel early in the morning.'

'Begging your pardon, sir — !' he began aloud.

'I know,' Cheviot repeated. He turned his head and smiled. 'But I can't do it, Joe. Not, that is, if I want to score a hit.'

'Sir?'

'This is how you would desire me to stand, isn't it? Sideways to the rail: thus? Right foot pointed forward, left foot sideways?'

At each movement Joe nodded eagerly.

'Whereupon,' said Cheviot, illustrating, 'I bring my right arm down and over, like this, stiffly stretched out towards the target? Isn't that the manner of it?'

'Sir, that's the only manner of it! I bet you,' exclaimed Joe, inspired, 'I bet you even my *pa* wouldn't think of another way!'

'Oh, but there is. You've seen it. You're thinking of form and not effect, aren't you?'

'Sir?'

'Some of the best pistol-shooting (I don't say all, but some) is done as you saw it. You don't consciously aim. It's like — like throwing out your hand and pointing with the forefinger. It can be done very quickly: like this! It's (what shall I call it?) a gift, a knack, a trick. You possess it, or you don't.' Cheviot paused. 'Is there anywhere I can wash?'

Joe the younger seized with pleasure at what he could understand.

321

'Just there, sir! Water laid on.'

In the left-hand wall, outside the rail and beside the door to the shop, there was a brownish stone sink, with a tap above it and a short metal pump-handle beside it. The small mirror above had been polished, the thin towel on the nail was clean.

Cheviot washed his hands and face with yellow soap, pumping up the water in gushes at a time.

The beaverskin hat fitted well on his head, since the bump had begun to go down. But his body-bruises, tightening now, hurt badly when he bent over the sink.

And the worst part, he was thinking bitterly, was that this duel — somewhere, anywhere; at some time; he didn't know! — need never have been undertaken at all.

He had accepted Hogben's challenge only to draw Hogben on, to make it part of a shooting-match and a wager. If he shot better than Hogben, then Hogben and Wentworth would tell him all they knew about Margaret Renfrew. But he need learn nothing more about the dead woman; his case was finished. What mattered was the duel.

If he lost Flora, after last night . . .

After last night, this morning, a few hours . . .

If he lost Flora, because of a foolish

challenge and a bullet through his brain . . .

Could that, perhaps, be the meaning of a brief but terrifying dream?

The big white-faced clock in the shop went on ticking. It was four minutes to nine.

Hanging the towel back on its nail, refusing to face the possibility of Flora being carried irresistibly away from him as though in dark water, he went back to the iron rail with its long shelf.

'Joe! If you please, Joe.'

Joe the younger, who had cleaned, polished, and hung up the last weapon used, scurried back. From the floor Cheviot took up the green-leather case, like a writing-case with a handle, he had brought with him from the Albany.

It was in fact a writing-case, though he had cleared out its contents for all the exhibits he meant to display that day, if he lived to show them. Putting the case on the shelf, he opened it and took out the small pistol with the lozenge-shaped gold plate let into its handle.

'Joe, have you ever seen this before?'

'Well, it's a Manton.' Joe was pleased again as he examined it. 'That's our mark: you see? Before my time, but then I'm very new. 'A.D.' Specially made, I bet.'

'Yes. For a man now dead. If you have a

bullet to fit this, will you load it for me?'

'Got to clean it first, though. Look at the inside of this barrel!'

'Very well, clean it. Then load it. But make haste!'

Cheviot tapped his fingers on the shelf as he looked behind him. Not Captain Hogben, not Lieutenant Wentworth, not even Freddie Debbitt had appeared. Freddie might at least have let him know the time and place of the actual duel: and, more important, the distance.

The front of the shooting-gallery, with a large bow window on either side of the door, resembled an ordinary shop. Through the panes, each oblong set in frames of white-painted wood, he could see out into Davies Street. He could see its long lines of stone hitching-posts, as everywhere else, and its iron tethering-rails. Nothing else.

The flighty October weather, alternately dazzling with sun or dark with cloud, floated its flash and shadow over the skylight. A smell of decaying earth clung to the gallery and to the street.

Joe, by the left-hand wall, was loading the small pistol. He poured in powder, to an exact measure, from one of the sealed metal flasks. He greased and dropped in the tiny pellet, from one of the various-sized bullet-boxes on the wall. Using a small wad torn from a newspaper, Joe carefully folded it, pressed and tamped down with a ramrod.

'Where shall I put up the wafer, sir?'

'This time, Joe, I need no wafer. I am only firing anywhere at the wall.'

The hammer clicked back. There was a light, stinging crack. Instead of studying the iron back-wall, Cheviot leaned over the barrier and seized Joe's arm.

'This is not large,' he indicated the pistol. 'But you smelled smoke? There's still a sharp and distinct smell of it?'

''Course there is!' cried Joe. His voice went up. 'There allus is!'

'Good. Now fetch me the bullet, please.'

'Sir?'

'The bullet I just fired. Bring it to me.'

Joe clumped back to the target-wall. His feet rattled among fallen and misshapen bullets. He studied them, picked up one, and returned.

'Take care, sir. It's still hot.'

Cheviot did not care if it burnt his fingers. The explosion of powder had burnt black that twisted pellet, driving its grains into soft lead and covering it. He nodded, putting away the bullet in the writing-case, and taking out a leather-covered book.

'Joe, I am neither mad or drunk. I have

cause for what I do. Be good enough to read a dozen lines: here. And another six lines: here.'

There was a pause, under the swift-moving, lightening-and-darkening sky.

'Well, sir,' said Joe, 'what's o'clock? It's plain enough.'

'But the weapon? In my stupidity, at first, I never thought it had yet been invented.'

'Not invented?' exclaimed Joe. 'Why, Mr. Cheviot, we've had it for years and years and years! Didn't you see the King's coronation procession eight — no, nine — years ago?'

'No. I — I was from home.'

'Well, *I* was only a nipper. But it put my father in poor spirits for days. I was no better, though I couldn't tell why. Crowds in the streets, everywhere, but not a cheer for the King. All quiet.'

'Yes?'

'The state-coach was beautiful. Like a dream. I never saw the King before or since, 'cos he won't come to London. But he was so big and bloated you couldn't believe him. He kept his eyes half-shut up, as though he didn't care. He did care, though. He would shift round and round, angry as fire, 'cos people didn't huzza. Anyways! Don't you remember the bullet-hole in the glass of the state-coach window? And, first off, nobody could tell how it had come there?'

'Yes! I seem to have read . . . no matter. Go on.'

'Not invented?' exclaimed Joe, annoyed and ashamed of himself for having been so much impressed. 'Why, sir, I've got one of 'em here!'

'You've got one? May I see it?'

Suddenly assuming his father's air, Joe opened a little gate in the barrier and marched out.

'Be pleased,' he said, 'to step into the shop.'

The white-faced clock ticked more loudly there. The atmosphere, of oil and wood, was pleasant to breathe amid the gun-racks. Though there were some few rifles, most of them were single-barrelled sporting-guns, their barrels polished and their wooden stocks a new, glossy brown. Joe reached up among them . . .

Bang!

Cheviot had been too preoccupied to hear horses in the street. What he heard then was the heavy slam of the street-door to the shooting-gallery, as three men strode in.

'Put it back!' Cheviot said quickly to Joe Manton. 'Put it back in the rack!'

In the open doorway to the shop stood Captain Hugo Hogben.

Like Lieutenant Wentworth, a little way

behind him, Hogben did not wear his uniform. He wore black with white linen, a hat stuck on rakishly, and a cloak over his arm. The other two wore ordinary clothes, though Freddie Debbitt's waistcoat would have shamed the rainbow. Hogben's little eyes turned away.

'The fellow's here,' he said to Wentworth, over his shoulder. 'Been practising, I see.'

Not once did he look directly at Cheviot, or speak to him, even when they stood full-face. Hogben's expression, between the feathery black side-whiskers, was impassive except for a very slight sneer.

'Hullo, Joe,' he said. 'It's a match for a thousand guineas. Now where's the fellow's money?'

He swung round and strode back into the gallery.

Freddie, moving past him and past Wentworth, came hurrying into the shop. He nodded towards Manton the younger, indicating that Joe should go on into the gallery, and Joe did so. Freddie, in something of a dither, addressed Cheviot in a low voice.

'Dash it all, Jack! Where have you been? Looked everywhere for you. After all! Got to tell you the terms of the — meetin', haven't I?'

'Where is it?'

'Just beyond old Vauxhall Gardens. T'other side the river, by Vauxhall Bridge. North-east there's an imitation Greek temple, and a flat space with trees all round it. Know the place?'

'Yes,' replied Cheviot, who didn't. 'At what distance do we fire?'

'Twenty paces.' Freddie gulped a little, eyeing his companion, because this was much shorter than the usual distance. 'Agreed?'

'Agreed. The time?'

'Five o'clock this evening.'

'In the *evening*?' That took him aback; for some reason Cheviot drew out his watch and opened it. He looked out of the shop-window. 'I never heard of a meeting in the evening. Besides! Let's see: today is the thirty-first of October . . . '

'All Hallows' Eve,' said Freddie, trying to make a small joke. 'Eh? When ghosts walk, and evil spirits ride the wind.'

'At five o'clock, Freddie, it will be nearly dark. How are we to see each other?'

'I know, I know!' Freddie sounded querulous. 'But those are Hogben's terms: conveyed through Wentworth, of course. Never been done before; but nothing in the code against it. We looked to see. Deuce take it, Jack, why are you worried?'

'Did I say I was worried?'

329

'No, but — ' Incautiously, Freddie's voice soared up. 'Damme, man, you're the better shot!'

From the gallery adjoining, addressed to empty air, Hogben's voice called out.

'Let the fellow come in here,' it sneered, 'and try to prove that.'

'Steady, Jack!' cried Freddie.

And Freddie was right. He must never again lose his temper with this Guards officer: not a fraction of an inch. Cheviot loosened his tense shoulders, nodded, and followed Freddie into the gallery.

There, looking out of one of the big bow windows towards the street, he saw Flora sitting in a carriage drawn up at the kerb.

The bay horses were harnessed to an open carriage: low-built, of glided dark lacquer and white upholstery. Flora, in a short fur jacket, her hands in a muff, an uptilted bonnet white-framing her hair, caught sight of him.

Flora pressed her fingers to her mouth, then threw them out towards him. Her eyes and lips said the rest.

Cheviot lifted his hat and bowed, hoping to return the message with his gaze. He dared not look at her for more than a second or two, or it would have unsteadied his aim. He had not expected her; it was a shock from which he turned away.

The preparations, under Hogben's loud-voiced orders, were nearly ready.

Joe Manton had loaded six duelling-pistols, setting each down on the shelf just two feet apart. It was impossible to compare them in any way to modern revolvers; the round bullet weighed about two ounces. Then Joe took up the box of 'wafers.'

These wafers, of the heavy material which afterwards they would call cartridge-paper, were white in colour, round, and something over two inches in diameter. On the back of each was a light coating of glue.

Carrying a wet rag in one hand and the wafer-box in the other, Joe went to the black target-wall. He wiped the wall clean of paper-bits. Turning back and forth to measure distance, he moistened the backs of six wafers. He banged them with his fist to a wall as thick as Vulcan's iron door. Like the pistols, they were each two feet apart, shoulder-high.

As Joe returned, those wafers became white and staring spots on the black. But, at thirty-six paces, they looked very tiny.

'Now, then!' said Hogben, stamping his feet as though about to begin a race. He addressed Lieutenant Wentworth. 'A thousand guineas. Where's the fellow's money?'

Wentworth, whose appearance out of

uniform seemed even odder than Hogben's, stood straight in astonishment. Finally he saw his companion was serious.

'Hogben,' he said, 'permit me to tell you that I'll not suffer such behaviour much longer. There's no need for this. In any wager, no gentleman is expected to — '

'Where's the fellow's *money?*'

Without a word Cheviot went to the left-hand edge of the shelf, behind which Joe Manton was standing almost against the wall. Mainly in banknotes, but with a number of gold sovereigns and some silver, he counted out the money beside Joe's elbow.

Still without speaking, he returned to stand beside Freddie with his back to the window.

Hogben cast off his cloak and threw it aside. For the first time he looked at Cheviot.

'Now, fellow!' And he jerked his head towards the shelf. 'Shoot first.'

Suddenly Cheviot took a step forward. Freddie, seeing the look on his face, leaped in front of him.

'Toss a coin! That's fair. Toss a coin!'

'As you please, Mr. Debbitt,' agreed Wentworth, fishing a florin out of his waistcoat pocket. 'Hogben, you were challenged to this match. It's your call: cry it.'

'Heads,' said Hogben, as the coin spun high in the air.

'Tails,' Wentworth announced, bending over it as it rattled down. 'What's your will, Mr. Cheviot?'

'Let *him* shoot first.'

Hogben, unruffled, settled his hat on his head. He took up the first pistol on the left-hand end. There was a muffled melodious click as he drew back the hammer to full-cock. He turned sideways, setting his feet into position.

The clock in the shop ticked loudly. No one must move, no one must utter a word of congratulation for a good shot or a word of condolence for a bad.

Hogben did not swagger. With his mind on the money, he was quiet and prudent. He took his time, which he could never have done in a duel. His right arm lifted, lowered, and straightened. He waited until the skylight grew bright on that tiny wafer.

Whack!

A streak of fire, a report echoed back in iron concussion. The wafer, struck dead-centre, flew to pieces or disintegrated in flame.

In a leisurely way Hogben put down the first pistol and moved on to the second.

His second shot clipped the upper edge of the wafer; it split, with tearing edges, but still stuck to the wall as the bullet clattered down and rolled.

His third shot was a complete miss.

The flattened bullet freakishly bounced back and bumped along the floor halfway towards those who watched. Hogben stood for a moment with his head down, the black hairs at the back of his neck bristling over the collar, but still unruffled. Acrid smoke-haze thickened round them; he waited until it had lifted.

With his fourth bullet he got more than an edge of the target. His fifth and sixth shots were straight on the wafer. In fact, the sixth wafer flashed into flame as it vanished.

Hogben put down the last pistol, straightening his shoulders still more.

'There!' he said jauntily, with one eye on the notes and gold. 'Beat *that*, fellow.'

It was first-class shooting. Everyone knew it. But no one said anything, as Hogben washed his hands and face at the sink, and Joe Manton jabbed and scratched with his wet cloth to clean the target-wall. He put up six new wafers.

Whistling between his teeth, Captain Hogben lounged with arms folded. Joe began the business of cleaning and reloading the six pistols. It seemed to take an interminable time, while the clock ticked and Hogben whistled 'A Frog He Would.'

'Your turn, Mr. Cheviot,' said Lieutenant Wentworth.

Cheviot's throat felt dry. He did not look out at Flora. Freddie touched his arm; he hesitated, and walked to the barrier at the left-hand side.

Whereupon Freddie, despite the rules, jumped and cried aloud to his Maker.

Whack! — Whack! — Whack! — Whack! — Whack! — Whack!

Cheviot, in fact, was not moving and firing as fast as it seemed to his startled companions. But the stunning concussions rolled back. The black-powder smoke, spurting and clouding, blotted out heads, faces, and the barrier as well. Six shots were fired in as many seconds.

In the street, bay horses stirred and clattered. Cheviot put down the last pistol and joined Freddie in the window. Smoke presently lifted, gushing out of skylight and window.

Each of the six wafers, shot squarely in the middle, had burnt or disappeared. Except for a few white adhering bits, and a few bits floating up with the smoke, the target-wall was as clean as when Joe had last wiped it.

The earnest-minded Wentworth, who had been regarding Hogben in a thoughtful way, spoke very politely to Freddie.

'I think, Mr. Debbitt, there can be no doubt your principal has won the match?'

'N-no! N-no! Deuce take it, none at all!'

'Very well.' Wentworth turned to Cheviot. 'Sir, we agreed to give you certain information — '

But Cheviot, coughing smoke out of his throat, stopped him.

'Sir, this information is no longer necessary to me. I absolve you from giving it.'

'That's good. That's damn good!' said Hogben, and laughed. 'Because you wouldn't have got it anyway.'

Wentworth's fair complexion flushed red.

You might have thought such shooting would have taken down the gallant Captain a little. At very least it meant that a duel at twenty paces would be fatal to them both. But Hogben remained as loftily superior as ever.

'Oh, I keep my promises,' he said, plucking up his cloak from the floor and throwing it round his shoulders. 'You've made the mistake, fellow. I said I'd *give* information. I didn't say who I'd give it to, remember? I didn't say to *you*.'

Here he opened his eyes wide, pleased at his own cunning, and laughed again.

'I'll give it fast enough to your superior

officers, What's-their-names, at Whitehall Place. I say, Wentworth. You've arranged with Debbitt for the time and place of the meeting?'

'Yes.'

'We're usin' my pistols?'

'Stop!' said Freddie, seizing at his own smudged face. 'I forgot to mention — '

'Any pistols,' Cheviot interrupted curtly, and went over to wash at the sink.

'Then that's settled, fellow,' grinned Hogben, 'and *you're* settled.' He shouldered towards the door. 'Coming, Wentworth?'

'No.'

'Coming, Debbitt?'

'Yes, yes! That's to say, not with you. Got no horse. 'Nother appointment. Jack, old fellow! Congratulations, and shake hands. There!' Freddie lowered his voice. 'No doubt about this evening. You'll wing him. Meet you there. Goodbye!'

Outside the window, Flora was standing up in the carriage and contemplating Cheviot uncertainly. He waved and smiled at her as he finished washing.

The door slammed as Hogben strode out. He mounted a white horse and galloped south towards Berkeley Square. Freddie followed him. Stopping only to lift his hat, bow deeply to Flora, and pay her (it seemed) flowery compliments, he hurried north towards Oxford Street.

With no notion of the thunderbolt to fall in the next few seconds, Cheviot paid the modest charges asked by Joe for the use of the gallery, and received Joe's compliments. Leaving Joe sweating with relief, he retrieved the green writing-case from where he had left it below the barrier.

Lieutenant Wentworth had also drifted towards the sink, examining a grimy face in the looking-glass above. Cheviot, murmuring something polite to him, opened the front door.

'Good day, sir!' called Joe Manton the younger. 'I thought, for a while, there'd be trouble here. So help me Harry, I did!'

Abruptly Wentworth yanked down the metal handle. Water splashed into the sink, and out over his clothes. His face, reflected in the mirror, was twisted into a look nobody would have cared to see.

'Mr. Cheviot,' he said, with his countenance smoothed out again, 'may I have a word with you on a matter of the most vital import?'

18

The Trap by Vauxhall Gardens

The door was partly open. The air, though tinged with autumn decay, was mild and mellow. Cheviot held the door open.

'Yes? What is it?'

He turned back with reluctance. Flora, whose fear of the proprieties would not let her step down from the carriage and enter a shooting-gallery, made a mouth of impatience. Cheviot's head ached; he had had less than half an hour's sleep, and a terrifying dream.

'Sir,' said Lieutenant Wentworth, 'it may be that I betray a trust. Or doubt a friend. But it is my duty to speak out. Did you mark nothing strange in Hogben's manner?'

Cheviot made a gesture with the writing-case.

'Frankly, sir,' he said, 'I grow weary of Captain Hogben. Even if we kill each other in the duel, as seems likely — '

'In my opinion,' said Wentworth, 'there will be no duel.'

'*What?*'

They were now alone in the gallery. At first mention of that word 'duel,' flat and ominous, Joe Manton slid out from the gate in the barrier and disappeared into the shop.

Wentworth splashed water on his face, dried it without troubling about soap, and moved closer. Out of uniform he seemed less a soldier than, say, a student: correct, formal, yet far less haughty, like a man who has gained much experience overnight.

'What do you tell me?' Cheviot demanded. 'No duel? No — no danger?'

'I did not say that. There may be very great danger. For you.'

'But Hogben . . . ?'

'Oh, Hogben will risk nothing. There are many who will tell you that he never gives fair play.'

Flora had said that. Cheviot looked out of the window. Flora stood holding at her hat, the wind whipping her skirt against her knees, while her lips formed the words, 'What is it? Why do you stay?'

'But what can Hogben do?' Cheviot insisted. 'You yourself will be there, I take it? And my own second?'

'Yes, if Hogben is there. I can tell you no more, sir; I don't know; I only suspect. I have tried to be the man's friend, but it won't do. If we are not there — '

'Yes?'

'Someone else may meet you in the twilight. And Hogben is much desirous of your death.'

Cheviot, realizing he had forgotten his cloak, fetched it from the ledge of the bow-window. The open door creaked and swayed. Hogben's image rose up, grinning, still with all the honours and an ace of trumps up his sleeve.

'Someone else may meet you in the twilight.' The twilight of All Hallows' Eve.

'Lieutenant Wentworth,' said Cheviot, twining the cloak round him and with his hand again on the knob of the door, 'I thank you deeply for your warning.'

He bowed, closed the door after him, and hurried across to Flora.

Even while he sprang up the step, and Flora made room for him to sit down, neither of them would speak what was upper-most in both their minds. True, Flora began: 'What time did you leave me this morning?' but swallowed it back after four words as she noted the stolid back of Robert, the coachman. There were no footmen up behind.

'I have heard,' she said instead, 'you were an expert pistol-shot. I loathe to watch even practice. But how you showed it against

341

Captain Hogben!' Proud, intensely happy and yet uneasy, she added: 'There — there was no quarrel with him, I hope?'

'None whatever, as you saw.'

'But I heard nothing, dearest! Except the shots.'

'There was little else to hear.'

'I thought,' Flora said eagerly, and nodded towards a wicker hamper on the floor, 'we could go for a drive into the country, if it pleased you? There is food and wine in the hamper there. And we could be from London all day?'

'Yes! I must visit Scotland Yard, but only briefly. What should you say, Flora, to somewhere past Vauxhall Gardens?'

'The very place!' Flora's eyes shone. 'To be sure, the Gardens are closed for the season. And none but the vulgar people have gone there since my grandparents' time, though they still have fireworks and balloon-ascents.'

'Flora, don't use those words!'

She was appalled. 'Don't use . . . what words?'

'"Vulgar people.' It is time we understood — !' He gulped and checked himself.

'Jack! Have I offended you?'

'No, no! You could never do that; I spoke from vapours; pardon me. There is a Greek temple, I think, north-east of the gardens?'

'Oh, there is!' She lifted her voice. 'You heard, Robert?'

'My lady,' said the coachman. 'I heard.'

The carriage clopped away towards Berkeley Square, with the mild air in their faces under a changing sky. From under the short brown fur jacket, its seams outlined in blue-and-white, Flora slipped her arm through Cheviot's. Because she wished so much to speak of themselves, as he did, she would not do it.

'To Scotland Yard, you said?' she went on with unnatural brightness. 'I daresay it's all those people you captured at Vulcan's. You never told me, you know. But all sorts of rumours are going round, and the most tremendous praise for you.'

'For *me?*'

'Well, and for your police too.'

'Ah, that's better! That's what I hoped!'

'But do tell me! If the police attack a gaming-house, aren't the punters supposed to be as guilty as those who keep the house? Aren't they arrested too?'

'In theory, yes.'

'And yet they say you didn't arrest any of the punters! You shook them by the hand, and congratulated each on his prowess as a warrior, and assured them their names would never be mentioned in the affair. Is that true?'

Cheviot laughed. It loosened his taut nerves to roar with laughter.

'My dear, could I arrest those who had assisted me?' he pointed out. 'Besides, it gave me a helpful suggestion. You should have seen Inspector Seagrave and Sergeant Bulmer in that broil. As one blackleg after another went down under a truncheon — '

'Not *all* of it, please!'

' — then Seagrave or Bulmer would haul the leg up to a sitting position, and cry, 'Here's Jimmy So-and-so; he's wanted for housebreaking,' or 'Here's Tom Crack-'em-Down: highway robbery, arson, God knows what.' I should have seen it before then: Vulcan had drawn in half the fraud-and-flash world to pack the house. When we rolled 'em downstairs into wagons — '

'Don't laugh! It is not funny!'

'Darling Flora, but it *is* funny. I was able to assure the punters this was no gambling raid, but the biggest haul of known criminals in years. Which it was. B, C, and D Divisions had to open their cells to accommodate 'em all. That's why I was so late.'

'Yes. You were late.'

The carriage had swept through Berkeley Square, where nursemaids in fantastic tall caps pushed perambulators in the garden under foliage still yellow-green. It had rattled down Berkeley Street, and left into the tumult of Piccadilly.

Flora, deep-dreaming, spoke again.

'Vulcan!' she muttered. 'Vulcan and that woman of his! Jack, what . . . ?'

'That was not pleasant. He's in a cell now.'

'Then I don't wish to hear a word of it. No; stop; tell me all the same.'

'The woman we released. But Vulcan had been — well, put to sleep, in handcuffs, in his office upstairs. By the time I found the key to the jewel-drawers (Kate de Bourke dropped the key-ring in the gallery), Vulcan was up and trying to destroy his ledger even in handcuffs. I never guessed he was carrying a pistol.'

'And that's where you got the bullet-hole in your sleeve. *Isn't it?*'

Cheviot's mirth had left him.

'That's not important. No,' he repeated, 'I never guessed he was carrying a pistol. He never tried to draw it when we fought across the table. Vulcan, in his own twisted way, is a sportsman. But Hogben — !'

'What *of* Hogben?' Flora asked very quietly. 'There is something more, as I well know. Surely it would be easier for me if I heard?'

'Don't trouble your head about Hogben. He has some ace of trumps up his sleeve, or thinks he has. I wish I knew what it was. That's all.'

He would say no more. The carriage turned down the slope of the Haymarket at its junction with Piccadilly, left into Cockspur Street, and down Whitehall.

'Flora, may I give an order to your coachman? Robert! Be good enough to stop at number four Whitehall Place. Don't drive into the yard; pull up at the gas-lamp outside it.'

'Very good, sir.'

And then, to Flora, as he got down from the carriage outside the red-brick house:

'I shall not be a long time. Afterwards, I hope, we can both laugh.'

But he was a long time. Flora, cradling her muff, felt the minutes as hours as she waited. The coachman's back was straight and unmoving. All about the carriage a rumble and rattle of wheels, the shouting of those who drove them, beat against a woman torn between intense happiness and intense apprehension.

It was, actually, more than an hour before he returned: apologetic but grim-faced as he climbed into the carriage, and gave the signal for Robert to go on.

'I am afraid,' he said, 'you must stay by me until this evening.'

'But what else?' Flora cried. 'That is no penance. Are we to — to laugh?'

'No, unfortunately. I should not keep you by me, yet perhaps that may be best. You see, I have promised to deliver Margaret Renfrew's murderer by eight o'clock tonight.'

The carriage, with its deep upholstery, swayed and rattled faster.

'And,' he added, 'I am excused one duty. Should there be any riot outside Pinner's, I need not command the division.'

'Jack,' a stifled voice answered him, 'I beg you to cease speaking riddles. Riot?'

'There is a tailor, it seems, named Pinner. I think that yesterday,' and he pressed his hands over his eyes, 'someone mentioned a tailor with a taste for making inflammatory political speeches. I've just heard of him from Colonel Rowan and Mr. Mayne. His shop is in — Parliament Street, they said.'

So far as confusion mattered, he was in a worse state than Flora.

As the carriage rapidly bowled south, gone was every vestige of Whitehall as he seemed to recall it in his other life.

Ahead loomed up a triangular wedge of buildings, smoke-clouded from piled chimney-stacks, dividing it into two streets. The right-hand street, he decided, could only be King Street since the left-hand one, along the river, must be Parliament Street.

He was right. Robert reined the horses left, where there were few wheeled vehicles and the house-fronts showed ancient, darkened, of stone or brick crumbling away. Most were shops — a tallow-chandler's, a mirror-maker's, a butcher's — amid some private houses which bore no brass plates or polished bell-handles.

'A crazy ruin,' he muttered. 'Look there!'

Across Parliament Street a small crowd had gathered round a small man, with a big chest and a shock of white hair, who was standing on a wooden box outside the door of a shop lettered *T. F. Pinner, Tailor and Cutter* above its window.

A policeman sauntered on the left-hand side of the street, eyeing the crowd but not interfering. The little man with the big chest and the white hair, a bottle of gin stuck in the pocket of his surtout, had worked himself into a fury.

'Don't you want the Corn Laws repealed?' he was shouting. 'You can't argue with starvation. *They* can't argue with it. Is there one man among you,' his arm went up, fist flourishing, 'who hasn't starved or seen his family starve?'

A voice yelled, 'No!' The crowd, small enough indeed, moved and shuffled. It spilled out across the roadway. Robert's back stiffened; his whip-hand drew back and up.

'Drive on!' said Cheviot, standing up in the carriage. 'Don't touch anyone. Drive on!'

'Then the only way to get it,' bawled the orator's voice, 'is by a Reform Bill and a Reformed Parliament. The facts, the true facts . . . '

They clattered past, the voice beginning to fade. Someone screamed at them; no more.

'But, Jack,' protested Flora, who was surprised rather than distressed, 'this happens every day. Where is our concern in it?'

'Not today or tonight, at least. All the same — '

He was still standing up in the swaying carriage, holding the handrail behind the driver. He could not go on speaking, because he was gripped uncannily by that past of which he was a part.

On the right, serene beyond antiquity, rose the towers of the Abbey. On the left, beyond Westminster Bridge, he saw another tower: squat and square, beside a huddle of carved and painted buildings stretching towards the massive stone of Westminster Hall. In five years all of this on the left, except Westminster Hall, would be gutted by fire, and perish. He was looking at the old Houses of Parliament, with a flag flying from the square tower to show Parliament was sitting.

And, glimpsed past Westminster Bridge and the square tower, flowed the Thames: too close without embankments, brown-coloured from mud and sewage, the kindly river that would yet bring the cholera.

'Jack,' said Flora, 'what on earth are you gabbling about?'

He had not known he was speaking at all. He sat down beside her and took her arm.

'Forgive me. That drunken tailor, I daresay, seemed to you oafish and ridiculous? And yet he's right. It will come about.'

'You? Preaching reform?'

'Flora, I preach nothing. I only regret the unhappiness I have caused you, and may still cause you, because of what I cannot explain. Meanwhile, we go to the country. For God's sake, if we can, let's forget all else.'

It seemed that they did forget. When they crossed Vauxhall Bridge, iron-built and comparatively new, the Surrey side of the river opened with a drowsy beauty of autumn. No life stirred in Vauxhall Gardens: the winding walks, the bandstand, the two statues of Apollo and one (a strange companion) of Handel.

But it was pleasanter to be alone. The carriage presently reached an open space, surrounded by trees. Against the trees at the back of it gleamed the thin white marble of a small semi-circular temple with a statue inside. Since the temple was after the Greek fashion, the statue must be given her Greek name of Aphrodite.

Robert swung the horses round and came to a stop near the temple. He wound the reins round the whip-stock, put on the drag, and climbed down to make Flora a formal little speech.

Her ladyship, he said, doubtless would not require him for an hour or two. Near the entrance to Vauxhall Gardens, he said, there was a public-house, the Dog and Vulture, and might he beg leave of absence for a time?

Flora made a little speech meaning that he could. They hardly heard his footsteps in the grass as he went away.

'And now, sir,' declared Flora, with a mock-prim air but a deadly coldness at her heart, 'you will be kind enough to expound all the hints you have been giving. Do you wish to drive me mad? I . . . What's wrong?'

Cheviot had been looking at the sky.

'The time,' he answered without thinking. 'It must be well into the afternoon. Later than I thought.'

It would have been easier to look at his watch. But he dared not do it.

'The time?' Flora echoed indignantly.

'Does the time matter?'

'No, no, of course not! Except — '

'Do you wish to eat or drink?' asked Flora, haughtily tapping the hamper with her foot. 'There is much here, if you find my company so tedious.'

'Stop that! Don't coquette. This isn't the time for it.'

'Oh, I know! But last night, or rather this morning, was so — so — '

'Yes.' He spoke with some violence. 'It was perfect and complete. Perfect and complete, I say again. That's why I must ask you: Flora, have you and I ever been married?'

'*Married?*'

'Yes. I am quite serious.'

'Well, really! What a question! If — if we ever have,' cried Flora, 'I must have made vows at the altar in a dream. Besides, you — you never asked me.'

'You're sure of that? *You* never thought it? Because I did. When I crept downstairs this morning, and let myself out without rousing the house, I wondered . . . '

'What *I* wondered,' she said, 'is how you could have left without awakening me. I always wake when you do. I put out my arm, and you were not there. It was dreadful. It seemed as though you had gone forever.'

'Flora, stop! Say no more — just for a moment!'

He lowered his head. Beside the wicker hamper stood the green writing-case. But he was not thinking even of that. The trees, which yet retained green in tattered foliage amid yellows and reds, whispered faintly round the Greek temple.

'No,' he said in a baffled kind of way, 'it can't be true. You are a prisoner in this age, and have always been of this age. Whereas I . . .'

'Yes?'

'Listen! Only three nights ago I promised to tell you all. I must do so, and yet you will not credit me. Just as at Lady Cork's, you will shrink back and think me mad-drunk though my eyes are clear and my speech unstumbling . . .'

'If you told me *what?*'

'Still I must say it,' he insisted, without seeming to hear her, 'because there are dreams and premonitions inside the mind, perhaps even inside the soul. And I think, Flora, that soon we shall be separated from each other.'

'No!'

Then she was in his arms, but not in the way of love-making. As he held her, it was more like a whispered and desperate quarrel.

'But what could separate us? You mean — death?'

'No, my dear. Not death. And yet, in a fashion, something like that.'

Flora cried out in protest. Whereupon, while he clung to her even more fiercely, there ensued one of those endless, aching scenes in which each person misinterprets the other's words; and it cannot be set right. Flora maintained he said he was going to die; and he retorted that he hadn't said anything of the kind. On and on it went, while the shadows deepened and heart-sickness grew.

'Then be pleased,' Flora sobbed, 'to say what you do mean!'

'Only this, as I have tried to explain. At some hour soon, at what seems an hour of victory and triumph, the dimension called time will move and change. All will dissolve. All! What is it about 'the unsubstantial pageant'? Never mind! But on this occasion it won't be easy. It will be terrifying.'

'I don't understand! I don't!'

'A dream I had — '

'Oh, dreams. Everybody knows dreams go by contraries!'

'One day, my dear, they will make dreams rather more complicated than that. No: perhaps I shouldn't have said a dream.' He drew his breath in deeply. 'Very well. You had

354

better hear the truth. When you once said I seemed like somebody out of another world, that was truer than you knew. I *am* . . . '

'*My lady! Sir!*'

Those two, locked away in their own world, had failed to hear the loud fit of coughing which had been going on at a distance for some seconds. When Robert the coachman felt that his tact would only strangle him, he gave a respectful hail instead.

Both of them lifted heads from a world lost.

A light, dazzling into Cheviot's eyes, made him blink and stare round. The light was lowered. But shadows were so heavy that he could scarcely see Robert, with a lantern in his hand.

The air felt misty and damp. The lines of the Greek temple glimmered white.

'Forgive me, my lady,' Robert called respectfully. 'But I thought you'd wish me to return. It's twenty-five minutes past five.'

Cheviot's hand went to his watch-pocket. 'Past *five?*'

'Yes, sir. Much more than that, too. That was the time I left the Dog and Vulture, and it's a bit of a walk from there.'

This was the point at which they heard hoof-beats on the road by which Robert had come from the pub. Horses, more than one and at the gallop, pounded hard and pounded closer. He thought there were three of them. The wink of a swinging lantern, held in the right hand of the leading horseman, brushed greenish-yellow foliage.

Then Hogben would be here, after all. The other horsemen must be Lieutenant Went-worth and Freddie Debbitt. On the other hand, if Hogben had sent someone else . . .

'Robert,' he said quietly, 'please get up on the box and drive Lady Drayton home as soon as may be.'

'Robert,' said Flora in a high but calm voice, 'you will do nothing of the sort. We remain here.'

The leading horseman swept into the clearing, with the others behind him. They rode lathered horses, blowing through the nostrils. As the first horseman held his lantern high, Cheviot saw what he had never expected to see.

True, the third horseman was Lieutenant Wentworth. But the second was Sergeant Bulmer. The first was Inspector Seagrave, with the silver lace glinting at his collar.

'Sir,' croaked out Seagrave, holding the light, 'can this coachman of yours drive fast? He'll need to.'

'What's this?' Cheviot demanded. 'What are you doing here? I expected to meet

Captain Hogben. I — I have an appointment for five o'clock.'

Seagrave and Bulmer exchanged glances.

'Then *that's* it!' the latter blurted. 'Well, sir, Captain Hogben made another appointment for five o'clock. As like as not, to be sure you'd be here and out of the way. His appointment was with the Colonel and Mr. Mayne at Scotland Yard.'

'With . . . ?'

'Sir! He's denounced Lady Drayton for murdering Miss Renfrew, and you for helping her. He's done that already, he and a Miss Louise Tremayne. They say they saw Lady Drayton fire; and the pistol fell out of her muff; and you hid it under a lamp. And they've got Mr. Mayne mor'n half convinced!'

Cheviot stood up in the carriage. His mind went back, vividly, to that passage at Lady Cork's house on the night of the murder. He remembered his impression that one of the orange-and-gold doors to the ballroom had opened and closed, with what might have been black hair in the opening . . .

He had been seen. He had been seen after all, and by Hugo Hogben.

19

Counter-Stroke

In the Whitehall Place office of Colonel Rowan and Mr. Mayne, at a quarter past six, question and answer had reached their height.

'You are prepared, Captain Hogben,' asked Mr. Mayne, 'to sign the statement of which two fair copies are now being made by our clerk?'

'I am.'

Mr. Richard Mayne showed neither satisfaction nor dissatisfaction; he was a lawyer; but his voice almost purred. He sat behind the scarred table, with the red-glass lamp burning in the red weapon-hung room. Colonel Rowan, however, stood by the table with a faint angry flush under his cheekbones.

'Be very sure, Captain,' he said curtly. 'Both Mr. Mayne and I are magistrates. This is a deposition under oath.'

Hogben, in front of the table with his arms carelessly folded, eyed him up and down. It was evident that he did not think much of a Colonel who had commanded the 52nd Light

Infantry. Hogben's face showed as much.

'What's the good of the clack?' he asked, opening his little eyes wide. 'I said it, didn't I?'

'And you, Miss Tremayne?' Colonel Rowan inquired with much politeness. 'You are prepared to sign a statement, too?'

Louise Tremayne, in a padded chair well back from them all and towards the windows, had come to a state not far from hysterics. After all, she was little more than nineteen. Clasping a muff of silver-fox fur against a silver-fox jacket, she raised a pale face in which the hazel eyes seemed enormous.

Even her turban, of dove-grey silk, added to that child-like appearance. And yet something stubborn and tenacious, something perhaps inherited from him she called her dear, good, kind papa, kept her from giving way to her feelings.

'I vow to you, as I have vowed before,' Louise told them, without blurring a syllable, 'that I did *not* see Lady Drayton . . . well! I did not see her fire a shot.'

The last three words horrified her, as though she could not imagine herself speaking them.

'Not that, no!' she insisted. 'Hugo saw that. The rest of it I saw with my own eyes, and I vow it. Indeed, I tried to tell Mr. Cheviot yesterday. But I did not see Lady Drayton k-kill anyone.'

'Careful, m'dear!' Hogben dropped his arms and spoke threateningly. 'You said to me — '

'I didn't!'

'Captain!' And Colonel Rowan snapped it like an order. Hogben stiffened by instinct, then sneered when he remembered. 'If you please,' Colonel Rowan added, 'we will not have this young lady intimidated.'

Mr. Mayne, seated at his ease and very bland, held up a deprecating hand.

'Come, my dear Rowan,' he said. 'There has been no intimidation here. We have seen to that. But there is evidence, I fear; yes, a great deal of evidence. Do you now so greatly favour our own Mr. Cheviot?'

'We have not heard his side of it.'

'True. True. But he lied to us, my dear Rowan. Can you doubt it? Do you imagine Captain Hogben and Miss Tremayne have spun this story out of whole cloth, especially since every word they say confirms what I have already suggested?'

Colonel Rowan hesitated, and Mr. Mayne went on.

'Not one word did *he* say about that pistol or any other pistol. He lied to us, in the most serious matter which can affect a police-officer. As a barrister — '

'As a barrister, then, you already prejudice the case.'

'Pardon me, Rowan. It is you who prejudice it. You like Mr. Cheviot because he is of your own sort and kind. He is well-mannered. He is quiet. He is modest — to you. He never strikes until first he is struck; and then, I grant, he strikes back quickly and hard.'

'Another English principle,' Colonel Rowan said politely, 'which I commend to your attention.'

'*But*,' replied Mr. Mayne, tapping the table, 'he is a man of notoriously loose morals. Either he shielded his mistress, Lady Drayton, who is known to have hated Miss Renfrew; or else, being himself entangled with Miss Renfrew and wishing to be rid of her, he himself planned the whole crime.'

Here Mr. Mayne spread out his hands.

'I say this with evidence, Rowan. When we have fair copies of the statement — ' Hearing a pen scratch, Mr. Mayne scowled and craned round. 'Tush, tush, Henley, have you not yet finished making the copies in longhand?'

The green lamp was burning on the desk of the chief clerk in the corner. Behind it Mr. Henley lowered his pen.

'With all respect, sir,' Mr. Henley answered in his hoarse, heavy voice, 'it's not easy when my hand shakes like what it does. And, again with all respect to the Captain and his lady, this can't be true.'

'Henley!'

'Mr. Mayne,' said the chief clerk, 'I was there!'

Alan Henley could be unobtrusive when he liked. But he could seldom hide his strong, forceful personality. The heavy face with the thick reddish side-whiskers, the brown eyes glowing, was thrust out past the lamp.

'If I was there, which I was,' and the pen seemed small in his fist, 'I should have seen it. If a pistol dropped out of the good lady's muff, and Superintendent Cheviot hid it under a lamp, wouldn't I ha' seen it?'

'No.' Hogben, the inarticulate, got out his words fast enough. 'And I'll tell you why, clerkie. Your back was turned. You were shifting a dead 'un over on her back, face up. Weren't you, fellow? Yes or no?'

'Yes or no, Henley?' Mr. Mayne asked without inflection.

Beads of sweat glimmered on Mr. Henley's forehead.

'It may be,' he said, 'I shouldn't ha' seen that.' He nodded towards the half-fainting Louise Tremayne. 'But, as the young lady tells you, Lady Drayton fired no pistol from her muff. Why, I watched her! And the muff had no bullet-hole. And she couldn't ha' done it.'

'Not even,' Mr. Mayne inquired quietly, 'by turning the muff quickly sideways, thus,' his hands illustrated, 'and firing through the opening at one end, so that there would be no burns of powder?'

'I — '

'On your oath, Henley, do you swear that could not have occurred?'

Mr. Henley began to prop himself up on his thick ebony stick. He stumbled and almost fell. His gaze shifted away and dropped.

'Well . . . ' he said uncertainly.

'Then you cannot swear it?' Mr. Mayne demanded.

'No, sir, I can't swear on my oath as — '

'Then your testimony is valueless. You have only half a dozen lines to write. Sit down, my good Henley, and complete them.'

A slight smile twisted Hogben's mouth, ineffable and superior, as the chief clerk slumped down and picked up the pen. It was Colonel Rowan who suddenly held up his hand.

'Listen!' he ordered.

For five or six seconds nobody spoke. There was no noise except for the dogged scratching of the chief clerk's pen. Louise Tremayne put her face in her hands. Perhaps only Colonel Rowan's quick ear had caught the faint roaring sounds very far away. In any case, he plucked up a hand-bell from the table and rang it with loud clangour.

The door to the passage was instantly opened by a sergeant, with the numeral 9 on his collar.

'Sergeant!' said Colonel Rowan. 'What's the latest report from that — that small disturbance in Parliament Street?'

'Sir!' said the newcomer, saluting. 'No rioting yet, sir. But the crowd's a-getting bigger. The point is . . . '

'Yes? Continue?'

'Well, sir, it's not only that tailor-cove, Pinner. They've got more'n half a dozen speakers. As soon as our lot persuade one of 'em to shut his potato-trap, another bobs up in another door with people holding torches all round him.'

'Who is in attendance, Sergeant?'

'Inspector Blaine, sir. Sergeant Crossley, too, and his constables ten to nineteen. There's complaints from the 'Ouse of Commons, sir.'

Mr. Mayne interposed. 'I tell you, Rowan, we can spare no more men!'

'Not from our division, perhaps.' Colonel

Rowan smiled coldly. 'But with your permission, Mayne, C and D divisions have provided eighteen more. Sergeant! They may join the others. No violence unless it be unavoidable.'

'Yes, sir.'

'Sergeant!' Mr. Mayne called in a different tone. 'As you do this, will you be good enough to step out into the street and fetch in two witnesses for a deposition? Any passers-by will do.'

'Very good, sir.'

As the harassed officer opened the door to go out, there were sounds of hurry and turmoil in the passage. Evidently the police were active that night. Not a minute later they heard, through closed window-curtains, a carriage smash at a gallop into the yard and pull up.

Nor was it long before the sergeant, number 9, ushered in two witnesses. One was a seedy man in a battered white hat, the other a shrunken elderly gentleman on his way to the Athenaeum Club. Both were far from sweet-tempered.

'Gentlemen, gentlemen,' protested Mr. Mayne, soothingly, 'I shall detain you but a moment. (You have finished, Henley? Good.) I humbly beg you, my dear sirs, merely to affix your signatures as witnesses to two copies of a document. Captain Hogben?'

Hogben scratched his signature with a bold flourish. So did the others. The copies were sealed and attested, the witnesses bustled out with as little ceremony as they had been bustled in. Mr. Mayne beamed.

'Though it is scarcely essential,' he continued, 'may I ask, Miss Tremayne, whether you will give Captain Hogben your muff?'

'My muff?' cried Louise.

'If you will. And let him show us how Lady Drayton held the muff, sideways, so as to fire the shot?'

'*Yes!*' struck in a new voice. '*By all means let him show that.*'

The voice was not loud. If anything, it was quiet; too repressed, too quiet.

In the open doorway stood Superintendent John Cheviot.

His face was pale, his jaws clenched hard except when he spoke. Under his cloak he wore black, as Hogben did, except for soiled white linen and a gold watch-chain with seals. He carried by its handle what resembled a green writing-case.

But the effect of that quiet, almost agreeable, tone was so sinister that it left in the room a faint chill. Louise Tremayne repressed a scream.

Just behind him stood Flora Drayton; and, beyond her, Sergeant Bulmer. Cheviot bowed for Flora to precede him into the room. In dead silence he pushed out another padded chair, not far from Louise. With a slight nod to all the others, Flora sat down. She was more pale than Cheviot; but just as composed, her head up.

Cheviot made a slight and cryptic gesture to Sergeant Bulmer, who nodded and closed the door. Cheviot softly crossed the room to the table behind which sat Mr. Mayne. Amid the drift of papers there still lay, a sardonic reminder, Colonel Rowan's silver-handled pistol.

With a look of distaste, without speaking, Cheviot transferred it to the desk of the chief clerk. In its place he put down the green writing-case.

The eerie silence was broken at last by Mr. Mayne.

'You come rather late, Mr. Cheviot,' he said.

'Yes, sir. That is true. A certain person,' Cheviot answered, 'took the most elaborate precautions to make sure I should not be here at all.'

He turned briefly, and glanced at Hogben. Hogben laughed in his face. The laugh, behind closed teeth, clashed badly against the quiet and the hard courtesy of the two Police Commissioners.

'Surely, Mr. Cheviot,' remarked Mr. Richard Mayne without expression, 'it was rather brazen of you when you promised to delivery to us the murderer of Miss Renfrew by eight o'clock tonight?'

'Sir, I do not think so.' Cheviot removed his cloak and hat, putting them carefully in a chair. He returned to the table. 'After all, it is only a quarter to seven.'

'Mr. Cheviot!' interposed Colonel Rowan, with an almost pleading note in his voice. 'Captain Hogben has made a statement, now copied and attested . . . '

'I was aware of it, sir. May I see the statement?'

Mr. Henley handed over a copy.

There was a small fire burning in the grate of the mantel-piece, beside the big moth-eaten stuffed bear with one glass eye. Nobody spoke while Cheviot slowly read the statement through. Flora Drayton, still with her head up, looked from Colonel Rowan to Mr. Mayne and to Captain Hogben; she did not look at Louise.

'I see,' remarked Cheviot in the same cold, calm voice. He put down the pages on the desk. 'Captain Hogben, of course, is ready to answer questions concerning what he has testified?'

He faced Hogben. Hogben, arms again folded, looked in his eyes with calmness changing to surprise.

'Questions, fellow? From *you*, fellow? Damme, not likely!'

'I fear that won't do,' Colonel Rowan said quietly.

And Mr. Mayne, for all his prejudices, was iron-fair.

'Indeed it won't do!' he agreed, and rapped his knuckles. 'You have accused Lady Drayton and Mr. Cheviot of a conspiracy to do murder. Pending further notice, he is still the Superintendent of this division. Should you refuse to answer his questions, your deposition becomes suspect.'

'*That* fellow?' demanded Hogben, and then controlled himself. 'Ask away!' he said.

Cheviot took up the statement.

'You state, here, that you saw Lady Drayton fire the shot?'

'Yes! Disprove it!'

'You further state that the weapon was a small pistol, with a lozenge-shaped plate in gold let into the handle, and bearing some initials? You saw this, you say, when it fell from Lady Drayton's muff, and I picked it up?'

'Yes!'

Cheviot unfastened the writing-case, took out the pistol belonging to Flora's late husband, and gave it to Hogben.

'Is that the pistol you saw?'

Hogben's eyes narrowed, fearing a trap.

'You need not hesitate,' Cheviot said in the same bleak tone. 'I acknowledge it as the pistol in Lady Drayton's muff. Do you identify it?'

'Yes!' Hogben said triumphantly, and handed it back.

'Did you smell smoke? Either at the time of the shot, or afterwards, did you smell powder-smoke?'

'No!' Hogben blurted. 'Funny thing. I — ' He stopped, shutting his mouth tightly and warily.

'Did you hear the shot?'

'I . . . '

'Since you refuse to answer, we will ask others who were present. Miss Tremayne: did *you* hear the shot?'

'No!' said Louise, startled. 'But, to be sure, the orchestra was . . . '

'Mr. Henley! Did you hear the shot?'

'N-no, sir. As I said. But, as this young lady tells you . . . '

Cheviot turned to the two Commissioners of Police, putting the small pistol on the table.

'Mark it, gentlemen. No sound of the shot; and, which is far more important, no smell of powder-smoke. The latter fact, in my density, I failed to note at the time.'

A convulsion of creaks and cracks went through Mr. Mayne's straight chair.

'Mr. Cheviot!' he said, lifting his hand. 'Do you *admit* Lady Drayton killed the deceased woman with this pistol here?'

'No, sir.'

'But you admit the pistol was in Lady Drayton's muff? That it fell to the floor? That you hid it under a hollow-based lamp?'

'I do, sir.'

'Then you lied? You suppressed evidence?'

'I did, sir.'

'Ah! And in that event,' Mr. Mayne asked in a silky voice, 'may I make so bold as to ask why?'

'Because it would only have misled you, as it has misled you now.' Cheviot's voice, so repressed that the nerves ached for it to grow louder, was having an uncanny effect on them all. 'Because that pistol had nothing whatever to do with the murder of Margaret Renfrew. Permit me to prove as much.'

With no change in his expression he went to the closed door, knocked once on it with his knuckles, and returned.

The door was opened by Sergeant Bulmer,

ushering in a small, bustling man, in a brightly coloured waistcoat and with dark bushy side-whiskers. His knowing eyelid gave him a man of the world's appearance, yet his pursed-up mouth indicated that never, never would he say too much on any matter.

'Mr. Henley,' said Cheviot, 'can you identify this gentleman?'

'Why, sir,' the chief clerk returned, with a grimace, 'that's the surgeon I fetched three nights ago, when you desired to have the bullet removed from the poor lady's body. That's Mr. Daniel Slurk.'

Mr. Slurk gravely removed his hat and approached the table.

'I am rejoiced to see you, gentlemen,' he said to the two Commissioners. He did not sound rejoiced; his tone was guarded and irritable. 'Superintendent Cheviot, I may observe, has summoned me from home at a most devilish inconvenient time. I — '

Cheviot's gesture stopped him.

'Mr. Slurk. Three nights ago, the twenty-ninth of October, did you go to number six New Burlington Street, and in my presence extract a bullet from the body of Miss Margaret Renfrew?'

'I extracted a bullet from a woman's body. Yes.'

'Did this bullet cause her death?'

'It did. The post-mortem examination has since proved — '

'Thank you. Could you identify the bullet?'

'If I saw it,' replied Mr. Slurk, stroking his bushy whiskers and letting droop a knowing eyelid, 'yes.'

Cheviot opened the writing-case again. From a piece of paper, wrapped up and marked in ink, he took out a small pellet of round, smooth lead. It shone under the light of the red-glass lamp as Cheviot held it out in his palm.

'Is this the bullet?'

Pause. Then Mr. Slurk nodded and handed it back.

'That's the bullet, sir,' he declared, preening his whiskers.

'You are sure?'

'Sure, sir? The bullet did not strike bone; it is unflattened, as you may remark. There is the scratch, rather like a question mark, made by my probe. I observed it at the time. There is the distinct marking left by my own forceps. You would wish me to swear to it? I am cautious, sir; I must be so. Yet I would swear.'

'Mr. Mayne!' said Cheviot.

Catching up the gold-mounted pistol and the small bullet, he thrust them across the table under the barrister's nose.

'You need be no authority on pistols, Mr. Mayne,' he continued. 'In fact, you need never have touched one. But take these, sir; thank you! Now try to fit the bullet into the muzzle, as I myself did three nights ago.'

Mr. Mayne instinctively jerked back. But, challenged, he took both of them. After a pause he cleared his throat.

'This — this won't do!' he cried, with a wavering sound in his tone. 'The bullet, small as it is, is much too large to fit into the barrel of the pistol.'

'Consequently,' Cheviot demanded, 'the bullet could not possibly have been fired from Lady Drayton's pistol?'

'No. I allow it.'

For the first time Cheviot raised his voice.

'And therefore,' he said, pointing to Hogben, 'that man has been telling a pack of lies under oath?'

It may only have been the tension which held them, like a drumming in the ears; yet it seemed to some of them that they could hear, distantly, a very faint roaring noise. Both the women had stood up from their chairs.

Hogben, dropping his arms, glanced quickly at the open door. Sergeant Bulmer stood in the doorway, his lips drawn back from his teeth.

'One moment!' interrupted Colonel Rowan.

Throughout this Colonel Rowan, who had moved back from the table, had been listening with a look of satisfaction on his thin, handsome face. Now, however, he was frowning and biting on his lip.

'I entirely agree,' he remarked, as a hush fell on the room again, 'that the bullet could not have been fired from that weapon. But . . . may I see the bullet, Mayne?'

Mr. Mayne passed it to him.

'You seem to be a person of some reflection, Mr. Cheviot,' the barrister said. 'And, as for myself, I — I appear again to have been too hasty. Mark you, sir! This does not in any way lessen the charge against you of suppressing evidence, or . . . '

Once more Colonel Rowan interrupted.

'In my opinion,' he announced, 'we have here more than a question of a bullet fired from Lady Drayton's pistol. This bullet was not fired from any weapon at all.'

'Oh yes, it was,' said Cheviot.

Colonel Rowan drew himself up.

'I may say, I think,' he replied with suave courtesy, 'that I have had *rather* more experience with firearms than even yourself, Mr. Cheviot. This bullet,' he held it up, 'is smooth and unblackened by powder-burns.'

'Exactly, sir. So I found it three nights ago.'

'But any bullet, fired from any pistol,' said Colonel Rowan, 'is burnt black by powder grains into soft lead by the time it leaves the muzzle of the weapon!'

'Again I praise your correctness, sir,' Cheviot declared in a ringing voice. He dived once more into the writing-case, and held up a tiny, flattened, black-crusted pellet. 'Here, for example, is a bullet I fired from that pistol at Joe Manton's shooting gallery this morning.'

'Then may I ask, with all restraint, what the devil — ?'

Cheviot replaced the flattened missile in the case.

'But it is not so, Colonel Rowan, with *every* weapon,' he said.

'You mock me, Mr. Cheviot!'

'No, sir. I should not mock one who has ever stood my friend. Consider, Colonel Rowan! No noise! No smell of powder-smoke! Finally, no bullet burnt black by the powder! What sort of weapon alone could have fired the shot that killed Miss Renfrew?'

Colonel Rowan stood motionless. As illumination came to him, his pale-blue eyes turned slowly . . .

'You have it!' Cheviot said. 'I confess myself blind and obtuse to it until last night, when I exposed a rigged roulette-wheel at

Vulcan's gaming-house.'

'Vulcan's?' asked a bewildered Mr. Mayne.

'Yes, sir. In the midst of exposing it, I realized what might also be done by the impact of a powerful spring released by the immense force of compressed air.'

'Powerful spring? Compressed air?'

Cheviot took from the writing-case a leather-bound book. He flipped over its pages.

'Allow me to read two very brief passages from a volume entitled *The Fatal Effects of Gambling* — and so on, published by the firm of Messrs. Thomas Kelly, etc., in 1824. It deals with the clumsy crime of John Thurtell, who killed a blackleg named William Weare by quite literally punching out his brains with the muzzle of a pistol. This, or the part dealing with false gambling methods, need not interest us.

'But here, in the appendix, is the testimony of a rogue named Probert. True, or false, Probert's words are illuminating. Thurtell, he says, had also intended to murder a man named Wood. Remember it: Wood!'

'But I still demand to know — ' began Mr. Mayne.

Cheviot, finding his place in the book, swept on.

''*Probert*',' he read aloud, "*was to go*

home early at night, and keep the landlady and her daughter drinking belowstairs after Wood was gone to bed; and when he was supposed to be asleep, John Thurtell, disguised in a boat-cloak, was to enter the house by means of Probert's key of the street door, proceed to Wood's room, and shoot him through the heart with the airgun'.'

The stillness in the room, despite the faint distant tumult, was like a cloying physical presence.

'An air-gun,' muttered Colonel Rowan, and snapped his fingers.

'Wait!' said Cheviot.

''He was then'' Cheviot went on reading, ''to place a small pistol that had been discharged, in Wood's right hand, so that it might appear as if he had shot himself'.'

Cheviot lowered the book.

'Crime, or intended crime,' he asked, 'surely does go on repeating itself, does it not? Afterwards, Thurtell could have found himself an alibi.'

And Cheviot snapped his fingers towards Sergeant Bulmer in the doorway.

'Now what, exactly, does an air-gun of this age look like? We find the answer on page 485. Permit me to read again!'

Over flickered the pages.

'Here we have it! 'The air-gun',' Cheviot

read, "*resembled a knotted walking stick —*"

'A — a what?'

"*A knotted walking stick*'," Cheviot read inexorably, "*and held no less than sixteen charges. It was let off by merely pressing one of the knots with the finger, and the only noise was a slight whiz, scarcely perceptible to any one who might happen to be on the spot*'."

Cheviot closed the book and dropped it.

'Sergeant Bulmer!' he cried. 'Show us what you have found, in the place where it must be.'

Bulmer's hand reached outside the doorway. He entered the room carrying an object which drew all eyes, and Mr. Mayne jumped to his feet.

Cheviot pointed to it.

'We sought the explanation of an apparently impossible crime. But there never was an impossible crime. The assassin fired his shot in full view. With my own eyes I saw him lift the weapon to fire, when I thought he meant only to point. If you accept my innocence, he was the only person standing in a dead straight line to the victim.'

Drawing the breath deeply into his lungs, Cheviot faced the two Commissioners of Police.

'The murderer, gentlemen, is your own chief clerk — Mr. Alan Henley.'

20

The End of Death-in-Waiting

To Flora Drayton, standing up on trembling legs with her hands moist from being inside the silk lining of the muff, the staring faces before her seemed to swim in a murk of red and green light.

She could not see Cheviot's face, and was glad she could not.

But clearly she saw the face of Mr. Alan Henley. Mr. Henley, his fleshy lips open and his brown eyes bulging, had turned a sickly colour from terror. He tried to prop up his stocky figure on the thin ebony stick; but he stumbled, and nearly fell face down across the desk.

Cheviot's voice, dominating them all, still rang out.

'I will offer further proof. When I first met Mr. Henley in this room three nights ago, I marked him (without suspicion, I allow) as something of a ladies' man, a dasher, a lover of good food and wine. He had bettered himself from his original beginnings, and he strove to fly higher.

'He limped, as he limps now, on that same thin ebony stick. The walking-stick-cum-air-gun, which you see in Sergeant Bulmer's hands and which was found in Mr. Henley's own locked cupboard in this house, he never dared carry at his duties here. Colonel Rowan, an experienced Army man and a sportsman as well, would at once have recognized that thick knotted cane for what it is.

'Three nights ago, when I was bidden to visit Lady Cork's house on what seemed a matter of stolen bird-seed, he was ordered to accompany me as a shorthand writer. Had he not been so ordered, he would have suggested the same excuse to go.

'But what followed, and to which Lady Drayton herself can testify — '

Briefly Cheviot swung round towards Flora.

She could not bear to see him. He seemed coldly inhuman, the light-grey eyes wide and hard. To Flora, in her cosy and sheltered and gas-lit life, it was as though someone had squeezed her heart with fingers; she could not bear to look on.

But Cheviot had turned back.

'As Lady Drayton and I left this house,' he went on, 'Mr. Henley was already on horseback. He must ride on well ahead of us, you see. But first he stopped by our closed carriage. Very conspicuously, in the light of a carriage-lantern, he permitted me to see the thick and knotted cane he had exchanged for his ebony one.

'If *I* recognized the disguised air-gun for what it was, his plan would have been frustrated at the beginning. But, clearly, I recognized nothing. God help me, no! With its iron ferrule-cap fitted on, as you see it now in the hands of Sergeant Bulmer, I did not even recognize it when he boldly and cynically allowed me to examine it just after the murder.

'But, to return to the time when he sat on horseback by Lady Drayton's closed carriage, and he gave me a certain warning. I marked his uneasiness then, as I had already marked the sweat that ran down his head (why?) when Colonel Rowan had been saying that the clothes of someone shot at a fairly short distance would bear powder-burns.

'Sitting on horseback, Mr. Henley said to me, '*Look very sharp when you talk to Lady Cork. And to Miss Margaret Renfrew too. That is, if you do talk to her.*'

'It was the first mention, in this affair, of Miss Renfrew's name. Why?

'And how did Mr. Henley come to know so much of Lady Cork's household? When he was there, I noted, he was treated almost as a servant. He was scarcely noticed. Lady Cork did not know him. Miss Renfrew herself did not seem to know him. But recall this:

'When Flora and I entered Lady Cork's house, we were greeted by Miss Renfrew on the stairs. Her mood was strange, wild; it seemed unreadable. But all agree it was defiant — and it was *ashamed*.

'On those stairs, and in this humour, she spoke certain words with great intensity. She spoke them after a group of young men had passed her and gone up.

'*"What puppies they are,'* said Miss Renfrew. '*How little amusement they provide! Give me an older man, with experience.'*

'She was not looking at me. No. Her eyes, with a most strange and cryptic look, were fixed at a point past my shoulder. Much as it may distress you, Lady Drayton, I beg you to speak. Who was standing just behind me on those stairs, and followed us up?'

At first Flora, through dry throat and lips, could form no words. She too was remembering that scene on the stairs.

'It — it was Mr. Henley,' she faltered out. 'But I had forgot him.'

Cheviot swung back.

'We all forgot him,' he said. 'Yet look at him, even now! He is likeable, as none can

383

deny. He has much virile charm. He has raised himself, doubtless from what you would call low beginnings, to the position of chief clerk to the Commissioners of Police.

'When or where he first became acquainted with Margaret Renfrew: this I cannot prove or even say. But is it remarkable that a lonely and pretty woman — denied affection, denied love to her passionate nature by some mysterious repulsiveness which all could feel yet none define — is it remarkable she should have fallen victim to an older man who had learned the craft of flattery?

'More! Does it surprise you that *his* head was turned?

'He was bettering himself, as he strove to do. This infatuated woman, for a time at least, would steal money for him. She would steal Lady Cork's jewellery for him. And why? So that he could line his pockets, so that he could win money across Vulcan's gaming tables; and become in his own eyes the 'true gentleman' he wished to be.

'Nevertheless, there was a matter on which he had not reckoned.

'He had not reckoned on Miss Renfrew's soul, as deeply and damnably snobbish as any about her. Offend snobbery, and you are undone. Recall her, all you who knew her! Physical passion, the balm of compliment and flattery, would hold her enthralled for a while. But then . . .

'Then she would become ashamed of having robbed Lady Cork. But this only in part. Most of all, she would be horrified at having taken as a lover someone whom she could never proudly display. A crude man, in her eyes. A man of uncertain grammar and manners as clumsy as his walk; in short, a man of low origins. *That* was why she was ashamed. *That* was why she had become ready to betray him, as well he saw and knew. And so, to protect his own fierce respectability, he shot her with the air-gun before she could speak.'

Cheviot paused.

Mr. Alan Henley, behind the desk with the green-shaded lamp, uttered a bubbling kind of cry. He had not uttered a word. But he jerked his right hand, with the head of the stick in it, and papers flew wide.

'Stop!' said Mr. Mayne.

As though emerging from a kind of mesmerism, Mr. Mayne rubbed his forehead and thrust out a round face.

'You speak with persuasion, Mr. Cheviot,' he said. 'But this man,' he nodded towards Mr. Henley, 'has served us faithfully, according to his lights — '

'Agreed!' said Colonel Rowan.

'And the evidence against him must be complete.' Mr. Mayne struck the table. 'Your producing of the air-gun, there, is legal proof which may be taken into court. Always provided this unburned bullet *is* an air-gun bullet — '

Mr. Daniel Slurk, who had been tapping the brim of his hat against his teeth, allowed one eyelid to droop still further.

'Sir,' he said to Mr. Mayne, 'I could have told you it was fired from an air-gun. As a surgeon, sir, I have some small experience of bullets.'

'But you did not so tell Mr. Cheviot?'

'I am a cautious man, sir. I was not asked.'

'Very well!' And Mr. Mayne stared at Cheviot. 'But it is little of legal evidence to say, 'A woman looked thus.' 'A man spake thus.' Have you any proof that Miss Renfrew stole Lady Cork's jewels, or that Henley ever laid hands on them?'

'Yes!' said Cheviot, and opened the writing-case again.

'Here,' he went on, 'is a letter written by Lady Cork, and delivered to me by hand at the Albany early this morning. It contains the substance of a conversation I had with her late last night. Lady Cork actually saw Miss Renfrew steal the diamond ring which appears in a list I produce. Lady Cork knew

Miss Renfrew was prepared to confess; she is willing, as you see, to testify in a court of law.'

Once more he attacked the writing-case. A handkerchief, knotted round some objects within, he untied and flung out; glittering jewels rattled and rolled across the table under Mr. Mayne's eyes. Beside them Cheviot thumped down two accountbooks.

'Here,' he continued, 'are the jewels themselves. Any of my men can tell you I found them at Vulcan's gaming house; and Lady Cork has identified them. Now look in these accounts!' He riffled the pages, pointing. 'See whose name is written opposite the description of this, and this, and this, and this. All five of the stolen pieces. The name, in every case, is Mr. Alan Henley.'

'This,' said Mr. Mayne, after a pause of examining, 'would seem — '

'Complete,' said Colonel Rowan, and swallowed.

'And you divined all this, Mr. Cheviot,' demanded Mr. Mayne, lifting his eyes, 'from the very beginning?'

'No, sir. No, as I have been attempting to tell you! My eyes were opened, only yesterday afternoon, by a remark made by Miss Louise Tremayne.'

'*I* made such a remark?' cried Louise. '*I*?'

She drifted forward towards him, all hazel

eyes and broad quivering lips, as though she would put her hand on his arm.

Flora flung her muff into the chair behind her. At that moment she hated Louise and quite seriously believed she could kill her.

'You were suggesting,' said Cheviot, not without sardonic humour, 'that *I* might be Miss Renfrew's lover.'

'But I never truly thought — '

'Never, Miss Tremayne?' he suggested gently. 'In any case, I denied it. I said something to this effect: 'Listen! The first time I ever heard that woman's name — '

'And there I spoke no further. I remembered when I first *had* heard her name, and who had spoken it: Mr. Henley. Past events, in their true shape, took form clearly. At the same time, I was looking straight down at this table and at Colonel Rowan's silver-handled pistol. That particular weapon, I see, has been put on Mr. Henley's desk at the moment . . .'

(Alan Henley stiffened. None saw this except Cheviot.)

' . . . and I recalled, with much distinctness, there had been no powder-smoke in the passage when Miss Renfrew was shot. There had been no noise, no powder-mark on the bullet. I did not think of an air-gun until Vulcan's spring-and-compressed-air mechanism exploded in the roulette-table.

'But the sequence of events on the night of the murder must now be clear. This small pistol,' and Cheviot took up the weapon with the gold lozenge set into the handle, 'was only intended as a dummy and a cheat.

'Who borrowed the pistol from Lady Drayton? Officially Lady Cork; but, as we know, it was Miss Renfrew who in fact borrowed it and kept it. Mr. Henley, as we also know, arrived at the house nearly half an hour before Lady Drayton and myself.

'It would not have been difficult for him to steal the small pistol from the room of a half-distracted woman who was ready to confess. Wherever he killed Miss Renfrew, none must suspect his thick and knobbed cane of being an air-gun.

'There must be a dummy pistol, fired, to account for the death. It is the same device, you will note, which the late John Thurtell meant to use in the murder of Wood. I doubt that Henley fired a shot inside the house. More probably it was in the garden, into soft earth. He then had time to go back into the house, hide the pistol under a table in the upstairs passage near Lady Cork's boudoir, and sit down quietly in the foyer.

'Lady Drayton, before the murder, found the discharged pistol. For good reasons which she explained to me, but on which I need not dwell, she concealed it in her muff.

'In the boudoir, while I was questioning Lady Cork in the presence of Miss Renfrew and Mr. Henley, matters all but boiled over.

'By the Lord, you should have seen Miss Renfrew's demeanour then! You should have seen how often and how furtively she glanced at Henley, who was (apparently) unconcerned and busy at his shorthand. But, again, you should have seen her demeanour when she marched out!

'He knew he must kill, and kill quickly. The opportunity was provided.

'I think, Colonel Rowan, you would have seen the truth in our positions in the passage if Mr. Mayne had not so persistently suspected Lady Drayton and myself. Consider!

'Henley and I left the boudoir, closing the double-doors behind us. We turned round. Lady Drayton was standing about a dozen feet ahead of us, well to our right, her back turned. Miss Renfrew opened the passage-door of the boudoir, and came out.

'Now what happened? Two seconds earlier, Henley had lifted his cane as though to point. I did not see him remove the ferrule-cap. Probably he meant no harm — until he saw Miss Renfrew. I thought nothing of it; why should I?

'Miss Renfrew walked across diagonally, as though to the ballroom. She turned, and in the middle of the passage she walked towards the stairs with her back to us. If you had listened to the testimony of Lady Drayton, which I included in my report, you might have seen the truth. What was that testimony?'

Flora herself could not remember. Her mind was too confused. But Cheviot, putting down the small pistol on the table, spoke clearly.

'Flora Drayton,' he said, 'told me this. *'She,'* meaning Miss Renfrew, *'was well ahead and to the left of me. I felt a wind, or a kind of whistle or the like, past my arm. She went on a little and fell on her face'.'*

At last Flora remembered, and all too vividly. The terror of the night was returning.

'In other words,' said Cheviot, 'she felt the bullet pass her on the left. Henley, with a direct-sightline to his victim, pressed the knob of the cane. Any noise was hidden from me by the loud waltz-music. That small bullet, which at a longer distance would not even have been deadly, struck Miss Renfrew through the heart. She took two steps and fell dead.

'It was the last act,' Cheviot said. 'But it was not the last link.'

'Not, you say,' Mr. Mayne asked in an unexpectedly high voice, 'the last link?'

'No,' Cheviot suddenly pointed. 'You think Alan Henley has been your faithful servant?'

'Yes!' Mr. Mayne and Colonel Rowan spoke at once.

'He is not.' Cheviot shook his head. 'Though I did not stress it in my second report, so much was evident from my visit to Vulcan. Someone had warned Vulcan I should be there, else he could not have packed the house with so many blacklegs. Who warned him?'

'Well?'

'I — I counted it strange,' Cheviot muttered, 'only a coincidence perhaps, that there should have been so many resemblances between Vulcan and Alan Henley. Both are self-educated men: though Vulcan, save for his rings, has achieved near-perfection of manner. Both have a physical disability caused by accident: Mr. Henley a lame leg, Vulcan a glass eye. Both are inordinately vain, especially of their power over women.

'Vulcan, in his study or office, could not help mentioning this. He remarked on the strangeness that some men, even with natural disadvantages, should have this power. He added, meaning himself, that he knew such a man. And I, with my eye on the two walking-sticks propped at the far end of his private roulette-table, said, 'So do I.'

'He is quick-witted. He guessed I meant Mr. Henley. It was as though an arrow had struck home.

'In fact, he tested me by referring to it later. Should the police make any attack on his gaming-house, he said that he would be warned beforehand. And I replied, without surprise, that I was aware of it.

'Then Vulcan knew. He knew I meant the chief clerk to the Commissioners of Police. Again the arrow struck home.

'Your faithful servant? No, I think not! Mr. Henley had assisted Vulcan far more than in pledging jewels there. How far he may be associated with the owners of other gaming-houses, a matter at which I only guess, it will be your duty to inquire. But faithful? Never!'

Again, from Alan Henley's thick throat, issued a wordless cry.

He did not deny; he did not speak. His left hand reached out, in a tentative way, as though he would seize the medium-bore silver-handled pistol and turn it on himself. But he could not do it.

In his staring eyes was reflected the image of the hangman. He pressed his hands over his face. The ebony stick clattered to the floor. He fell headlong across the table, amid flying papers, in a dead faint.

Flora, her throat choked, saw another figure loom up. Captain Hogben, his cloak over his right arm, was backing against Mr. Henley's desk. Hogben's body was partly obscured by the green-shaded lamp. His own right hand went snaking out . . .

'Is it not ironic — ?' Mr. Mayne was beginning, when Cheviot cut him short.

'Ironic?' he cried. 'Have you seen no worse irony?'

Whereupon, to those who listened, Cheviot seemed to take leave of his wits.

'I, as Superintendent of C-One of the Criminal Investigation Department! I, who prided myself on my knowledge of scientific criminology? I, because I never dreamed they had been invented, was deceived for two days by a common air-gun, when any gunsmith of the year 1829 could have told me.'

They were staring at him. Behind Sergeant Bulmer, who stood rock-like with the thick and knotted cane, the doorway was crowded with policemen. The other sergeant, with the collar-numeral 9, fought his way through them.

Breathing hard, Sergeant 9 straightened up and saluted.

'Sir!' he said to Colonel Rowan. 'The riot's begun. That tailor, who's drunk, set fire to his own house. The devil knows why he did, but it's crazed 'em. There's six hundred men a-fighting in Parliament Street, and the truncheons are out. They've attacked our men, and spilled round into King Street . . . '

'We shall deal with it,' snapped Colonel Rowan. 'Meanwhile, Mr. Cheviot, have you gone mad? What is this you speak of 'C-One'? 'Criminal Investigation Department'?'

Cheviot laughed.

'Your pardon,' he said. 'I could not even remember Mr. Fulford's biography of King George the Fourth; and the fact that a bullet-hole from an air-gun was found in the glass of the coach-window. That was in 1820. Air-guns must have been known long before then. But it took Joe Manton the younger to remind me.'

'A biography of the King?' echoed an astounded Mr. Mayne. 'But the King is yet alive! No biography of His Majesty has yet been written.'

'No, sir,' agreed Cheviot. 'I had also forgotten that Mr. Roger Fulford's account will not be published for more than a hundred years.'

'Good God!' breathed Colonel Rowan. 'Mr. Cheviot! Control yourself, lest we think you a staring lunatic.'

'Perhaps I am,' Cheviot retorted. 'But there

is one more reckoning to be settled. It is not at all concerned with Mr. Henley.'

And he pointed to Hogben, whose hand still moved along Henley's desk.

'I mean that man there,' Cheviot snapped. 'Captain Hogben has sworn and is perjured. It was done before a magistrate. He will pay. And the penalty for that, in this age — '

This was the point at which Hogben acted, in what seemed all one movement.

Hogben's right hand swung up the silver-mounted pistol. His left hand whipped the long black cloak off his other arm. As it billowed out, he threw the cloak over Cheviot's head and into his face.

Making a dart for the door, he saw it was full of policemen. Instantly Hogben charged between Flora and Louise. There was a bursting crash of glass and flimsy wood as he dived, left arm protecting his face, through the lower part of the window.

They heard him hit the ground sideways, and roll. He was up in an instant. Carriage-horses screamed, whinnied, and reared up. But there was no horse for Hogben to take; he and Louise, like Cheviot and Flora, had come there in a carriage.

In the dim light of the gas-lamp, out there at the entrance by the crooked tree, they saw him running hard for Whitehall. Cheviot, who

396

had disentangled himself from the cloak, whipped round to those in the doorway.

'Let every man stand where he is!' he shouted. 'This is one prisoner I take myself.'

Running to the window, shielding his own face against glass-edges, he ducked his head out, swung his legs through, and dropped outside. They saw him running hard after Hogben as the latter, at the entrance, turned left and south down Whitehall.

Even as Hogben had acted, Sergeant Bulmer flipped off the iron ferrule-cap of the air-gun and swung it up to fire. But he could not find, on the handle of the cane, the knob you pressed to discharge it. As Cheviot disappeared through the window, Bulmer flung down the air-gun on the floor.

'Sir,' he said to Colonel Rowan, 'I've never disobeyed the Superintendent yet. But I'm disobeying him now. And *I've* got — '

His hand went under his coat to the hip-pocket. Then *he* vanished through the broken window.

Alan Henley still lay face down across the desk. The others stood motionless. Colonel Rowan, Mr. Mayne, Mr. Slurk, Louise, Flora . . .

They heard no noise except pounding footsteps as Bulmer ran hard across the freezing mud. Then even these died away.

There was nothing except, very faintly and distantly, the roar of a fighting mob.

'No!' Flora cried. And, after a pause: 'No!'

It was like a prevision, a rending of heart and a knowledge of what had happened when it did happen.

Very clearly, and not too far away, they heard a pistol-shot.

You might have counted one, two, three, possibly four; and, with the same clearness, there was another shot.

Afterwards, only silence.

Very slowly Colonel Rowan walked to the shattered window, put his head out, and looked down towards the left.

'Bulmer!' he called, though Bulmer could not possibly have heard him. 'Bulmer!'

Far to the south, a red light of fire flickered in the sky.

Colonel Rowan, pale-faced, drew his head back from the window and turned round. In his scarlet coat, with the buff facings, his shoulders back, he returned to the desk as though in a dream.

They were all in a dream. It went on and on, but it could not last. Mr. Slurk's hat dropped from his fingers and bounced on the floor. Louise Tremayne had cowered down in the chair. Only Flora stood straight, her chin up and her eyes as though very far away.

Presently they heard footsteps returning. The person who returned, with dragging steps, was Sergeant Bulmer. Nobody urged him; nobody called from the window; nobody dared.

Silently, his face dumpling-dull under his tall hat, he fought his way through the group in the hall as he entered by the front door. He appeared in the doorway, not quite seeming to understand. In his hand, loosely held, was a pistol stamped with the crown and broad-arrow. Its reek hung in their nostrils.

'Yes?' asked Colonel Rowan, clearing his throat. Anger burnt him. 'What happened? Where is — where is Superintendent Cheviot?'

Bulmer seemed to ruminate heavily.

'Why, sir,' he said, 'the Superintendent's not back.'

'I know that! Where is he?'

Sergeant Bulmer lifted his head.

'What I meantersay, sir,' he said heavily, 'he's not ever a-coming back. What I meantersay: he's dead.'

Again the eerie silence coiled round the red and green lamps.

'I see,' muttered Colonel Rowan.

'Hogben,' said Sergeant Bulmer, with a violent effort, 'Hogben never meant to run far. Hogben, he stopped and turned. And you know the Superintendent. Went for Hogben, he did, with empty hands. So Hogben up with the pistol and fired in his face.'

Once more Sergeant Bulmer made a violent effort to speak.

'Well,' he said, 'I wasn't far behind. The Superintendent told me never to carry a loaded barker. I swore I wouldn't. But I had one. I leaned close, so I couldn't miss. I shot that bastard Hogben between the eyes. And, by God, I'm proud I did.'

Nobody spoke until Mr. Mayne burst out.

'It was Cheviot's own fault,' he cried, with the wrath of shaken nerves. ' "Fire burn and cauldron bubble!" He always quoted that, about Margaret Renfrew. He never knew, he never guessed, it applied far more to himself.' Then Mr. Mayne was stricken. 'Lady Drayton! I ask your pardon! I never meant . . . '

His voice trailed off.

Flora, still standing motionless, did not look at him or speak. Only her lips quivered, and began to quiver uncontrollably, as the roar of the mob rose and flames were painted bright in the sky.

Epilogue

'O Woman! in Our Hours of Ease — '

When Cheviot saw Hogben turn round, black against the line of fire and struggling distant men, he knew what would happen as soon as light glinted on the silver mounting of the pistol.

He said one word — '*Flora!*' — as Hogben pulled the trigger.

Something struck him very hard in the head. Or so it seemed, though he saw no fire-flash and heard no report. The single notion left in his brain was that it seemed odd to be falling forward, instead of backwards, if you ran into the impact of a heavy bullet.

Then darkness; nothing more.

How long the darkness lasted he could not tell. There were movements, tremors, ripples at its outer edges. There were sensations through his muscles, in his heart and nerves. A thought crept into his brain and astonished him.

If he were dead, surely, he could not think. And certainly he could not hear.

'Superintendent!' said a voice.

401

Cheviot raised his head, which ached badly and blurred his sight. He was kneeling, oddly enough, against the door of some cab.

'I couldn't 'elp it!' a voice was saying over and over, a little distant. ' 'Ow could I see, in the sanguinary fog, if a car comes smack out o' them gates and smack across me incarnadined front bumper?'

'That bullet!' Cheviot said. 'It must have missed me!'

'What bullet?' asked the voice close in his ear. And he recognized the voice.

He raised his head still further, in the open door of the taxi. All about him was white October mist. His hat was a soft hat, a modern hat. Through the mist gleamed the lights of a pub on the left.

Ahead of him, as he peered round, towered up the tall iron gates — open arches — of the western entrance between Scotland Yard Central and Scotland Yard South. Locked with the front of his taxi loomed another car atop which ran the glowing panel with the black letters POLICE.

'Don't you see the sign there?' the police-driver was demanding of the taxi-driver. 'Don't you know no public vehicles are allowed beyond this arch?'

'Steady, Mr. Cheviot!' said Sergeant Boyce, who assisted Inspector Hastings in the Night

Duty Room at the back of Scotland Yard Central.

'Er — yes.'

'You had a bad knock on the head,' Sergeant Boyce went on. Like all the night-duty force, he was of the uniformed branch. 'You had a bad knock on the head when the cars hit and your head struck the door-handle. But the skin's not broken; it's only a bump. Take my arm and step down.'

Cheviot took his arm and stepped down on a solid pavement.

Time had slipped back; time had slipped into place.

'I didn't dream it!' Cheviot said.

'No, no, 'course you didn't. By the way, your wife 'phoned half an hour ago, and said she'd be here to pick you up and take you home in the car. Don't frighten her! She's in the office now, and — '

'Didn't dream it!' said Cheviot.

'Easy, Superintendent!'

'The murder mystery was all solved,' Cheviot went on, still dazed. 'All solved in every detail. But the rest of it, in many parts, I'll never know and I can never learn. I did live in 1829. The past does repeat itself! I never even saw an engraving of the old Houses of Parliament — '

'Now listen, Superintendent.'

' — I never read a description of Joe Manton's shooting-gallery, or knew its number in Davies Street. Parts of my real life here, and parts I never dreamed, are all confused together. I can never sort them out. If only she . . . she . . . '

Light footsteps rapped across the pavement from the Night Duty Room, hurried out under a smaller arch, and a woman's figure loomed up.

'All right, sir? Here's your wife.'

Cheviot's wits cleared. And so, with a kind of inner cry, did his heart.

A woman's arms went round him as he seized her in turn. Through the mist looked up the same blue eyes. The same mouth, the same fair complexion, the same golden hair under a modern hat, were just as they had seemed before they faded.

'Hello, darling,' said Flora.

We do hope that you have enjoyed reading this large print book.

Did you know that all of our titles are available for purchase?

We publish a wide range of high quality large print books including:
Romances, Mysteries, Classics
General Fiction
Non Fiction and Westerns

Special interest titles available in large print are:
The Little Oxford Dictionary
Music Book
Song Book
Hymn Book
Service Book

Also available from us courtesy of Oxford University Press:
Young Readers' Dictionary
(large print edition)
Young Readers' Thesaurus
(large print edition)

For further information or a free brochure, please contact us at:
Ulverscroft Large Print Books Ltd.,
The Green, Bradgate Road, Anstey,
Leicester, LE7 7FU, England.
Tel: (00 44) 0116 236 4325
Fax: (00 44) 0116 234 0205

STRANGER IN THE PLACE

Anne Doughty

Elizabeth Stewart, a Belfast student and only daughter of hardline Protestant parents, sets out on a study visit to the remote west coast of Ireland. Delighted as she is by the beauty of her new surroundings and the small community which welcomes her, she soon discovers she has more to learn than the details of the old country way of life. She comes to reappraise so much that is slighted and dismissed by her family — not least in regard to herself. But it is her relationship with a much older, Catholic man, Patrick Delargy, which compels her to decide what kind of life she really wants.

DUMMY HAND

Susan Moody

When Cassie Swann is knocked off her bike on a quiet country road, the driver leaves her unconscious and bleeding at the roadside. A man later walks into a police station and confesses, and they gratefully close the case. But something about this guilt-induced confession doesn't smell right, and Cassie's relentless suitor Charlie Quartermain cannot resist doing a little detective work. When a young student at Oxford is found brutally murdered, Charlie begins to suspect that the two incidents are somehow connected. Can he save Cassie from another 'accident' — this time a fatal one?

SHOT IN THE DARK

Annie Ross

When an elderly nun is raped and murdered at a drop-in centre for drug addicts, the police decide it's a burglary gone wrong. Television director Bel Carson sees pictures of the body, and is convinced that this was a ritualistic murder, carried out by a sadistic and calculating killer. Then he strikes closer to home, and Bel determines to track him down. As she closes in on the monster, she senses that someone is spying on her home. And, in a final, terrifying twist, she finds herself caught in the killer's trap . . .